For my mother, Delores Meyer, with love…who always told me to never give up and never stop writing. I miss you so, mother! I hope they have books in heaven for you to read.
This book is also for my sweet brother Jim Meyer, who passed away on May 27, 2015. He was a great singer/musician/songwriter and a loving brother. If you'd like to listen to some of his songs, go here:
http://tinyurl.com/pytftzc

Other books by Kathryn Meyer Griffith:
Evil Stalks the Night
The Heart of the Rose
Blood Forge
Vampire Blood
The Last Vampire (2012 Epic EBook Awards Finalist)
*Witches * Witches II: Apocalypse*
Witches plus Witches II: Apocalypse
The Calling
Scraps of Paper-*1st Spookie Town Murder Mystery*
All Things Slip Away-*2nd Spookie Town Murder Mystery*
Ghosts Beneath Us-*3rd Spookie Town Murder Mystery*
Witches Among Us-*4th Spookie Town Murder Mystery*
What Lies Beneath the Graves-*5th Spookie Town Mystery*
Egyptian Heart
Winter's Journey
The Ice Bridge
Don't Look Back, Agnes
A Time of Demons and Angels
The Woman in Crimson
Four Spooky Short Stories
Human No Longer
Night Carnival
Forever and Always
Dinosaur Lake (2014 Epic EBook Awards Finalist)
Dinosaur Lake II: Dinosaurs Arising
Dinosaur Lake III: Infestation
Dinosaur Lake IV: Dinosaur Wars
Dinosaur Lake V: Survivors
*All Kathryn Meyer Griffith's books here:
http://tinyurl.com/ld4jlow
*All her Audible.com audio books here:
http://tinyurl.com/oz7c4or

~

Egyptian Heart video *on You Tube (but with old cover):*
https://www.youtube.com/watch?v=cogCNYKzPqc
More of My You Tube book videos*:*
https://www.youtube.com/results?search_query=Kathryn+Meyer+Griffith

For my mother, Delores Meyer, with love...who always told me to never give up and never stop writing. I miss you so, mother! I hope they have books in heaven for you to read.
This book is also for my sweet brother Jim Meyer, who passed away on May 27, 2015. He was a great singer/musician/songwriter and a loving brother. If you'd like to listen to some of his songs, go here:
http://tinyurl.com/pytftzc

Other books by Kathryn Meyer Griffith:
Evil Stalks the Night
The Heart of the Rose
Blood Forge
Vampire Blood
The Last Vampire (2012 Epic EBook Awards Finalist)
*Witches * Witches II: Apocalypse*
Witches plus Witches II: Apocalypse
The Calling
Scraps of Paper-*1st Spookie Town Murder Mystery*
All Things Slip Away-*2nd Spookie Town Murder Mystery*
Ghosts Beneath Us-*3rd Spookie Town Murder Mystery*
Witches Among Us-*4th Spookie Town Murder Mystery*
What Lies Beneath the Graves-*5th Spookie Town Mystery*
Egyptian Heart
Winter's Journey
The Ice Bridge
Don't Look Back, Agnes
A Time of Demons and Angels
The Woman in Crimson
Four Spooky Short Stories
Human No Longer
Night Carnival
Forever and Always
Dinosaur Lake (2014 Epic EBook Awards Finalist)
Dinosaur Lake II: Dinosaurs Arising
Dinosaur Lake III: Infestation
Dinosaur Lake IV: Dinosaur Wars
Dinosaur Lake V: Survivors
*All Kathryn Meyer Griffith's books here:
http://tinyurl.com/ld4jlow
*All her Audible.com audio books here:
http://tinyurl.com/oz7c4or

~

Egyptian Heart video *on You Tube (but with old cover):*
https://www.youtube.com/watch?v=cogCNYKzPqc
More of My You Tube book videos:
https://www.youtube.com/results?search_query=Kathryn+Meyer+Griffith

Prologue

Some women wait all their lives to find their one great love, if they're lucky enough to find it at all. I traveled to Egypt and three thousand years into the past to find mine. It was my destiny...as was everything that happened to me that summer the University sent me to Egypt on a grant, to search for the lost necropolis I was sure existed beneath the desert sands not far from the three Pyramids of Gizah. Here is my story....

Chapter One

My mother had warned me before I'd bought the plane tickets, "Maggie Owen...these days with all the strife going on, Egypt isn't a safe place for anyone, much less a woman. Why can't you put this trip off for a while and go some other time? Next summer maybe?"

"Because the grant is for *this* year, *now* Mom. Maybe next year it won't be offered. And next year I won't have a published book out. That's why the College Board chose me. This is my chance. All I know, is that if I don't go now, I might never get to go. This is the time."

My book on deciphering ancient hieroglyphs wasn't a best seller but it had made the college look at me differently. It had helped that I'd filled the book with full color reproductions I'd drawn and painted myself from photographs of Egyptian artwork and hieroglyphs from the ancient tombs.

Kathryn Meyer Griffith

My series of Egyptian themed original paintings from the book were on display at local art galleries all over town and my reputation as an artist and published writer was growing.

I'd beaten out ten other professors who'd wanted overseas grants for research this summer. Fate wanted me to go and I wasn't going to argue with fate.

"Okay. But I'll worry about you every day." My mom's face had shown her concern and I understood her fears as I put my arms around her that last night before I left.

"I'll be careful," I'd promised her. "Just take good care of Snowball." Snowball was my cat. A puffball of white with such an ugly little pug face, she was cute. I'd had her fourteen years and hated leaving her. But I knew Mom would take good care of her and give her the love she needed. And Snowball wouldn't be lonely because Mom had three other cats.

"I will. She's going to miss you. though. Like us."

"I know. I wish I could take her. But she's too old and the desert is too hot for her. It gets up to a hundred and twenty in the sun this time of year."

"Glad you're going to Egypt and not me. I don't believe I'd like living on the sun."

"Very funny." It was different for me. Heat didn't usually bother me. And if you wanted something bad enough, I figured, you put up with a lot more than a little heat.

I'd dreamed of being an Egyptologist and college professor digging in the sands of Egypt—

Egyptian Heart

been beckoned to Egypt—for as long as I could remember; as if it'd waited and held a great secret for me. As if I'd lived there before. Ever since I was a child, I'd been lugging home library books full of colorful pictures and stories of the ancient land. I wanted to walk the same ground and gaze upon the same antiquities that those earliest Egyptians once had. Descend into the tombs, decipher the hieroglyphs and unearth the scrolls that would reveal the ancient peoples' loves, fears and lives. Their secrets. I was looking for something.

Then I was there. In Egypt. The ancient people used to call it *To-mery* and it was as sultry and mysterious as my colleagues at Boston University warned me it would be. The sun was a ball of fire pulsating above and baking every living and inanimate object on the archeological dig. The desert around me was endless and dusty, the tents were airless and cramped and I couldn't understand what the natives were saying, though I was trying to learn the language.

The desert sand crept into my suitcases, into my bags and like a mischievous thief, invaded the clothes I wore. The grains were fiery hot and everywhere a rainbow of earth toned colors sparkled beneath the sun's rays. The sun burnt my flesh and brought tears to my eyes; sand mixed with the trickling sweat on my body and built up in the creases and crevices, making me sticky and uncomfortable minutes after rising in the morning. During the day the sand swirled around my head in a cloud like a living thing, tugging at my hat and my loose clothes and often making it difficult to walk.

And those were the good times.

The bad times were when the vicious sandstorms would roar in from the horizon unexpectedly and roar away as swiftly, leaving destruction and gritty sand behind everywhere. Our tents had to be securely tied to the ground or they'd blow away. All my books, clothes and personal items had to be placed in huge plastic bags and roped together to keep out the sand. So I lived out of trash bags, picked granules out of my food and kept myself bundled up in lightweight clothes to protect my skin from sunburn. It was like living in an oven.

But I didn't care about any of that as I strode across the rocky plateau in long steps, away from the pyramids beneath the blazing noonday sun. The heat, the primitive conditions and the complaining natives the University had hired for the summer dig, didn't bother me. Being there was heaven. Magical.

My family had given me a lavish Bon Voyage party with cake, gifts and everything before I'd left the States. My two brothers and three sisters had been happy but uncertain for me. Unlike me, they were all married with children and had solid, normal lives. They would have preferred I'd found a boyfriend, gotten married and had a couple of kids, kept teaching and painted my pretty pictures from home, too, instead of gallivanting across the world looking for dead bones.

But, hey, the goodbyes had been said. I'd packed and the plane left the next morning. Nothing would have stopped me. Not even the pathetic look on my mom's face. And I didn't have a boyfriend or

Egyptian Heart

anyone else to miss or miss me. I was alone. I was always alone.

You chase them off, Mom said. *It's that old soul behind those emerald eyes of yours, honey. A soul that has experienced many lifetimes and suffered and knows too much. It glares back out at people and frightens them off.*

My mom was a whimsical, perceptive woman and an exceptional watercolorist, who in some ways, I took after. But she believed in reincarnation, eternal love and all sorts of weird things I could never accept. Me, I didn't believe in anything but hard work and myself.

We make our own destiny, I told her.

And she'd just laugh at me. *That's what you think. Just wait. Life has a way of surprising a person. Give it time. It'll knock you on your butt someday all right.*

"I'll be back in three months. That's not that long."

"So much can happen in three months, Maggie," she'd whispered and the words would later return to haunt me.

I had no idea how true they were going to be.

But standing in the desert weeks later, I wasn't thinking about my mother, my cat, my family or my lack of love affairs. I was thinking of Egypt and the *lost necropolis.* A forgotten and undiscovered Egyptian graveyard, a city of the dead and those who'd served them, buried under the sand near the Great Pyramids. The burial ground where perhaps Nefertiti, wife to the heretical and ill-fated pharaoh Akhenaton, and her children, who'd lived three thousand years before, might be buried. His remains, they believed, had been found, but his wife's and family's hadn't.

I'd first begun to suspect the lost city might exist three years ago when I'd come across a very old book, supposedly copied from some ancient scrolls found in an unknown tomb. I hadn't thought anything of it until my translating of the text began to veer away from what the book was reflecting. I'd always had a gift for deciphering tomb paintings and hieroglyphs.

My translation was different and I believed the original manuscript had been misread. A disparity here and there with key pictograms changed the meanings. In the last three years I'd searched and found more references in other books and ancient texts about this mysterious necropolis and I began my quest to find it. It was the reason I was here. If what I suspected were true, it could be the discovery of the century. And I would be the one to make it. It would make me famous.

I found a large square stone in the shade of a few straggly trees, and settled down on it, sighing softly. My hat provided shade and the limestone felt cool on my legs through my white cotton slacks.

I'd been working at the dig all morning, it'd been hotter every day as Egypt's summer moved in, and I was exhausted. I was where I'd always wanted to be, doing what I'd always dreamed of, but with no one to share it with, I found myself suddenly lonely.

My family, colleagues and friends were thousands of miles away.

Egyptian Heart

Staring out over the sand and the waves of heat, my loneliness brought me strange thoughts and a startling hallucination. I saw myself dancing, floating over the sand, with a man. And somehow I knew that he wasn't just any man, but the man I would spend my life with. He was tall and strong but I couldn't see his face; couldn't tell who he was. The figures were too misty and the illusion faded too quickly. Shaking my head, I tried to clear my mind. Must be heat stroke. Now I was seeing things.

But I wondered what it meant. I didn't usually daydream about suitors.

Sure, when I'd been younger I'd had dates and my share of boyfriends. I'd come close to falling in love a couple of times, but never had. I always pulled back at the last moment, something deep in my heart and soul kept me from loving anyone completely.

As if I was waiting for something or someone who was yet to come.

I wanted someone who would love me the rest of my life, protect and cherish me. Be the center of my world. Love the things I loved. He'd come someday, Mom said. I was beginning to have my doubts. But my someday lover still lived strongly in my heart.

He'd be smart, strong willed, sure of himself and wouldn't need to challenge and control me. But he'd also be tender. His touch would set my flesh and blood on fire, yet we'd be able to talk of many things. And, most importantly, he would love me more than life itself. If need be, he would fight to the death for me.

Kathryn Meyer Griffith

And sitting there in the hot sun of Egypt, he'd never seemed so real. I could almost feel his warm hands on my skin, could almost see his loving smile and thoughtful eyes. As if he were near. Nearer than when I'd been at home. How odd that here I was in Egypt searching for something that would make me rich and respected in my college circles back home but I was spending my time

daydreaming about love. I should be thinking of my job and the lost tomb.

My eyes scanned the pyramids and the desert in the distance. Outside the big cities, the people were nomads and truly followed the old ways. It was a land that in many ways lived in the past.

There were rules to follow, especially for a woman. Egypt was a country of Islam, usually a peaceful loving religion, yet foreign women needed to dress modestly and keep their bodies properly covered. If a woman dressed skimpily, I was told, she was putting herself in danger.

So I wore gauzy but opaque shirts with long sleeves and baggy cotton pants in sun friendly colors and I pulled my long silver-blond hair into a bun and kept it covered with a wide-brimmed straw hat. Dark sunglasses hid my eyes from strangers. I kept my fair skin covered and watched the tone of my voice. I was humble. I was cautious. I tried to be invisible. I'd learned my lesson the first few days I was here.

I'd caught one of the workmen staring at my face one morning and there was fear in his.

"Your eyes, mistress," he'd muttered in an anxious tone. "Such a pale strange shade of green.

Jinn eyes." He'd averted his gaze quickly then, and had hurried away, but not before I'd seen he'd been frightened of me. Of my eyes.

The peasants were superstitious. They hadn't changed in thousands of years and were afraid of anything different and of what they alleged was bad magic. In their history a Jinn was like a genie and most of them were evil. They caused mischief and grief in a person's life if they attached themselves to you. The peasant thought I had a jinn's eyes...maybe that I had a jinn inside me. Afterwards, I recalled that the workman had been wearing a blue amulet around his neck and had tattoos on his arms—two things that were supposed to protect a mortal from the malevolence of jinns.

Since that morning I kept my eyes hidden if possible. I didn't want trouble.

I wiped the sweat from my face with a rag kept tucked at my waistband and peered up at the three pyramids in the far distance. The largest was the final resting place of the mighty King Rhufu, the middle pyramid was Khafre's, Khufu's son, and the smallest was Menkaure's, a later and lesser successor. Khufu's pyramid towered above me at four hundred and fifty-one feet.

Contrary to what people think, most of the pyramid builders hadn't been slaves but had been free Egyptian citizens who'd toiled for love of their pharaohs and their gods. They ate bread and garlic, drank beer, wore mustaches and had generally died in their thirties from cancer, accidents and parasitic diseases. It didn't sound like that great of a job to me.

Looking at the massive stones that formed the pyramids, it was hard to imagine that the people of those ancient times had been small compared to today's humans. Between four and a half to five and a half feet being the average, even for men. I would have been considered a very tall woman at five foot eight. The people's sun-weathered skin had been different hues, from a dark ivory to cinnamon brown and their eyes a soft amber to deep ebony. Very fair skin and green or certain shades of blue eyes would have been rare and looked upon with mistrust.

Most of the common people wouldn't have been able to read or write.

The pyramids aged beneath the sun, waves of heat churned around them under the cyan skies. It didn't rain much in this part of Egypt and I sure could have used a gentle rain to cool me down. The heat was the worst I've ever experienced and I knew it could get worse.

A lone, dark bird flew above me and circled. To the Egyptians it would be considered a bad omen. A string of balking camels, led by a turbaned old man, trudged their way past a group of chattering tourists and ventured out into the desert. I watched the shaggy beasts until they plodded past our colony of tents, my home these last few weeks, and became a line of dots on the horizon.

Catching sight of the tents reminded me of the joys of tent living.

But, truth was, I was beginning to feel comfortable behind the flaps of my canvas house. It was cozy, even if it didn't have running water or a bathroom. Water came in plastic containers and the bathroom was a bucket. Odd thing was, living in a tent made me feel closer to the ghosts of the ancient people who'd once lived out on the sand in tents as well.

My eyes flicked back to the far away pyramids. There were always tourists around them. Oohing and aahing. Climbing. Taking pictures. Like ants everywhere. Oh, if only those stones could talk. The things they'd seen over the millennia: the lovers who'd met beside the huge structures or walked, kissed and wept tears in their shadows and the history that happened all around them.

I was woolgathering again. I couldn't seem to help myself. Since I'd arrived I kept hearing ghosts whispering on the breezes around me of long ago passions and secrets. I couldn't make out what they were saying but they haunted me. My fingers dropped to sift through the glittering grains at my feet. Something about this place, the humid heat, the exotic smells in the air and the warmth of the sand brought out the long dormant erotic side of me. I hadn't felt so alive, so sensual, since I'd been a teenager. My skin tingled it was so strong at times.

Egypt had cast a spell over me. That was it. It was bringing the woman I could have been, but never had been, out in me. I found myself staring at the men in the excavating crew and having the oddest thoughts. What did their tanned bodies really look like underneath those desert robes and headdresses and, at the end of the day, I mused, which ones were going home to please wives or lovers under the Egyptian moon.

Kathryn Meyer Griffith

The past. Love. Yearning. Passion. I saw them everywhere.

Sunstroke. That's what Jehan Es-senusi, head of the digging crew and Egyptian guide, would say if I told him about it. Sunstroke was his answer to all temporary lapses of sanity or unexplained illnesses. He was forever warning me not to stay out in the midday sun too long.

Makes a person crazy, he'd say, making air circles by his ear with dirty fingers.

Not that I'd confess to Jehan the peculiar ideas and emotions I'd been having. I didn't like him, though educated and knowledgeable, he'd been recommended and hired by the University to lead the workers. Otherwise, he was an enigma and made me uneasy with his emaciated tallness, sooty beard and mustache and shifty black as obsidian eyes. He had this way of scrutinizing me, as if he was a vulture and I was a mouse.

He never looked me in the eyes and never said much, or got too close, but there was something unsettling about the man. I couldn't stand his hungry eyes on me.

I would have gotten rid of him, but Jehan was the best guide around. He knew everyone and everything. When we needed something, information or permits, he could get them when no one else could. The men never questioned him.

They seemed afraid of him.

I sat there, remembering late last night. I'd been dressed for bed in a long nightgown and robe, making notes on the day's discoveries, as I usually did, and heard someone outside my tent. I went out to check and it wasn't hard to mistake Jehan's tall, bony figure limping away.

I called his name into the darkness but he didn't answer. The experience left me with an uncomfortable suspicion that Jehan had been spying on me. It hadn't been the first time, either. Someone had been shadowing me for weeks, yet I could never catch anyone at it. So it'd been Jehan all along.

In the corner of my vision, he was glaring at me. In his robe-like *galabia,* decorated with arcane amulets, flapping in the wind around his tall form, and in his *tarha,* the standard desert headdress, he reminded me of a sinister desert sheik out of some romance novel, or out of another time. His face's expression, except for the cunning lift to his mouth, cold and his blue eyes gleamed in the sun. Why is he looking at me like that?

Sayed, the other workmen's supervisor, happened to be standing next to me. Glancing at Jehan and then over at me he whispered, *"Es-senusi ...evil man. I* caution you, missy, to stay away from him. He uses *bad* magic. See the blue amulet around his neck?"

I nodded at the clean-shaven Egyptian beside me. Sayed and I had become friends the last few weeks. He was fair to the workers he supervised and respectful of me.

Educated in America, Sayed's English was almost as good as mine and he'd been invaluable to me, with the local people and their customs; knowing the workmen as well as he did. From the beginning, Sayed treated me as if I were his daughter. He'd always had a smile, a genuine twinkle in his brown eyes, and advice for me, whether I wanted it or not. He was a good man and I trusted him. So when he talked, I listened.

I never got the sense he was holding anything back from me or lying like Jehan.

"Why don't you and the men like him?" I'd wanted to ask that for weeks.

Sayed stared at me, amusement in his gaze. "You, with all your learning and knowledge of our country and the ancient times, really don't know?"

I had a hunch, but for a twenty-first century woman, it was too crazy to speak out loud.

"Jehan Es-senusi is a sorcerer," Sayed finally gave in and spoke the words I couldn't.

"There's no such thing." Though the bizarre notion had occurred to me many times over the last few weeks. The way the man acted, the amulets and tattoos; the fear in the other workmen's eyes when Jehan was around. "I don't believe in sorcerers or magic." I laughed uneasily. "You're a smart man, Sayed, don't tell me you believe in all that mumbo jumbo?"

"Believe?" Sayed's eyebrows rose and there wasn't humor in his gaze anymore. "I know for a fact that he practices dark magic. He's a follower of the secret ancient priests of Amon. It was said that they had the power to reach out and snatch a person's soul from their breast or take their magic from them. They were very powerful.

"And everyone knows Jehan has the evil eye, so no one dares cross him."

I knew the legends about the infamous priests of

Egyptian Heart

Amon. In their time, they'd defied the very pharaoh, Akhenaton, whose family we were searching for beneath the sands. The story was that the priests had used their magic to bring Akhenaton down because he worshipped one god and forced Egypt and his people to worship the same—and the land of many gods and the priests of Amon had fought him bitterly over it.

Sayed claimed that Jehan was a disciple of those same priests, which would explain a lot of things. But I, a modern woman who didn't believe in the supernatural, dark or otherwise, still couldn't accept the magic part.

"If it's true, Jehan is some powerful magical priest and everyone knows it," I said, "why is he here working on a University dig and taking orders from me? Shouldn't he be off leading a chant in a temple somewhere?"

Sayed smiled at me with his slightly crooked front teeth and replied thoughtfully, "No one knows why he's here. He's a wealthy man and doesn't need money. There must be some other reason. I'm looking for it. In time I'll find out and then I'll tell you.

"Yet for now, heed my warning and stay away from him, Miss Owen. I see him watching you. Perhaps he sees something in you...some magic...he desires for himself. He's waiting for something. Something to happen."

Shaking my head at the absurdity of the conversation, but knowing enough not to mock an Egyptian's religious beliefs, I replied, "Thank you for the warning, Sayed. I'll stay away from him if I can."

I didn't mention Jehan's spying on me. I was a big girl and could take care of myself, there was no use dragging Sayed into it. I'd just stay clear of Jehan. Which wouldn't be difficult since I had pretty much avoided him from the beginning.

My eyes wandered to the spot where Jehan had been skulking. He was no longer there.

"Please wear this." Sayed handed me a silver chain with a tiny blue amulet of an Egyptian beetle, a sacred scarab, carved into its face. A delicate thing that got lost in the palm of my hand.

"It's a gift from me to you. It's very old," he explained. "I've been saving it for years and now I know it was meant for you. It'll protect you from evil magic and harm, from Jehan, and lead you to the one you are fated to love. Wear it always. Never take it off."

As if it had been dug up from an ancient tomb, the necklace appeared authentically old. If it were real, it would be priceless. I wanted to ask where he'd gotten it. I wanted to give it back. The problem was: to not accept a gift from an Egyptian was considered rude, so I smiled at the man who was becoming my friend and slipped the chain around my neck. He'd given it from his heart and I wasn't about to hurt his feelings. I needed his goodwill and guidance too much.

The necklace had a cold feel against my skin and when I put my hand up to caress it, an eerie vibration tingled through my fingers. I had a strange premonition at that moment that this necklace was more than it seemed to be. Then I chided myself for

Egyptian Heart

becoming as superstitious as the Egyptian peasants I worked with every day.

"Never take it off," Sayed repeated, as if he really wanted me to remember that.

"I won't." It was the least I could do when he'd given me such a lovely gift.

With another smile, Sayed strolled away. "I need to get back to the digging site now. I think we're close to discovering what we're looking for. I will come for you if it is so."

"I'll be waiting," my voice trailed behind him as he vanished around the tents in the direction of where we'd been digging the last three and a half weeks.

I knew I should be following him. I needed to be digging, too. Instead, I lingered there in the sunlight and stroked the scarab hanging from my neck. For some reason, touching it brought me comfort. I studied it and wondered where it had come from and who had worn it before me. A peasant or some ancient Egyptian princess? If only I knew.

Nothing happened that day or for a few days after that. I worked at the site and heeded Sayed's warning to stay away from Jehan; though he continued to follow me around and stare at me from a distance, he never bothered me.

Then we unearthed the first of the burial chambers, a series of rich tombs surrounded by a huge common graveyard where slaves and laborers were buried. As the days went by and we kept digging, we eventually discovered the sprawling dead city beneath the sands just about where the

scrolls had said it would be.
    And everything changed.

Chapter Two

The University was ecstatic and allowed me to hire more workers so the digging could progress faster and more antiquities could be uncovered and catalogued.

A week later on a bright, hot morning we broke through into an antechamber of an unusual tomb. Not the one I'd actually been searching for, yet a significant discovery in its own right. According to the hieroglyphs on the walls, it belonged to someone who'd once been very important. Intrigued and excited, I couldn't get enough of the tomb or the past that it represented and I spent both my days and my nights below ground, examining, tagging and sketching pictures of what we'd found. I wore a mask across my mouth and nose for a while to protect me from any deadly mold but soon, finding it was safe, took it off.

The archaic ambience of the chamber of the dead was where I wanted to be more than any other place I'd ever known in my life. It was as if the tomb drew me to it. As if there was something or someone there that had once meant something to me. So strange. I felt as if I belonged there, in the ruins of a mummy's crypt in the center of a long dead city. The strength of my emotions confused me, but I figured it was the excitement of being in a real tomb.

The find, though not the tomb I'd been looking for, is still everything I'd hoped it would be, I e-mailed my mother that week. I had my wireless Internet laptop computer with me and extra batteries if I couldn't find a place to plug in. If I could find a signal. Mom and I e-mailed every couple of days. She kept me up to date on the home front and I kept her up to date on my progress. Then she piggybacked the e-mails to the rest of the family so everyone knew what I was up to. Mom said some of them read like history lessons, but she didn't mind. She liked history. I guess I couldn't stop teaching, even now.

Mom, today we found the tomb's Book of the Dead *and I began deciphering it. Remember, I told you about how* The Book of the Dead *is the story of that tomb inhabitant's life and death? This tomb belongs to a man they'd called Ramose Nakh-Min. As written in his* Book of the Dead, *he'd been of high rank and was the "overseer" of chariots" and "messenger to foreign lands" under the great pharaoh Akhenaton and his queen, Nefertiti. Three thousand four hundred years ago! So, not the tomb I was looking for, yet it's close and a fantastic find.*

Though Akhenaton was pharaoh, the real powers behind the throne, the commander of Akhenaton's armies, Haremhab, and the Priests of Amon schemed to dethrone him because, more a priest than a warrior, he was unpopular and didn't want to fight Egypt's enemies.

Egyptian Heart

When the Hittites, barbaric border enemies of Egypt, attacked, Akhenaton prayed to his one god for help instead of leading his armies against the invaders. He set his queen, Nefertiti, aside for one of their daughters and Haremhab and the Priests rose against him. Strange thing is, no one ever found Nefertiti and her daughters' tombs. History doesn't know what happened to them.

But Ramose Nakh-Min served Akhenaton and his queen to the end, whatever that end was. Maybe this is why Ramose's tomb is here with the lesser graves. As his pharaoh, he'd also died in great disfavor. Fantastic, huh, Mom? Got to go. Talk to you tomorrow. P. S. Give Snowball a hug for me and tell her I miss her. I miss all of you.

And the more I translated the writings in Ramose's *Book of the Dead* and the hieroglyphs on the walls of the tomb, the more I came to believe that the man in the sarcophagus had truly followed his pharaoh into disgrace. This was not the tomb of a public hero. This was a tomb that had been meant to be lost.

The days flew by and I was filled with the urgent need to learn as much of Ramose Nakh-Min as I could. But it wasn't easy. The tomb, once we'd discovered the sarcophagus, had begun to creep out the workmen. I don't know why. I couldn't get any of them to talk to me about it.

Mom, from the moment we broke the seals and crossed the threshold of Ramose's tomb the workers have been behaving curiously. At first they hesitantly entered and worked in the main burial chamber, though they were skittish and frightened, but when we found Ramose's mummy it became worse.

They crowd in the passageways and spout gibberish of dark magic being strong in the tomb, and now they refuse to go anywhere near Ramose's sarcophagus. I knew these were superstitious people but I had no idea they'd go this far.

Sayed says they're just spooked. Black magic has an aura, he says, and they can see it.

Nonsense. I don't know what I'm going to do. Most of the workers have walked out and left us. I'm continuing now with a small crew of men who respect and follow Sayed. The university has promised to find me more men. Until then, I'm pretty much alone here.

Just as curious, we haven't seen Jehan in days. I've told you about him…the guy I disliked who was following me everywhere?

I'd written my mother that I considered the whole dark magic thing ludicrous, but even I felt an eeriness as I stood in the dusty and lantern lit chamber beside the gilded sarcophagus with my dirty hands on it. It was all so familiar… the tomb and the man in it. There was a humming in the air; a feeling that it'd just been sealed up minutes ago, not eons. It was unnatural.

And the feelings had grown stronger with every day I spent exploring the tomb. I became obsessed with the remnants of the occupant's life. Who he'd been and what he'd done all those millennia ago. And suddenly the other necropolis—the reason I'd come to Egypt in the first place—didn't matter as much to me. Neither did the outside world or my

Egyptian Heart

old life back in the States. I forgot all else. My world closed in on itself until there was only the tomb. I hated to leave it. Going back to my tent at night to sleep or to e-mail my mother, family or friends, or writing in my journal, was too much time away.

Mom, sorry I haven't been e-mailing you as much lately, but I've been so busy. The cataloging of the tomb is going well. Sayed says that tomorrow we'll have new workers coming in to help. About time. I almost hate to share the tomb. It's been nice having it to myself.

I quit keying in words, got up and gazed through the open tent flap into the night. I thought I'd heard something or someone outside the tent. I was in my pink nightgown and robe that modestly covered everything but was made of silk edged in white and blue lace. I'd worked all day in the tomb and, exhausted, was going to get some sleep and be up at dawn to go at it again.

Yet I lingered and listened to the whispering outside on the wind, the compelling words in my ear, in my heart, urging me to listen to what they said: *come to the tomb. Come to the tomb...right now!*

Dizzy for a moment, I blinked and found myself in the tomb, standing beside Ramose's sarcophagus. Someone had lit a lantern. At least there was light.

"How did I get in here?" I rubbed my eyes and shook my head. "I must be dreaming, that's it. But this is so real." I squeezed my eyes shut. Maybe if I kept them closed long enough I'd wake up.

But, eyes shut or not, I could feel I was still in

the tomb. I could smell the dirt, the dust and the mold. I could feel the slight heat from the burning of the lantern.

Opening my eyes, I was alone and, yes, in the tomb. The workmen who hadn't run off were asleep out on the desert in their tents. My trembling fingers brushed across the golden engraving on the sarcophagus. By the length of the coffin I believed the mummy must have been a tall man for his time. I'd only been able to decode a small part of the surface inscriptions so far and I'd been eagerly anticipating being able to finally lift the massive lid and see what we'd find underneath.

No matter the mystery of how I'd gotten into the tomb in the middle of the night without remembering it—perhaps I'd sleepwalked. I had been working awfully hard the last few days. Exhaustion could do funny things to a mind. I had to get back to my tent. I wasn't dressed to meet people and sleep was what I needed…look…I was hallucinating. Grabbing a lantern, I turned to leave as shadows danced on the stone walls. Murmurs and rustlings drifted on the stale air and as I moved I glimpsed an object, a link or two of shiny silver I'd not seen before, sparkling on the lower base of the catafalque. Curiosity got the best of me.

I stooped down, reached out and pulled at the fragment of chain and a miniature compartment at the base of the sarcophagus was revealed. With my fingernails I pried open the tiny drawer and yanked its contents out into the light probably for the first time in thousands of years.

It was almost an identical match to the amulet

Egyptian Heart

hanging around my neck. The one Sayed had given me weeks ago. In the lamplight, I compared the two necklaces and they were the same. Almost. A luminescence had begun to emanate from the sarcophagus's necklace. It was *glowing.*

I didn't have time to think about why the scarab had turned into a lightning bug before I heard someone move behind me. I swung around, the shimmering amulet in my hands.

"Jehan, what are you doing here?" I was startled and couldn't hide it. He'd disappeared weeks ago and no one had seen him since. Now he just appears out of nowhere?

"Miss Owen," the thin man in the blue robes greeted me, moving closer. "What are you doing here alone in the middle of the night?" His eyes glistened in the lantern's pale illumination and he was out of breath as if he'd been running.

"I was just going back to my tent." I didn't feel I had to explain anything. I had to leave and get away from him. Those ferret eyes of his and that knowing smile made me uneasy and I pulled my robe tighter around myself.

"You found it." He was looking at the necklace in my hand with a greedy expression.

Then I knew what he'd wanted all along, why he'd hired on at the dig and why he'd been shadowing me.

"Found what?" I played dumb as my hand closed around the necklace. Whatever I had in my hand, I realized, was unique, special and priceless. And Jehan wanted it badly. I inched towards the entrance.

Jehan moved along with me and cornered me in.

I remembered what Sayed had confided about Jehan. *He has much magic but he wants more.* I didn't have any magic, didn't believe in magic and I was tired of playing games. I only wanted to return to my nice private tent and get some sleep. "What do you really want, Jehan?"

"What you have in your hand and the special talents you have."

"What are you talking about? What talents?" I glared at him. My look must have unsettled him a little because he stepped back, but never took his eyes off me.

He seemed surprised. "You really don't know, do you?"

"Know what?"

He sighed as if he didn't believe me. "You possess great power and you do not even know it." His voice was a husky rasp as his fingers reached out, stopping inches from my arm as if he were afraid to touch me. "Haven't you felt the difference since you came here to Egypt? She releases it. Feeds on it. Do you not feel it?" His eyes bore into mine. Trying to hypnotize me. Fat chance.

"I don't know what you're talking about." But, in a way, I did. Egypt had done something to me. There was something happening. I just didn't know what it was yet.

"Ramose," Jehan went on, gesturing at the stone coffin, "has been dust and worms for thousands of years, but what you are exists now. You, special one, with your fair skin and hair...those magical eyes...own powers that coupled with mine, would make us almost indestructible."

"I'm not interested."

"You should be. There are things in this world you cannot comprehend trying to harm you and events that will happen that you cannot stop. Come with me, be with me and I will teach you, protect you."

"No." All I had to do was look in Jehan's eyes and I knew him for what he really was. He was ruthless, selfish and cruel. There was no way I would ever join forces with a man such as he.

Besides, I had the feeling he was hiding something from me. That he meant me harm.

My palm where I clutched the antique amulet was beginning to burn. I glanced down and the radiance, stronger than ever, was seeping out between my fingers and growing brighter.

Jehan's ravenous eyes were on what I had in my hand and I knew it was the amulet that he coveted beyond anything. I wasn't going to let him have it, not until I learned its secrets. I didn't trust him and my mistrust served me well.

I was prepared when he threw himself at me and tried to take the amulet. We fell to the ground and wrestled for it. Feeling the scarab between my fingers I raked it down along his face. He cried out and pushed me violently away from him. There were scratches and blood on his left cheek and anger in his eyes.

He tried to snatch the amulet again and I shoved him with my feet, using a self-defense move I'd been taught in my karate classes; he stumbled away from me across the chamber landing against the wall in a murky corner.

And that's when it happened.

I'd unintentionally put my hand up to my neck, the two amulets touched and a light filled the dark tomb, blocking out everything else for a moment. I shut my eyes and the world spun. It was a good thing I was already on the floor.

When I opened my eyes again, Jehan was gone. The tomb was gone. My first surge of relief that I'd escaped the full confrontation turned slowly into confusion at my new predicament.

I was alone out in the middle of the night desert under a huge, shining moon, sitting in the cool sand.

There'd been no moon tonight that I could recall.

There was nothing in my hand and the necklace I wore pulsated brightly around my neck as the other one had been doing. Then the incandescence faded and the scarab grew dark. The thought that the two necklaces had merged together occurred to me and was as quickly dismissed. Solid objects didn't merge into other objects. But I didn't have time to fret about it because I had other problems.

I rose to my feet and slowly twirled in a circle. *Where was I?*

The distant pyramids were silhouetted against the moon, but there was nothing else around me. No tents. No people. No dusty SUVs. There weren't the far off lights of Cairo on the horizon or the lights of the communities that usually nestled up along the base of the pyramids. Lights I had always been able to see from our camp.

At night the desert could get cold and I was

shivering in my silk nightgown and robe as the wind pulled and pushed at me, my loose hair blowing. I didn't have a lantern but was grateful for the moonlight and wondered why I felt so strange. Why did even the air around me smell and taste differently—and why was there a full moon when there should have been no moon?

Then I heard the distant voices of people, many people, flowing on the night breeze. And they didn't sound happy. They were screaming and shouting. Horses nickered and metal clashed against metal.

Not knowing what else to do, I headed towards the commotion through the moonlight, my arms snug around my shivering body. I kept looking for our tents. For anything that would tell me I was where I should have been. The more time went by the more fearful I was becoming. All I could think of was to keep moving and walking.

Maybe this was a nightmare and I'd wake up soon.

I trudged through the sand for what seemed like forever, tracking the clandestine noises. At times, sure the people were over the next moonlit dune and at other times the sounds were so dim that I thought it was all my imagination.

Coming to the top of a hill I gazed down in amazement at the scene before me. It was some sort of village of closely packed and primitive looking mud and stone buildings laid out in a rambling pattern. I didn't know there was a village out here. I'd never heard of there being one. But I could smell cooking fires and food and could see flickering dots of light in the distance that looked like torches. And the shouting had begun again.

I was tired and freezing. The desert could get cold at night. But working in the tomb the last few weeks nonstop, not getting much sleep, and now this bizarre night adventure still didn't keep me from running towards the promised warmth of humanity and lights. They'd have a phone I could borrow and I could call someone at the dig, Sayed perhaps, to come get me.

There was no one in the village. It was a ghost town. I knocked on doors but no one answered. One door stood open and I peeked inside. Everything was empty and dark. I could smell food in the air, feel the warmth as if fires had recently been snuffed out, as if the people had just left.

Advancing through the darkened alleyways and inspecting the settlement in the moonlight I thought of what I'd seen so far. Everything seemed so *old.* So poor. There were no signs of electricity, telephone wires, cars, or modern conveniences. No signs of the twenty-first century. I knew there were backward places like this in Egypt. But this village bothered me. Something wasn't right.

Beyond the outskirts, the yelling had resumed. The noises were louder this time so I headed out of the village in their direction. I had to find people and help. I needed a ride into the nearest city to find out what had happened to my camp.

Within minutes I came across hysterical people running past me.

"Wait!" I cried, trying to catch up with them and get their attention. But they were terrified animals stampeding around me in the dark and I

couldn't stop them long enough to ask questions. "Why are you running away like this...what's wrong?"

I caught a shadowy child in my arms. A girl. "What's happening?"

She began speaking a fast-tongued gibberish I couldn't understand. I didn't speak Egyptian, though I'd picked up a couple of words here and there at the camp, but it didn't sound like any dialect I'd ever heard. I couldn't make sense of it.

"Slow down, please don't talk so fast." I felt a burning at my throat and glanced down to see my necklace was shining again. It lasted only for a moment.

And slowly the girl's words began to be understandable.

"Run...*run!* Ramose's soldiers have come to take us back," the girl groaned. "They will surely beat or kill us if they catch us."

Beat or kill? "No one," I reassured the girl, "is going to hurt you."

"Ha! Escaped slaves, when found, are *always* beaten," the girl hissed before she wrenched free of my grasp and merged back into the crowd of rushing people.

Slaves? "I'm not a slave! No one's a slave these days," I yelled to the empty air. The girl, as most of the stampeding people, had left me behind.

Then bellowing men on horseback were bearing down on me and, as were the rest of the escapees, I had no choice but to move and get out of their way. I heard the crack of the whip long before I felt its sting on my back. I screamed, thinking: *how could I feel pain if I was in some hind of a wacky nightmare?*

Maybe, my mind tried to grasp at a sane explanation, I'd gotten caught in the middle of an action scene for an old Egyptian movie and they didn't know I had wandered in by accident? But I didn't see any cameras or lights. Didn't you need camera and lights to make a movie? It didn't make any difference, there by mistake or not, barefoot or not; I was running for my life. I scrambled after the others.

The horsemen—who looked like soldiers, though it was hard to see details in the moonlight—were rounding us up like stray cows. I peered back once or twice. They not only had whips, but spears. Spears?

The whole time I raced around trying to evade the soldiers, my thoughts were going crazy. I could have sworn that girl had said the men behind us were *Ramose's* soldiers. Was it a coincidence that Ramose was the same name as the name on the sarcophagus in the tomb we'd found? I didn't want to think about that.

The girl had said they were slaves…in the twenty-first century? I guess it could be possible that modern day Egypt still had slaves. I remembered seeing a movie about the global slave trade. So slavery, mostly for sex, still existed. But the sex trade abducted children and young women and there were old men and old women in the group fleeing the riders. Yet, I couldn't ignore the other strange things I'd seen and experienced. There was no doubt in my mind that something was very wrong.

My thoughts scattered when I heard another horse and rider breathing down my neck and the bite of another whip. The pain exploded through my arm and it took all my courage not to cry out again.

If this was a dream then it was way too real.

I tumbled to the ground to dodge the horse's hooves, muffling my howls of outrage, then quickly jumped to my feet and darted another way.

I forgot everything but escaping the men on the horses, whoever they were. Avoiding the whips and capture, nothing else mattered. But there was no place to run or hide out on the moonlit desert. The light was bright enough to see objects as large as people and there was no getting away. Some of us, still free, doubled back to the village but that didn't work, either.

I'd seen the men on horseback up close. They *were* soldiers dressed in armor and leather as they might have been in ancient times. I recognized the costumes. Their sharp faces had been so angry as they'd glared down at us and their mastership of their mounts and their weapons had been professional. These were real soldiers, it came to me, not actors.

This was no dream. This was no movie. Somehow *this was real.*

As hard as I tried to get away, within minutes, I was corralled in with the others and herded like chattel across the desert. I was ready to collapse. I'd been run to the ground so many times, had been jostled, hit and prodded along until I no longer felt human.

I wanted to rest; crumple to the sand and sleep. I wanted a blanket. I was so cold. Food and water, I was so thirsty and hungry. I wanted to scream and swing at the soldiers, tell them that they'd made a big mistake and I wasn't any slave, didn't belong there, but I wasn't that foolish, to call more attention to myself than my unusual appearance already had.

I was blond and light skinned while the others were darker skinned Egyptians. I wore a silk robe and nightgown when the others were dressed in what seemed like rags of rough linen. I already stuck out like a lemon among a pile of walnuts.

No I wasn't that foolish.

I tried to figure out a way to escape.

The soldiers marched us, a ragtag bunch of crying women, children and a few old ones, numbering around twenty or so, onward through the night. They never let us slow down or rest; whipping the ones who lagged behind or fell to the sand.

I couldn't help but overhear, and understand, what little conversation went on among the prisoners and found myself more confused and frightened with every step.

We should not have run away…they will kill us now for sure. I am an old man, I can no longer work in the fields or cut the stones…they will work us to death. I will die…what will they do to my children, they are so young…better we die here out on the sands than return to that house.

My fellow prisoners didn't seem like people from my time. This didn't seem like my time. My

Egyptian Heart

fingers brushed across the amulet at my neck. What happened to the other one that had been in my hand in the tomb? And why did the one Sayed gave me glow at times? I had to place my hand over it often or someone would have seen the strange light. It was a good thing sudden warmth always preceded the glowing. It gave me time to cover it.

I suspected the necklaces had something to do with my present predicament and thought I knew what that was but, somehow, I couldn't get my scholar's mind around it. It was too preposterous. *There's only one necklace now. The two became one. It sent me back to the past and it's allowing me to understand these people's language; they to understand mine. But why?*

Nah. Crazy, crazy.

My mind shut down every time someone spoke of the punishments that awaited us. This wasn't happening, I kept telling myself. Some malignant vapor in Ramose's tomb has made me delirious and is causing me to hallucinate all of this. Soon I'll wake up. I wished it'd hurry up.

As dawn began to take over the darkness we arrived at the high wooden gates of what appeared to be a large compound. All of us were hustled into a courtyard, down a path and shoved into a low to the ground building of large uneven stone blocks. We were locked in.

There were no windows and only a faint light that snuck in between the gaps of the stones. I could hardly see the person next to me. The air was stale and dusty and there were no bathroom breaks. When we had to go we did it in a corner that everyone avoided. I could smell the others and thought they could all use a bath. I guess I didn't smell so good, either. Fear and physical exertion made a sour sweat.

"When will they give us food and water?" I asked a young woman who was sniffling and wiping tears off her grimy face. She protectively clutched a small boy asleep in her arms.

"Ha! When they feel like it. If at all. The last batch of slaves put in here was left to starve. That was their punishment." The woman leaned against the wall and stared into space, resigned to whatever was to happen.

Others were weeping or praying or had already fallen asleep. I wondered if I slept if I'd wake up in the tomb, in my own tent or in my own bed in my cozy Boston apartment with Snowball curled up beside me. The snow would be dancing against the windows and I'd be snuggled under clean blankets on my soft bed. I could get up, shower and have sweet hot coffee and warm cinnamon buns with butter for breakfast. I'd call my mother and tell her about the awful nightmare I'd had, about going back in time and being mistaken for a runaway slave. She'd laugh and tell me my imagination was running away again. I was always dreaming.

Oh, please, please let this be a dream.

I crawled into an inky corner and huddling on the dirt floor, fell into a fitful sleep. My body and mind too tired to work anymore. If I were truly blessed I'd wake up somewhere else and I didn't even care where. Just not where I was.

Chapter Three

I'd finished a second cinnamon bun and was eating fresh cool strawberries with whipped cream. The coffee was hot and strong, the way I liked it and I was feeding Snowball tiny bits of pastry. She had a real sweet tooth for a cat. She even loved a lick or two of chocolate, though I didn't give her much of that because it was bad for her.

So it was with a violent start that I awoke from that beautiful fantasy of breakfast and my cuddly pet to find myself still locked in a prison with smelly strangers I felt so much pity for. Most of them were barely skeletons and some of them were sick. Someone's coughing had awakened me. Oh, for a medical kit and some water. A big bottle of cough medicine. I wanted to help them but there was nothing I could do, I'd never felt so helpless. I didn't like it.

Rubbing my puffy eyes, I had no idea how long I'd been out but I knew I was in the same mess I had fallen asleep in a hostile twilight zone and clad only in my torn and dirty nightclothes, my hair one long tangled mass on my head. Something skittered across my scalp and I scratched at it. Fleas, just what I needed.

I dragged fingers through my hair, then spit on them and wiped my face using the edge of my robe to dry it off. I tried to straighten myself up a little. I was glad my robe had a zipper down the front, which kept it closed over my flimsier nightgown, at least my body was covered.

I must look a sight. There were scratches on my arms and legs and blood encrusted slashes where the whips had gotten to me. My whole body ached, throbbed or hurt. What with the hunger and thirst, I was in misery. My body wasn't used to such unkind treatment.

The sun must be up outside because I could see more around me than when I'd fallen asleep. Though my nightclothes were a mess, I looked around and noticed that I was better off than most of the others. They were wearing less, barely enough rags to cover themselves, than I. The children were all but naked.

In comparison, my outfit was modest, but way out of place. I caught a few of them staring at me as if I'd just been dropped off a spaceship.

I was locked up in a strange land, though I was sure—or almost sure—that once I actually talked to someone and explained who I was and how I'd gotten here, that they'd lead me to a phone or give me a ride into a nearby city where I could call. Easy.

I ignored completely the nagging little voice in my head that kept reminding me that I wasn't in my own time anymore. I rehearsed what I'd say in my head over and over. I was in denial but still told myself to try and not use contractions when talking to anyone here. Ancient Egyptians probably never used contractions. Oh boy.

Rubbing my fingers over my necklace, I thought what a story I'd have to e-mail Mom when I got back to camp. She'd never believe it. Heck, I didn't believe it.

I tried speaking with a gray-headed woman propped against the wall beside me. "Hello ma'am, are you awake? Can I ask you a few questions?"

In the dimness, I could see the woman peering at me. She made a clicking noise in her throat and asked slyly, "Who are you? I have never seen you before."

"Maggie Owen." I put my hand out to shake but the old lady shied back from it as if I had the plague. "I'm a professor at Boston University here on a college grant for the summer. I'm just a visitor." I didn't feel like going into much more than that because the woman behaved as if she wasn't all there and I wasn't sure she understood what I was saying. It must be the fear. She was shivering and mumbling to herself. Poor thing. What was she so afraid of? I wanted to put my arms around her but I knew she wouldn't allow that. She was frightened of me, too. "What do they call you?"

Her look was unfriendly but she answered anyway. "What do you want to know?" She hadn't given me her name.

"Where are we?" Simple enough.

"You do not know where you are?"

"No. All I know is that I was rounded up with you and the others and brought here. I am not a slave. I don't belong here." Oops, contraction.

Watch that.

I thought the woman was going to laugh at me, but she didn't.

Her voice grew low and serious and unexpectedly sympathetic. "We are slaves in the house of Ramose Nakh-Min, great warrior and General Haremhab's most trusted commander."

She stopped and I stretched out a hand to touch her shoulder. "Slaves?"

There must have been something in my manner that softened her because then she really began to talk. "Ramose is a fair master, but he has been away from his home for a long time, fighting for the general and our pharaoh in foreign lands. Some of us thought he would never return, that he was dead, and his guards were abusing us. They beat one of us to death, one too many, so some of us fled in fear of our lives.

"We fashioned a home out on the desert and we were happy." The woman released a weary sigh. "Then Ramose, who is not dead, returned and sent his soldiers to fetch us back.

"Now we will be harshly punished."

"And what pharaoh would you be speaking of?"

She looked at me with surprise on her dirty face. "Why, the great Akhenaton."

I didn't know what to say for my mind was numb. It was one thing to think I was in the ancient past, it was another to have it confirmed with words. What she'd told me couldn't be true. *It couldn't be.* Ramose Nakh-Min was a mummy in a tomb underneath the Egyptian sands, far from the shadows of the Great Pyramids. And Haremhab and

Egyptian Heart

Akhenaton had been dead for over three thousand years.

"How many children does Pharaoh have now?" I needed to know.

"Five daughters. He had six but his favorite, Meketaten, died a year past. Not one son."

Her voice settled to a whisper and she leaned close to my face. Her eyes were full of fright as if just talking about the living god would put her on his radar. "He is truly a cursed man, our pharaoh. That is what he gets for forsaking our gods. He has no sons to follow him." Apparently she didn't care much for Pharaoh. Since she was a mistreated slave, I imagine she wouldn't. Then as if she'd already said too much, she turned away and fell silent. Slaves were used to keeping their resentment to themselves. No matter what I did or said she wouldn't say another thing.

Unfortunately, it gave me a chance to reflect on my situation. Most of Akhenaton's reign had been a dreadful time for Egypt. So much infighting and intrigue as Haremhab and Pharaoh's army plotted to overthrow Pharaoh and the Hittites threatened the borders of Egypt. I knew the country would soon plunge into strife and war. Dark days. Not a good time for visiting ancient Egypt or to be in Ramose's household.

You can't fool yourself any longer, Maggie, you've been thrown back to another time in the distant past. No, that couldn't be right. I was in Egypt, in the year *2007,* not 1350-something B.C.

I decided that it didn't make much difference. I was in a bad fix no matter what. I must keep my head. Think. Prepare. And it kept me from dwelling on that whole time traveling conundrum. It was giving me a worse headache than I already had.

I should try to escape. When the door opened I could make a run for it. But where? On the other side of the gates was an endless burning, waterless desert. I didn't know where I was, or where I could run to be safe. I had no car, food or water and no shoes. The hot sand of day would burn my feet and my fair skin.

Or I could wait until someone opened the door and try to explain that I didn't belong there, wasn't a slave and that I needed to speak with their superior. But I'd dealt with our guards already on the trek there and knew I wouldn't find any understanding with them.

I scooted around, peeked out between the crevices, and examined my surroundings. Outside people were bustling about in archaic dress scurrying from place to place. The look of the household was like something out of a movie on ancient Egypt. It was amazing.

There were animals. I could hear camels bellowing and birds squawking and people giving orders or others muttering among themselves; hawkers at the gates sold their wares. The heavenly aroma of freshly baked bread and summer flowers wafted on the air to torture me. I could see the heat dancing over everything. Men on horseback rode by dressed in ancient Egyptian clothes or leather armor. If I wasn't in early Egypt or dreaming, then my delusion was beautifully detailed. Oh boy.

I slid down against the wall and closed my eyes,

trying not to lose what was left of my mental health, trying not to weep. My stomach growled incessantly.

I would have done anything for a sip of water and a couple of Ding Dongs or a large orange or apple. I was so thirsty and hungry. I should have eaten that ham sandwich sitting on the table in my tent last night. I should have eaten that bag of Fritos. But I'd been too busy writing my day's report and e-mailing. I smiled in that dark place. I never did finish Mom's e-mail the night before and never turned off the computer.

Oh, well. One dead computer battery. And those things aren't cheap, either.

The door to our prison opened and light flooded in. Soldiers, the same kind that had rounded us up last night, began to drag or shove us out into the blazing sunlight. I clutched my arms around my body and forced my legs to move.

The heat hit me with the force of a fist. The sun was a huge glittering ball above us and the air was thick with undulating waves of heat and pesky insects. It had to be over a hundred degrees in the shade. Not that there was any shade. I put my hands above my eyes until they adjusted to the sunlight and I began seeing what was around me. Then I didn't want to.

The soldiers, three of them, paraded us around the trampled down dirt of the courtyard. They pushed and goaded us as if we were evil criminals they'd caught sneaking out of prison. They began demanding names and firing questions at us one at a time. I was far back in line.

Amidst the interrogations, I found myself gawking around like a tourist in Disneyland. Off to my right stood a magnificent alabaster palace shining bone-white in the sun, surrounded by elaborate gardens and shrubbery.

We weren't on the desert anymore, but on the edge of it. I could see sparse green grass and the blue sparkle of water—oh, that water looked so good—beside the palace, a pond and stunted trees.

Our guards were busy with one of the other slaves so I turned to the elderly woman I'd talked to before, cowering behind me. "Do you know whose palace that is?" I pointed a finger at the white monstrosity.

"Lord Ramose's, of course. Do you know nothing, silly one?" In the light of day the old woman looked used up, shrunken, her leathery face a mask of wrinkles. Her hair was dull and thin and her brown eyes glittered with panic when she lifted them from staring at the ground. She could have been as young as thirty or as old as fifty. I couldn't tell.

She had her hands gripped so hard around my arm, I was afraid she'd cut off my circulation. Like most of the slaves, her teeth were bad and she was covered in unhealed wounds. The life of a runaway slave seemed to be hard on a person's health. I felt sorry for her, but then I felt sorry for all of us, me included. The guards had whips and weren't afraid to use them at the slightest provocation.

"You mean Ramose Nakh-Min, who is loyal to Pharaoh Akhenaton?" I wanted to see if the woman was as crazy this morning as she'd been last night.

Egyptian Heart

"Who else? We are here at his household and, as I told you, we are his slaves. Soon to be dead ones, by the looks on their faces." She cocked her head at the soldiers and there was hopelessness in her expression. "Ramose's soldiers have shown no mercy and have no pity. The best we can pray for is no torture and a quick death."

"It will be all right," I comforted her, patting her bony shoulder. "No one is going to hurt you. I will not let them."

The look on her face as she tilted it towards me was disbelieving. "You are crazier than I thought, young one. They *kill* slaves who do what we have done and you are as doomed as we are. And you are telling *me* not to worry?

"Though," she squinted at me in the glaring sun, "you are dressed strangely...and you look strange with that ivory skin and pale hair and those eyes of yours, the color of grass. You may not belong here as you said but you are going to be punished the same as me. You cannot save yourself, much less me." She hid her eyes against my arm and began to weep silently.

I patted her shoulders, trying to comfort her, and took in the other detainees. I was different. I towered above the other women and most of the men, with white skin, light hair and *jinn* eyes. The others were short and shades of brown.

Worse, the soldiers had noticed me. One was coming towards me. *Uh, oh.* I laid my hand over the amulet and waited. I had the feeling that he wasn't coming to help me.

"Who are you?" the soldier demanded. He was

as tall as I, and dressed in a short dusty kilt, a leather jerkin, leather boots, and a sword and dagger were strapped to his thick waist. His beard was ebony, his skin a pale shade of nutmeg and his eyes distrustful. He looked at me as if I were an apparition or a demon.

The old woman had disengaged herself from me and stepped away to stand behind someone else. Smart woman. The soldier was still looking at me.

All I could do was appeal to his humanity. "Hello, perhaps you could help me? I do not belong here. My name is Maggie Owen. I am an archaeologist working at the Boston University dig a distance past the Khufu Pyramid." I put my hand out for the man to shake, but he merely looked at it and then at me and stepped back.

My nervous uncertainty and hunger made me start babbling and I couldn't stop myself. "I am here by mistake. I am not a slave. I was lost out on the desert last night when you rounded all these people up. I am so glad to finally be able to talk to you about this. But, truth is, I guess I need to speak to your superior."

"Enough! Be silent! You never speak unless asked to speak," the soldier hissed at me, reached out with the butt of his whip and slammed it against my head. I went down like a dropped sack of rocks.

I must have blacked out because when I came to other soldiers were standing around staring at and talking about me as if I weren't lying on the ground in front of them, my mouth hanging open and my hands cradling my head. Blood trickled down along the side of my face and was sticky between my

Egyptian Heart

fingers. I couldn't believe what had happened, my mind was still trying to process it, but I wasn't talking without permission again anytime soon.

One of the soldiers stooped down and grabbed a handful of my blond hair. I tugged the strands away from his dirty grasp and hoped it wouldn't make him angry. It didn't. He seemed confused and then I saw the apprehension in his eyes.

"She is different from the others," he said, *"look at what she is wearing and look at her skin, so fair and untouched by the sun...her hair...as silver and pale as moonlight—"*

"Could be she is a house slave," replied another heavier soldier with darker skin than the others, *"she is dressed in nightclothes."*

"A bed slave is more like it," another one snickered.

I didn't know whether to be offended or frightened. *This wasn't happening.*

"Please?" I tried again, dragging myself to my feet and trembling. My head hurt and the world was spinning but I had to make them understand I wasn't one of the runaway slaves. My life might depend on it. This time my voice was more respectful. "There has been a mistake. I am an American, not anyone's slave. Can I please see the man in charge—"

The whip handle lashed out again and would have caught me on the other side of my head if I hadn't jumped quickly out of its way. I lost my balance and went down. I stayed. The ground seemed safer. This time I couldn't stop the tears and looked up through them at the three men tormenting me as if I was some circus freak.

Had they no heart or compassion and why couldn't I get through to them?

One of the soldiers prodded at me with his boot and I recognized lust in his eyes. Shuddering, I realized I could be beaten, raped or worse. Anything they wanted to do to me, they could do. This wasn't my time, my safe world and there was no one to help me. To them I was a no one, a worthless slave.

"Look at those eyes of hers...that evil green color," the man who'd pushed me with his boot said.

The soldier with the whip breathed, *"Jinn eyes."*

"She came from the desert," another soldier offered. *"She could be one. I have heard men talk of the desert jinns that appear out of nowhere to bewitch and destroy a man."*

"We should kill her now before she puts a spell on us."

"No, she belongs to Ramose."

"She is trouble."

"Jinn eyes. She is evil."

And all three soldiers edged away from me. One of them had short hacked off hair. The worst haircut I'd ever seen. Another looked as if he barely had an IQ of eighty. They would have made perfect B grade movie extras. If I wouldn't have been so scared, bleeding from cuts, bruises and now a knock on the head, I would have laughed at the whole scene. It was so absurd.

But, I have to get away from them and here, was all I could think of.

Then one of them stepped forward and kicked me. Oh, how the twenty-first century woman in me wanted to hit back, fight back but I knew that would be signing my death warrant. I had to be smart and play along until I saw my chance to escape. I hadn't cried out but slowly pulled myself to my feet and faced them, making sure I kept my evil jinn eyes lowered.

To the soldier that had kicked me, I spoke in a soft deferential voice, "I am no slave. Please, allow me to speak to Lord Ramose." I'd heard him say the name, heard the old woman say it, so the man who was their master and lived in the palace behind me had to be a man called Ramose. Not the same Ramose in the tomb I'd found, but another one.

"Please?"

I heard the slaves around me gasp. A slave didn't ask to speak to the lord and master. The other slaves had moved away from me. Their faces were full of disbelief and pity, but none stirred to help me. No one would risk his or her own skin for a suspicious stranger. Most had lived as sheep for so long and knew if they wanted to stay alive they must remain sheep. I felt no anger at them for that decision. I couldn't blame them. They'd been starved and beaten all their lives and they feared the whip and the sword. They were right to.

The soldier with the whip grabbed my arms roughly and shook me. His face near mine was ugly with belligerence and his lips were a tight line. "You ask too much, talk too much, slave, and need to be taught a lesson. Perhaps my men and I shall enjoy you in front of these others and then beat you and you will finally learn your place."

It didn't make any difference that I'd warned myself not to agitate them or that I needed to do as they told me to stay alive. When the soldier's dirty hands tried to rip my robe off, survival instinct taking over, I kicked him as I'd been taught. Hard. Then I jerked away and ran. No way was I going to let some sadistic brute rape and beat me. I'd die first.

The other men began yelling while the slaves were stone.

The soldier tackled me from behind and we tumbled into the dirt. I had to use the defensive moves I'd learned in my old life regardless of what he'd think of them. I had to protect myself.

The soldier hurting me wouldn't stop unless I stopped him and I was fighting for my dignity, my body, as well as my life. I had no choice but to fight and fight I did. I thought I was holding my own against him when abruptly, he ceased attacking me.

A heavy silence had suddenly settled over everything. No one spoke and nothing stirred. I was on the ground and glanced up to see frozen slaves and soldiers alike. For a moment I thought something weird had occurred again.

My hand went to the amulet, but it was cold and dark. It wasn't that.

Then the soldiers bowed and everyone else fell face forward in the dirt. Ground statues. Hadn't I also seen this before in those old movies?

No one moved, except for one man.

He was high up on an exquisite snow-colored horse, peering down at me, curious interest mingling with disapproval in his eyes. Even on horseback he seemed larger than the other men. His skin was lighter than any of the others around but yet not as pale as mine.

He wasn't dressed in rags or soldier's gear as everyone else, he was clad in rich gold cloth which shone in the sun like the jewels around his neck, arms and fingers.

There was color smudged above his jet-black eyes. His hair, covered in a swatch of dazzling white pleated linen, what I could see of it, was just as dark. The saddle he sat on and his bridle sparkled with silver. It was easy to see he was a person of wealth and power.

He was the most beautiful man I had ever seen. But his eyes, full of intelligent arrogance, were flat and cold. Here was a man who cared for little.

The man on horseback flicked his hand in a bored and curt gesture, in the sun the rings twinkling with tiny rainbows.

"What is going on here?"

The soldier with the whip spoke up, careful to keep his eyes down. "I am teaching this slave a lesson, my lord. She is one of the ones who ran away and we rounded up last night on the desert. She defied me."

"It looked to me she was teaching you a lesson," the man on the white horse chuckled softly as he stared down at me. "She is quite a fighter for a woman and a slave at that. It also looked to me as if she was defending herself."

"She was inciting a riot among the other slaves," the soldier, embarrassed, blustered. "I had to put her in her place, my lord."

I couldn't help it, my mouth opened and the words spilled out, "I did not incite any riot! I told him that I don't belong here...I'm a professor at Boston University...an American...not a slave...lost out on the desert...this is all a terrible mistake." Oops, contractions again.

The lord on horseback barely smiled. I thought I caught a glimmer of surprise and a shadow of compassion in those ebony eyes. But the emotions sped by like quicksilver leaving unreadable slate blackness in their place and I couldn't be sure I'd seen them or not.

This was a man used to hiding his feelings and hiding them well.

I sensed the dread, the awe, the others around me had of this man. The slaves' bodies were quivering. I was the only one standing with my head up, watching.

My dirty, tear-streaked face lifted upwards so I could feel the breeze and meet the horseman's gaze. Our eyes met and locked for a long moment. I wouldn't back down, wouldn't drop my eyes. Instead of angering him it seemed to further amuse him.

He had to be Lord Ramose, owner of the house and surrounding lands and, if my worst fears were found to be true, the Ramose next in power over all the Egyptian armies behind the mighty General Haremhab. It was an explanation for the way everyone was behaving.

If he were that Ramose then the last time I had seen him he'd been a mummy in a gold box in a

Egyptian Heart

dusty tomb.

I don't know exactly when I'd accepted that I was truly back in the past, as unbelievable as it seemed, and in Akhenaton and Nefertiti's time. I guess it'd been somewhere between when I'd been slapped up side of the head with the whip handle and when I'd looked up into Ramose's black eyes. I was in ancient Egypt. And as crazy as it sounded, I believed it.

"So you say you are not a slave?" Ramose scrutinized me. "I admit you do not act a slave and you are not dressed as a slave. Do all *Americans* dress in such fine fabrics?"

"Some, my lord." I wiped the tears from my face, knowing that I'd said too much without thinking already. Whatever I told them would be a risk.

I had to be extremely careful. As a suspicious stranger in this time and among these people, I couldn't let them know I was from the future. I couldn't let them know I knew things that I shouldn't be able to know. I'd be branded as touched in the head at best or an evil demon at worst. The ancient Egyptians had been as afraid of the supernatural as they'd be of aliens. I'd be dead, either way. I couldn't act too smart. I had to try to fit in. Not stand out.

I was afraid I'd blown that already.

"And I am not a slave, my lord. I am a stranger in your land. I was lost in the desert. I have come to you for help and instead your soldiers brutalize me.

"Is that how a guest to Egypt is treated? I'm throwing myself on your mercy. You are a man of honor, I have heard, and I know you will help me. *I am not one of your slaves.* Please believe me."

The soldier with the whip was practically snarling at me, his face furious. If Ramose rode away now without offering me his protection I was a dead woman.

Ramose reined his horse towards me and came close enough to reach down and almost touch my face. He studied me. I couldn't read his expression and had no idea what he was thinking.

"You are on my land and so you belong to me," he said softly. "But no one shall raise a hand to you again. You will be taken care of and your wounds treated—until I decide what is to be done with you."

He turned to the soldier who'd mistreated me and ordered him. "Have her brought to the house, Captain. Find a woman to clean her up and attend to her wounds. And, I warn you, do not lay another hand on her or I will have *you* whipped."

"Yes, Lord Ramose." The soldier hid his disappointment expertly, knowing his life depended on it.

Then Ramose spurred his horse and without another glance at me rode away through the gates, his guard and entourage falling in behind him.

I stood there speechless, aware that I was now out of the boat and into the rushing rapids. I watched Ramose ride away and worried what was going to happen to me now. At least I was safe from the Captain and his men and safe from gang rape and further beatings. Thank God.

The relief over that realization, and the aching of my battered body, was so great that an unforeseen weakness washed over me and I think I fainted.

The world blinked away and I entered a welcome emptiness. My last thought was: Please God let me wake up now and be home in Boston when I do. Please God. The thought of a warm bath, a plate of good-old American food and a cushy bed made me smile.

Chapter Four

I didn't remember anything after that until I awoke in a clean bed. More like a stone ledge covered in softness, straw under a blanket. I could smell the fresh straw. No pillow. Most of the ancient Egyptians slept like that.

The soldiers must have brought me here.

Ooh, my head hurt.

The amulet. Finding it around my neck, I sighed in relief. Maybe it wasn't magic at all and it hadn't been what had sent me here. Maybe it didn't have the power to send me back home. But maybe it was and maybe it did so I didn't dare lose it.

The room I was in was tiny and undecorated. Simplistically neat. White painted walls. Nothing in it but the bed, a small wooden table, a bench along one wall and a chamber pot in one corner. There was a big bowl on the table, some kind of a mug and a smaller incense bowl with a low flickering wick that gave the room a soft shimmering light source. There was a window high above me, the panes an inky mirror. It was night.

The pain in my back and head as I sat up reminded me of where I was. Still in ancient Egypt and in Ramose's possession. It hadn't been a dream.

Egyptian Heart

I weakly lowered myself onto the bed again. A sense of helplessness and desperation threatened to bring tears but I fought them off. Tears wouldn't help me now.

Things were sure different for a woman in these times. I couldn't count on my usual qualities and accomplishments to get me through. To keep myself safe I was going to have to pretend to be something I wasn't. I was going to have to be clever. And something I wasn't used to being. Quiet.

Someone had taken care of me. Tended to the cuts on my back and arms and the two broken lumps on my head. Wiped the blood from my skin and given me a sponge bath. I wasn't wearing my silk nightgown, but a plain beige sheath like gown. Nice soft material. My hair had been brushed. Except for not knowing what was to happen next, the pain, the gnawing hunger and thirst, I felt better.

My stomach growled and my eyes settled on the bowl on the table.

I slowly sat up again and came to my feet. A few dizzy steps and I reached it. There were fruit, dates and these funny looking pears, in the bowl. A piece of hard bread. There was cool water in the mug. I ate and drank so fast I nearly choked. It was the best food I'd ever eaten.

When the woman shuffled into the room I had just finished. I felt as if I'd gotten my brain back. My thoughts were clear for the first time in a long time. Food and drink cured a lot of things.

She was a small, scrawny woman with a shaved head and skin a light milk chocolate brown. When she shyly lifted her head I saw her eyes were almost the same shade. It seemed they took up most of her face, they were so large. And sad. Her other features were small and delicate.

She wore a coarse white robe and was holding a bundle of what appeared to be more clothes in her skinny arms. I thought, in those initial moments of our first meeting, that she was a nondescript diminutive being who blended into almost any background. She quivered like a thin twig in the wind. She was frightened of me.

I winked at her. I couldn't help it. What a pathetic creature. I wondered what had made her like that.

"I am Nefrure, a lowly slave in the house of mighty Lord Ramose." Not a smile, not a flicker of an eyelid. Nothing.

I smiled, trying to put her at ease. "I am Maggie Owen." It was best not to say too much and to talk as they did. No more contractions or slang from my time. I had to be careful how I talked for as long as I was here. "Are you the one I have to thank for cleaning me up and caring for my wounds?"

"Yes." Nefrure's expression unchanging. "Do not thank me. You have become my responsibility for as long as you are here. I did what I was told to do." Her eyes were downcast but I received an echo of the real woman underneath.

I thought I caught something, perhaps pride or defiance, lurking in the way she held herself. Held her head. Maybe I was wrong, but I didn't think so. She wasn't as simple as she tried to make people believe.

For as long as I was here. I touched the scarab

Egyptian Heart

at my neck. If it had somehow brought me here to this time...would it send me back? When? And why was I here? Was there something I was supposed to do or had this trip just been a wild mistake of fate? I remembered Jehan had wanted the amulet I'd found in the base of the sarcophagus. Wanted it badly.

It came to me then. Something Jehan had said in the tomb.

You have great power and you do not even know it. Egypt releases it. Feeds on it.

What had he meant? That I had some magical power I knew nothing of? And what did the amulets—both of them—have to do with it?

Sayed had given me the first necklace, so did that mean he'd known something about the magic it controlled as well? It was all too confusing. And Nefrure was watching me and waiting for a response like some tiny curious bird.

"Thank you for everything, Nefrure," I said to the slave. "For the care and the food. I was probably a mess when they brought me here."

Nefrure merely nodded, but there was a peculiar look in her eyes as she met mine.

"How long have I been here?" I'd wandered back to the bed, sat down and leaned against the wall, weary. Time travel, starvation, forced marches and beatings took it out of a person.

"You slept all day and a night."

That surprised me. "That long, huh?"

Once more Nefrure bobbed her head. She didn't seem to have much use for words. I was beginning to understand why. Everyone had his or her place in this time, and a slave's was at the bottom. Silent and subservient. That way they didn't call attention to themselves, which, I had learned the hard way, was not a good thing.

Was I a slave as well? I didn't really know. Yet. I looked up at the window and then met Nefrure's probing gaze. "I cannot just walk out and leave, can I? From this room?"

"Leave here?" The slave seemed baffled at the question. "Why would you want to?"

Nefrure came closer and set her bundle down on the edge of the bed. She was standing over me. I had the sense that under the slave's aloof exterior was a lonely woman.

"I do not belong here."

"Where would you go? All that is beyond is the desert."

"I know."

"And Ramose has made you my responsibility. If you were to leave I would be blamed. I would take the punishment meant for you."

That changed everything. I couldn't run away knowing Nefrure would be harmed for it.

"Then I am trapped. I cannot leave. Even if I could." I couldn't help the sadness that crept into my voice. What was I going to do now? I didn't have an answer.

The other woman's face softened. "Why are you thinking of escaping? You are smiled upon by the gods. Ramose has noticed you and taken an interest in you. It is a great honor. Any woman here would kill for such an honor.

"Ramose is a rich and powerful man. He has the favor of Pharaoh and owns all the lands you see here and more.

"Most importantly, he has not yet taken a lesser or greater wife. They say he has been looking for a special woman all his life and with this one only will he share his wealth, power and dreams."

In these times the ruling classes had lesser and greater wives. The lesser wife was more like a favorite concubine who was rewarded for her long term service while the greater wife was a true wife and was given all the authority of the household, second to her husband. She was the one that usually held his heart.

If Ramose had no lesser or greater wives, it explained the envy in Nefrure's eyes when she looked at me.

Smiled on by the gods, my foot. Ramose had merely taken a fancy to me. Heaven knew what kind. "I just want to go home, Nefrure." Yet as I said it, I knew I wasn't speaking the complete truth.

I wanted to go home because I was unsure of what was going to happen; what Ramose wanted. I'd lost the freedom and power to choose my own way. In a strange land with strange customs. I was scared.

I wanted to go home, but the opportunity to live among these people and learn first hand about their lives and times was a gift I couldn't turn away from. It was as if my life, all the hard work, the learning, the studying and the isolation had led up to this. For whatever reason I'd been thrown back in time, my scholar's brain pleaded, I should use it and soak everything in.

If I could stay away from whips, brutal soldiers,

stay out of danger and if I ever got back home…what a book it would make. What knowledge I could return with.

In a way, wasn't it worth the risks? Perhaps.

If the amulet was what had sent me here and *if* it allowed me to remain for a while. For all I knew, at any moment, it could decide to hurtle me back to my time in another burst of light.

I had the feeling that going back or staying wasn't my choice. It was up to fate. As long as I was here, though, I'd better have a good cover story to explain my ignorance of all the things I was going to be ignorant of. I shut my eyes, inhaled slowly and said, "I was brought here against my will, Nefrure. From a far distant place, yet that is all I remember. In the horror of being abducted I have forgotten almost everything about my land, my past life, except what I have told you and a few other memories. Memories that come and go.

"That is why I am unhappy. I am a stranger in this land and do not know its ways or customs. I do not know who I am. I am frightened."

That explanation would let me get away with a lot, I figured. You can't learn everything about an ancient people from books and old scrolls. Not every little detail. Being human, I was bound to make mistakes. Pretending not to remember would be a good, all inclusive excuse.

A small hand covered mine and when I opened my eyes Nefrure was perched on the bed looking at me and her expression was finally one of sympathy.

"I understand. I, too, was stolen away from my home and family in Nubia and forced into this life of slavery. I know how the heart breaks when you can no longer see the faces of those you love. When freedom is taken from you.

"I am sorry, Mistress. Sorry this has happened as well to you. But you have nothing to fear or worry over. Ramose has given orders for you to be treated as a royal guest. You are—"

"I know, smiled on by the gods. And call me Maggie. I am no one's mistress. Treat me as an equal, Nefrure. Because that is what you are. Let us be friends, please."

The slave hesitated, as if she wasn't sure of me yet, or that I was truly a friend, then said, "Maggie is an unusual name. I have never heard it before." The slave pronounced my name with an accent, which made it sound different somehow.

"It is short for Margaret. Everyone calls me Maggie."

Nefrure gave me a small smile. I was finally gaining her trust.

"What will happen to me now?" I thought it was time I found out.

Nefrure seemed taken aback. One of her thin eyebrows arched upwards. "If you are fortunate the master will have you for his bed or, if you are truly blessed, he will take you for his first lesser wife. As soon as you are well, that is. Lord Ramose is believed to be an honorable man and would not ask anything of you until you are completely yourself again. In that he is different from other Lords. It is said, he will not force a woman to his bed. Not that he needs to."

She added, "The salve I put on your wounds

will heal them quickly. Another day or two."

My mind had stopped taking in information at the words *the master will have you for his bed.* Not if I could help it.

Nefrure read my silence well. "There are far worse fates than going to a man's bed. You are lucky to be alive...Maggie. That soldier you angered is well known for beating slaves to death. He is a cruel man. He has tortured and killed many slaves for less than what I hear you did.

"And if you try to escape perhaps even Ramose's protection might be taken away." Nefrure was trying to warn me, help me in her own way.

What she was saying sank in and reminded me that I was in a dangerous position if I could be tortured or beaten to death for merely talking back or displeasing a man.

I must never forget that. Not for one second. I closed my eyes again. So tired.

"I cleaned and mended your nightclothes," Nefrure said. "An unusual garment. I have never seen anything like it. The material is unlike anything I have known before. The sewing of it. The delicate colors. That strange metal trim that travels down the center. What is this on the border?"

Half asleep I recalled that lace would be something Egyptians didn't have. Nor could they duplicate the subtle shade of pink the nightgown and robe were. "Lace," I replied with my eyes still shut, wondering how she'd gotten my nightgown off without using the zipper. Slipped it over my head most likely. What would she say if I showed her how the zipper worked? A faded smile. "Thank you for mending, cleaning and returning it."

Nefrure's voice was barely a whisper. "You must have been a very important woman in your land to own such fine clothes. It is a shame you cannot remember."

"Yes, a shame."

I heard Nefrure stand up and say, "You must get more sleep. You must get well. To be as healthy and pretty as you can be. They say Ramose can be very generous to a woman who pleases him.

"Tomorrow I will return to see how you are doing." Nefrure left quietly and I passed into sleep.

To dream of Ramose's tomb. I was lost deep in the burial chambers. My lantern kept getting dimmer and the shadows were closing in. Jehan was closing in. There were noises in the gloom. Growling and hissing. The ancient Egyptian gods were waiting to pounce on me the moment the light left.

They were hungry and mad at me for using their magic without permission or sacrifices.

Wazit, with her serpent head; Set, with his devilish face, pointed ears and forked tail and Osiris, God of the dead, with his mummified body.

Just when Sekhmet, lion-headed goddess of the desert, was about to devour me, I woke up. I was still in the small room with the white walls. Outside it was still ancient Egypt. Sunshine streamed in the windows, yet it was cool in the room.

I felt much better and stood up. No more dizziness. My headache was only a faint pounding behind my eyes. I gently ran my fingers over the lash cuts on my shoulders. They were healing nicely. Whatever medicine Nefrure had put on them was working.

She must have visited me again sometime during the night because there was more bread, fruit, a hunk of some kind of meat, a mug of wine and a pitcher of water on the small table.

I ate as much as I could and then explored. I wasn't surprised to find the door barred from the outside. I couldn't get out.

I am a prisoner, I thought wretchedly, as I watched the world go by through the window. I could see that my room was attached to the buildings that crowded up against Ramose's palace. Workers or slaves were scampering about everywhere, coming in and out of the main house. They seemed in a real hurry.

Sweet aromas of warm bread and sizzling meat lingered on the air. Was this just a normal day or was something big in the works? I didn't know. But my curiosity was engaged.

Nefrure returned later that day, as she'd promised.

"I have brought you clothes for tonight and face paint to make you presentable," she told me as she set a bundle of shiny cloth and a basket of what looked to be a collection of bottles, tiny pots, a knife, and other things on the table.

"Presentable for what?" I found myself smiling at her. There was more to this unimposing slave woman than she showed the world and if I became her friend,

perhaps I would learn what that was. She could

teach me so much of this world of hers.

I'd mulled it over since I woke that morning, feeling more like myself and able to better handle things, and had decided to look at this *visit* as an *adventure.* An invaluable way of gaining knowledge of these people and this time. As I'd thought before, this could make a heck of a story when I got back home.

"Ramose has asked to see you tonight. There is a celebration at the main house and I am here to help you dress for it. I thought that, being from another land, you may not know how to prepare for a feast."

"I do not." In fact, I did know a lot of how they dressed and what kind of jewelry and make-up the women had worn. I'd just never tried wearing any of it.

"Then, Mistress, I will make you beautiful."

"Not until I have a bath, friend, you will not." I smiled again. I was filthy. I could smell myself and I didn't smell pretty. It'd been over four days since water and soap had seen my body. I needed to submerge myself in scalding water. My hair was greasy and felt like it was full of teeny critters.

"A tub is on its way and hot water. I have perfumed soap for your body and your hair."

Nefrure was putting out the tiny pots of colored paints and dark kohl to outline my eyes with on the table, along with small bottles of what had to be perfume. The shiny cloth must be a garment for me to wear.

My eyes took everything in but I didn't want to touch a thing with my dirty hands.

A girl of around twelve, as close as I could guess, dragged in a large wooden tub. Dressed in a simple cotton robe, it hung on her skinny frame. Her eyes were a cocoa shade and so was her hair. Her skin, a sun-streaked brown, was darker than mine, but not as dark as Nefrure's.

The girl had bluish markings on one wrist and a blue shell amulet hanging from a string at her neck.

She observed me with a timid expression on her thin face. Either my skin, hair and eye color made her uneasy, or the gossip she'd already heard about Ramose and me did.

"What do they call you?" I asked the girl as she was leaving the room. She was a pretty thing, not much taller than four and a half feet. I towered over her she was so short.

"Ahhotpe, Mistress." Her eyes were on the floor, as if wary of me. Then she was gone.

"Ahhotpe is a good girl, Mistress," Nefrure spoke. "A hard worker and loyal."

"Is she your daughter?"

"No." Melancholy in her voice. "Yet she is like a daughter to me. I have seen her grow up and her family is as mine."

The girl returned with a large jar and then another and another. When she left for the last time there were five jars.

"Hot water. But not too hot." Nefrure busied herself pouring the contents of the jars into the tub.

I couldn't wait and, Nefrure there or not, I stripped off the garment I was wearing and slid in. It felt great to get clean.

I washed my hair twice and scrubbed my body,

except for my healing wounds, until it was red.

Nefrure gave me the gauzy white linen gown to put on. It fell softly to my feet and was tied up under my breasts with a golden belt. It was flimsy and revealed every line of my body. There were no underclothes. Egyptians rarely wore them because the summer climate was too warm. I felt as if I was half-naked. I was.

Nefrure sat me down at the table so she could do my hair and face. She didn't cut the length of my hair, which was past my shoulders, but trimmed it evenly and cut my bangs straight across. An Egyptian hairstyle I'd seen in endless books and tombs.

"Do I have to wear all this make-up?" I lifted a kohl pot.

"A woman does if she wants to be beautiful."

"Oh, well, can we tone it down a little?"

Nefrure gave me a strange look but nodded.

She'd outlined my eyes with the kohl and put emerald shadow above them to bring out the green. Dark pink color accentuated my lips. I could have been in a dream. Being fixed up like an Egyptian kewpie doll and going to a party with people that had been dead for thousands of years.

I was excited and terrified all at once. I wanted to go but I wasn't sure what Ramose was expecting of me. Information…friendship…subservience…sex…love?

It wasn't as if I'd left a husband or a boyfriend at home. I was a free woman. Well, free of love, that is. I loved no man.

And, not for the first time, I questioned if I were only sleeping and dreaming still in Ramose's dank tomb. Was this really happening?

As Nefrure prepared me for the gala I tried to draw her out. There were so many things I wanted to know. After a while, she dropped her guard and warmed to me for the first time and we really talked.

She told me she'd had a lover once, Henu, and had borne him three children, a girl and two boys. All sold away into slavery. She hadn't seen them since they were children. My interest in her and her life seemed to change her opinion. She was beginning to trust me.

When Nefrure finished, she took something from the basket wrapped in cloth and produced adornment for my hair and jewelry for my neck, arms and ears. Luckily, my ears were pierced, as were most Egyptians, and she was able to put long, dangly gold and beaded earrings on me the same hue as the dress. There were golden arm bracelets and something delicate and sparkling to circle the crown of my head and intertwine into the strands of hair.

I refused to take off my scarab amulet. "It is my protection against evil. I never take it off," I told Nefrure, and with a knowing glance, she said she understood.

When my transformation was done I stood up and spun around slowly. I was barefoot, but I felt like an Egyptian princess.

Me. Someone who usually dressed in plain black suits for work or blue jeans and a T-shirt for every day. Someone who rarely wore make-up. I had never cared before what I looked like.

Egyptian Heart

I wish I had a full-length mirror. I would love to see myself.

"Mistress, you are very lovely. You look like no other woman Ramose has ever known with that silver-white hair and snow skin...those green eyes of yours...he will be pleased." Nefrure spoke. "Ramose has asked you be brought to the main house as twilight becomes night. It is almost time."

"Is there to be many people at this gathering?" I was getting more nervous every second. I had to find a way to deal with Ramose and the other people of this time. Had to gain and keep control over my destiny. Be smarter than them.

I'd only met Ramose once for a few minutes and had no idea what kind of man he truly was. I hoped he was, at least, fair minded and nothing like that guard that had brutalized me that first morning.

Then again, it was Ramose who'd saved me. He must be a better man.

It was a shame that I hadn't had more time to decipher the hieroglyphs in Ramose's tomb and learn more about him and his place in history. Well, I was going to learn firsthand now.

"Many, many people. When Lord Ramose returned from Pharaoh's city days ago, he brought with him his friend and general, the great Haremhab. Lord Ramose is hosting this feast tonight in his honor.

"The household has been in turmoil, preparing, for the general goes nowhere without a large retinue and many of his soldiers. They have recently returned from a long campaign and are a rowdy bunch who have been out on the desert too long.

There will be much food, music and dancing girls."

The slave caught my hand and her voice lowered, "Be careful, Mistress. Terrible things happen at these revels when the men have had too much beer and honeyed wine. Watch out for yourself."

In answer, I picked up the sharp knife in its sheath that she'd used to cut my hair, tied it to my belt and hid it between the folds of my gown.

Nefrure's eyes widened. "You would not use that on Lord Ramose or any of his guests? You would be punished for even thinking of such a thing. I would be punished for the knowing of it."

"I will not use it unless I have to, I promise. And I would say you knew nothing of it if I did. Do not worry, you would be safe." I told myself I wouldn't use the knife at all. That carrying it with me was only to make me feel more secure.

The real truth was, I didn't know if I had it in me to cut another human being. I don't know what I was thinking.

"What is Lord Ramose like, Nefrure? What is it like being a slave in his household?"

"He is demanding, yet not cruel as many are. He is a better master than most. There is always enough food and a dry place to sleep. Not too many beatings—when the Master is here, that is. When he is away the soldiers do as they wish and they can be brutal. They delight in degrading and tormenting us. It has been much better since Lord Ramose returned. The beatings have stopped."

"I am glad to hear that." Then I had to dig. "What else is said of Lord Ramose?"

Egyptian Heart

Nefrure thought about that for a while and offered, "That he is a clever man. He reads, speaks many languages and admires wisdom and beauty. He is a famed warrior, and General Haremhab's most trusted commander, who has fought many battles in Pharaoh's name."

"And how does he treat women?"

"They say he has bedded many. Though he has taken no wives, he has many concubines. Makere is his favorite and has been for most of a year. She wants to be his wife so badly, but they say he has a heart of ice and that no woman has ever melted it. Not even Makere."

Then she murmured, "They say he waits for someone but that she has not come yet. He waits still and that is why he has never taken a wife."

I'd heard that before. "Who are *they?*"

"*Why* everyone."

"Ah, slave gossip."

I glanced at the darkening window and at Nefrure. The more I learned about Ramose the more nervous I was about facing him again. As if I had a choice since I'd been ordered to attend the night's festivities.

Let's see if a twenty-first century woman could outsmart an ancient Egyptian man.

"I guess it is time for me to go," I said and Nefrure led me from the room and out into the fading sunlight. It was hot but there was a breeze. The now waning full moon was riding up off the horizon.

I raised my face to the darkening skies to enjoy the breeze. It felt good to be outside again. The ambrosia of eucalyptus and fruit trees was heavy around me. The citrus smell of myrrh. Branches swished above my head and I could hear horses and camels communicating among themselves beyond the gates.

I could have sworn I heard a lion roaring far out on the desert and remembered that the Egypt of this time still had lions. Another reason why I couldn't escape out into the desert even if I was able to. Not to mention the cobras, scorpions and hyenas. I'd been lucky the other night not to have wandered into any of those dangerous predators.

I didn't feel like myself in all my exotic finery and make-up. The palace ahead of me was ablaze with torches. It seemed so alien. No electric lights, telephone lines or noisy cars.

For a moment I thought of my apartment back in Boston. All my comforts. I missed it and I missed my cat, Snowball. Would I ever see her again—or my family? I didn't know.

We walked under palm trees up to a door, and with a bowed head, Nefrure spoke respectfully to a guard. He took a torch from a bracket on the wall above him and lifted it high to get a good look at me. His contemptuous eyes took me in. "She *is* a beauty," he stated, touching my hair and flashing me a knowing grin. A little too friendly for me. I retreated a step.

"She is for Ramose. He has sent for her," Nefrure interceded quickly and the guard's expression changed to one of regret.

"Lucky man," I heard him grouse as I trailed the slave through the door and down torch lit halls of shining marble and granite, the stone cool on my bare feet. The flickering torches in their sconces lit our steps as we made our way.

I couldn't help but be impressed at the beauty and the opulence of Ramose's palace. Towering columns of white chiseled alabaster lined the passageways, announcing other chambers and rooms.

The walls were picture mosaics of multi-colored stones, carnelian, turquoise, lapis lazuli and obsidian; depicting palace life. Women and men conversing and loving together. Children running and playing around fowl-covered ponds. The pictures I'd seen over the years hadn't done the Egyptian artwork justice. I ran my fingers over the stones and felt the textures, drank in the vivid, fresh colors. Up close the paintings were stunning.

Ooh, I'd love to take some of these home with me.

Nefrure didn't bat an eye. She'd seen these halls most of her life and they didn't impress her. They belonged to the rich. Not for her or her kind.

The next hallway showed many Egyptian gods and goddesses. Obviously, Ramose, unlike his pharaoh, still honored more than the one god, Aton. There were marble statues of animals and people every few feet of our journey. All exquisite. I'd spent so many years looking at such statues in museums behind glass or in dusty books that it was astonishing to see them up close, to touch and stroke them.

Nefrure kept looking at me as if I were nuts. Touching and admiring everything like I'd never seen such things. I smiled at her. "They are just so beautiful. Ramose must be a very rich man."

"He is."

I could hear people laughing and talking and it grew louder with each step. My stomach twisted and I fought to keep from turning and running the other way. Was I really going to do this? Did I have to? Wasn't this just a dream?

We came to a large double door.

I looked at Nefrure, saw the caution in her eyes and knew, for her sake, I had to go in and face whatever was inside for me to face. She turned and placed a hand on my arm. "Please, whatever you do, do not displease any of them. Do not look them directly in their eyes. Do what they ask. They are bored and sometimes seek to hurt others on a whim for amusement. Please be careful Maggie."

The little slave's concern touched me. "I will be careful, Nefrure." Then seeing the fear in her and making the connection for the first time, I guessed. "What happened to your hair?"

Her fingers brushed the side of her bald head anxiously and her eyes were sad. "It was shaved off for displeasing one of them." She turned her head towards the voices and gave me a mocking smile.

"How did you displease them?"

"It was my fault. I brought the wrong food to the table and my hair was shaved off as a lesson, in front of everyone. They laughed and laughed as I cried. I am not to grow it back until the woman I offended says I may. I am not allowed to wear anything over my baldness. No scarves. No wigs. My hair was my pride, you understand. It was long, to my waist, black as a raven's wing. It was my only beauty. The woman knew this."

"I am so sorry, Nefrure." I took her hands in mine. She was shaking. "You are still beautiful. Your good heart shines through your eyes and makes you so."

Her look wrung my heart. It took so little to please her.

"So do not worry for me. I will be good and will not get you in any trouble. I will not attempt to run away." *Unless I can't help it,* I muttered to myself. "I promise."

I thought I saw tears in her eyes when she turned to leave. Drawing in a deep breath, I went through the doors.

Chapter Five

Though I should have just kept my head down as I entered the room, for the first few minutes, I couldn't stop myself and stared at the people in the massive banquet hall. Some were at lengthy tables, eating, gossiping and laughing; some were sprawled on the floor on bright pillows or on long low couches.

By the fine wigs, jewelry and clothes, they were the aristocrats of this time. By their posturing and condescending manner towards the slaves that waited on them, I could tell that they were haughty and full of themselves. Spoiled.

Dangerous then, to me—a powerless nobody in their midst.

There were scores of soldiers and most of them were already drunk.

I felt eyes on me from the moment I walked in and the whispers began. I must look so different from them with my blond hair and pale skin. Good fodder for more rumors.

I didn't know what to do or where to go and then there was young Ahhotpe taking my hand. She was dressed in fancier clothes than the last time I'd seen her and there were flowers in her hair but I recognized her. "I was sent to bring you to Lord Ramose," she volunteered and I gratefully followed her to the main table along the front of the room.

Remembering Nefrure's warning, I dropped my head and tried to take in the sights and people without actually meeting anyone else's eyes. Hard to do because there were men calling out to me, hooting and hollering, urging me to stop by their tables and talk to them. Yeah, sure. Talk.

Ahhotpe led me to Ramose and left. I looked up to meet the inquisitive eyes of a man dressed in a shirt of gold and a white kilt, an ornate linen headdress and, as most of the people around us, eye make-up. So much jewelry, he shone like the sun. He looked so different than the first time I'd seen him, I had to search his face to be sure it was the same man who'd rescued me from the soldier's whip. I wasn't, until he gave me that arrogant smile of his and spoke. Then I knew it was him.

"So the woman from the strange land cleans up well indeed. Have you been treated properly since first we met?"

This was going to be tricky. The room had hushed and everyone was watching Ramose and me. I felt like an actor in a play who didn't know their lines. Or the play. "Yes, my lord, I have been."

"I can see that you have. You look much better than the last time I saw you." His voice was husky. "Come sit by me and tell me more of your story and your home. How you came to be out wandering in the desert. My curiosity is great."

For a moment, I questioned if I was Ramose's slave or his guest. His manner towards me was friendly and courteous. Who was this man and why did he affect me the way he did? Whenever his eyes fell on me I couldn't take mine away. He mesmerized me. He said one thing, but I swore he was thinking, meaning, something else entirely.

I sat down on his left after room was made for me and that's when I noticed the woman on his right. She had caramel hued skin, high cheekbones accenting huge eyes that appeared to be some shade of blue, not the usual brown, and an ebony wig seeded with strands of gold and pearls. Her eyes were kohl ringed, her lips pouty and bright crimson, her face perfectly shaped. Her body, in her clinging blue silken gown, with full breasts and hips, was absolutely perfect. She was small compared to me. She couldn't have been over four foot eight or so. She was so beautiful. Next to her, I must look like a tall, pale ghost.

But there was something in the eyes, a hard cunningness that reminded me of a cobra. And there was an air of possessiveness when she looked at Ramose that told me she had to be Makere, his current concubine. Nefrure had spoken of her. Said she was sadistic to her servants and slaves. She thrashed them for the slightest misstep and sliced up their arms and legs to mar them for life. If a slave was too pretty or caught Ramose's eye, she'd scar their faces; make them ugly, so he'd never look at them again.

Makere was watching intently, and it made me uncomfortable.

There were other women around and they were all eavesdropping as well. I was the center of attention because Ramose was speaking with me.

"I was right, you were a rare jewel hiding beneath that layer of sand and dirt," he said. "The clean gown and trinkets do you much more justice than the shapeless nightclothes you had on when I first saw you."

I ignored the compliments and the interest in his eyes. Ramose was used to complaisant females falling over him, so I had to guard how I talked to him. Guard what I said. I could never forget where I was and when. I had to entertain him and teach him at the same time. Teach him that I was different. That I wasn't a slave or a whore to be bought for a night and then discarded.

"Thank you for sending me the clothes and the jewelry." I touched the cloth of my gown. "It is not me. The look, I mean. I feel overdressed. Like a kewpie doll." It'd slipped out before I realized I'd made a blunder. Already. So much for being guarded.

"Kewpie doll?" There was bewilderment in his voice as he repeated the words.

I figured I had to explain it. "Where I come from a kewpie doll is a prettily dressed up child's toy. Complete with painted face and fancy clothes. But thank you for sending me these garments and for helping me that day out in the courtyard."

"You are welcome." His hand moved towards me and his strong fingers stroked my hair. He leaned over and took my face into his hands. "I am a direct man. When I see something I desire, I take it. You can pay me back by coming to my bed tonight."

He was looking at me, but he still wasn't seeing me.

"My lord, I appreciate what you have done for me," I mouthed softly so he alone could hear, "but I would prefer not to. In my land, a woman has a choice of these things. And as I said before, I am not a slave, but a free woman. I will decide who I bed."

Ramose seemed startled by my rejection of him, my words; he pulled away and seemed to genuinely look at me for the first time. And see me.

"What strange ideas you have. Do all women behave as you where you come from?"

"Yes."

"The men allow it?" I could tell he was a little irritated but intrigued.

"Yes." I met his eyes and I caught the growing interest in their depths.

I also caught Makere glowering at me from behind Ramose.

"I was told," Ramose continued, "you do not recall much of your life before being found on the desert."

I liked the way he said *found*.

"That is true. I do not." I didn't like lying but there was no way I could sit there and tell this man that I was from the future. No way I could tell him or anyone there who I really was. Suicide would be easier.

"Then how do you know you were not a slave in your old life? How do you know what your life was like? Who you were?" Ramose picked up a piece of meat from his plate and handed it to me. Looked like chicken. Smelled like chicken.

"I remember some things," I replied, nibbling on the meat. A slave sidled up behind me and brought me a plate of my own food. I was hungry so I ate. It wasn't easy with Ramose studying me. Half the room slyly watching me.

I didn't dare glance at Makere again.

"You remember you are a professor at a Boston University and you are an American. Yet you do not remember how you got here?" Ramose's glance was sharp. He'd remembered most of what I'd said the first time he'd met me. Smart. I almost choked. I could have kicked myself for being so stupid and blurting all that stuff out that morning. But then that had been before I'd accepted I was truly back in the past.

I turned and forced myself to smile. "Yes, I am a teacher from America. And no, I do not remember how I got here."

A mouth of white teeth flashed at me. "I have never heard of this land *America.*"

"It is a far distant land. Over the waters." It was all I could think of at the moment.

"And you are an educated woman. You can read and write?"

"Yes," hesitantly. Good thing I could read and write, somewhat, ancient Egyptian.

"You are a respected woman in your land?"

"I am."

"You want to return?"

He had me there. I did want to go back but I wasn't sure how. Wasn't sure I ever could. "If I could, but I do not remember enough to do that, at this time. I would not know where to go or to whom." I tried to look sad. Lost. It wasn't hard.

"So, until you can remember, you are my guest for a while, living on my hospitality?"

I understood what he was getting at and annoyance flared up before I could stop it. It was my turn to lean over and say in a whisper to him, "I am and I am grateful. But that does not mean I have to pay you back by ending up in your bed tonight. Or any other night, for that matter, my lord."

Ramose laughed. "You have spirit, I will say that." His hand briefly caressed the side of my face, then pulled back. "Do you remember what they called you in this far distant land?"

I thought he was mocking me but replied sweetly anyway. "They called me Maggie."

He nodded. "Mag-gie. A pretty name.

"I am Ramose Nakh-Min. I own all this." He swept his hand around in a broad circle. "Everything and everyone." His meaning was clear.

Not me, I wanted to say, but held my tongue. Instead I gave him a begrudging smile. The beads in my hair tinkled and reminded me I was an Egyptian princess.

"Do you know you have the greenest eyes I have ever seen? Cat's eyes.

"And your hair," he murmured, twining his fingers in the strands, "is like soft moonlight. Your skin as pale as ivory. I have never beheld a woman like you."

There was something so charismatic about him that I had trouble remembering why I had to *not* obey him. He was so handsome, yet his face was the face of a dark angel you did not cross. Sharply contoured with a strong jaw, a nose arched and well formed, and the most beautiful dark eyes I'd ever seen, gleaming with wit and intelligence. His arms were muscled and his chest was broad and flat. His speech clear and educated. A knowing light glittered deep in his eyes. It spoke to me.

He was handsome, virile, attractive to women, and he knew it.

I'd never met a man like him in my whole life. It had to be the power.

There was music now in the center of the room and with all the people the noise level rose. I could barely hear what Ramose was saying. Then dancers—skimpily clad women in transparent gowns—glided out and started prancing around in front of Ramose, trying to get his attention. As he enjoyed the entertainment I clandestinely studied the people around us.

Sitting there with Ramose, Makere and the celebrating Egyptians, was for me, a scene right out of a much desired dream. It felt unreal. Dancing bejeweled women, singers, musicians and drunken revelers. Tables packed with exotic food and golden goblets of wine and beer. Drunken soldiers ogling me, and envious women gossiping about me. *Not an old movie.*

What would my stuffy colleagues back at the University say if they could see me now? Dressed like this in this setting? The thought almost made me laugh, but I kept it to myself. I wished that I had my drawing materials because I would have loved to sketch the gyrating dancers and the peacock guests. What a picture it would have made. Or I wished I had a camera. What would these people think of a digital or a video camera, I wondered.

Yeah, what I wanted was a snapshot of Makere.

If looks could kill. I'd never understood that phrase fully until I caught Makere's spiteful eyes on me. I had made an enemy and she wanted me to know it. Even though after his first interest in me, Ramose had cooled his attentions and had given his favorite most of his attention. Trying to make me jealous, I imagine.

Then again, Ramose wasn't stupid; could be he was aware that he was making her jealous and was cleverly distracting her. I was relieved. I didn't need Makere as an enemy. But what was Ramose up to and why was I still here at his feast if I'd turned him down?

To show me what I was missing, no doubt. To show me who was boss. I couldn't leave until he gave me permission. The feminist in me was rebelling, fuming inside of me, but the woman in me was flattered. For a while.

At times I would catch Ramose stealing looks at me, or he would say something in my ear or his hand would brush my skin. There was an overpowering physical attraction between the two of us that even I couldn't deny. It was as if I'd been sleeping all my life and was now waking. I had this bizarre urge to throw my arms around him and press my lips to his. Press up against him. I wanted him to touch me, hold me. Cherish me. It was the strangest thing.

Me? The woman who'd never needed anyone,

least of all a man? *Please.*

I fought it. There was no way I was going to start behaving like a loose woman on a first date. I had to remind myself who I was. Maggie Owen, educated college professor and liberated woman. I couldn't forget that I didn't belong here. My fingers grasped the amulet. It could hurl me back at any time.

I couldn't get involved with anyone here. Not anyone. Start something I couldn't finish.

But I'd never felt this way about a man and it unsettled me. Wrong time. Wrong place. Wrong man. Makere's man.

As if thinking of her made Makere respond, the other woman started a conversation with me. "So, lost woman from another land, what else can you do besides read and scribble? Can you sing or dance? Here, all Egyptian girls are taught to perform when they are children."

"No, I cannot do either." I could just imagine what Makere would say if I got up and did one of our modern American dances or sang one of the Beatle's tunes. And watching the Egyptian dancers slithering around the floor, I knew there was no way I could do their dances any justice. I was not graceful enough. Not uninhibited enough or nearly naked enough.

"You cannot dance?" Her voice sarcastic. "Oh, you are being too modest. Every woman can dance.

"So dance for us!" she commanded me.

I slid horrified eyes to Ramose and he shrugged. *This is between Makere and you,* it seemed to say.

"No." I didn't know if there was a title I should

be using for her. What did you call a lord's concubine? I didn't know. But I could tell she, having a short fuse, was getting angry.

Oh, oh.

"How dare you defy me." Makere stood up. "Dance!" Her pretty face turned ugly with her rage. This was a woman, I thought, who was used to getting her way all the time. She slapped her hand on the table. *"Dance."*

"No, thank you very much, I prefer not to."

Ramose's face was granite. I was on my own. I looked away, heart pounding, remembering what Nefrure had said about Makere's cruelty.

I had the feeling Ramose was waiting to see who had the strongest will. Makere or me.

Makere turned to Ramose and gave him her sweetest smile. "My love, make the new slave girl dance." She pressed her face close to his and ran her fingers along his neck. "Make her dance for us."

"Make her dance! Make her dance!" Other voices picked up the chant and soon half the room was demanding that I make a fool of myself. I was outnumbered and on the spot.

There was no way I was going to parade around in front of the whole hall shaking my booty. That was asking for trouble. Might as well stick a price tag on my butt. When I was trying so hard to stay under the radar. Sheesh.

Ramose did something that surprised me. In front of Makere, he took my hand and coaxed softly, "If I ask you to dance for us, would you?"

There was something in his voice that told me I had the right to choose and I did. "I beg your pardon, but no, my lord. As I said I do not know how to dance. Better it is left to the ones who are good at it." And at the last second I decided to appeal directly to him. "I wouldn't make you dance if you didn't know how. So please, do not make me dance *please?*"

"Then so be it. You do not have to dance."

I was so relieved, it almost didn't matter that Makere was furious. I guess she wasn't used to being challenged, and again I didn't dare meet her gaze. She'd turn me to stone for sure.

There was a commotion at the doors and a group of soldiers came shoving in, led by a heavyset man in soldier's leather and armor with uncovered head, sun-darkened skin, bushy eyebrows and a devilish mustache and beard. He was good looking in his own way, nearly as tall as me, not as tall as Ramose, but there was an attitude of brutish stubbornness to him and an air of absolute power clung to his muscled body.

Ramose stood and opened his arms to welcome the advancing man. "Ah, my friend General Haremhab! It is time you showed up. You have missed much of the entertainment, yet there is much left to see. The night is young. Come, sit by me."

The general strode up to us, threw his arms around Ramose in greeting, tossed a look my way, and then squeezed in between Ramose and I as his men sat themselves at a lower table.

I could tell the general had been drinking. He smelled like an opened beer can. Plates of food were brought for him and as he ate, like a pig; he conversed with Ramose on the latest military campaign but kept sending looks at me and Makere.

I didn't like the way his eyes raked up and down me as if I was a horse he was thinking of buying. He brushed up against me, while still conversing with Ramose, his eyes returning more often to me. They were the color of dry mud and his teeth were slightly rotten behind his curved lips.

"So, Ramose, who is this pale beauty you have seated me next to? A slave? Is she yours or a gift for me?"

It confounded but relieved me when Ramose responded, "No, Mag-gie Owen is not a slave. According to her, she belongs to no one. From a faraway land, she claims to be a woman of breeding and education who can read and write. My men found her wandering the desert, lost, a few nights ago and brought her here. Though the trauma of her experience has caused her to forget many things about her past. She is my guest here tonight."

I caught the gentle sarcasm in his eyes as he met my desperate look.

Haremhab had inched closer to me and put his brawny arm around my shoulders. "Well, if she is not yours, I claim her as spoils of war. She is the most beautiful woman here, Ramose, besides your lovely Makere, that is.

"But this one," the general peered at me with a drunken grin, "is unique. Look at her. Her hair, her skin. Eyes as green as new leaves. She is gorgeous and will warm my bed tonight. I thank you and Makere for having her here for me. Three months on the desert fighting Pharaoh's last war has made me hungry for a woman's soft company."

Egyptian Heart

"Perhaps I did not make it clear enough before," Ramose spoke carefully. "I claimed her before you arrived. She is mine and under my protection." I didn't like the way he was watching Haremhab or the way Makere was suddenly watching all three of us. Had I missed something?

A woman singing and playing some sort of lute had replaced the dancing girls. The song was ancient and haunting and an eerie backdrop for the drama unfolding with me as the main character.

"Ah, my friend, what matters a woman?" Haremhab exclaimed to Ramose. "Have we not shared many a one before battle? What a small thing to ask that we share this one. She will be returned to you when I am done. You know I have women waiting for me back in Amarna. I shall not need this one but for a night or two."

Haremhab tightened his grip on me and pulling me closer, laid his lips against my neck.

I shoved him away. "Don't do that!" Forgetting to speak like them. I knew I was in trouble. I knew Haremhab had more rank than Ramose. They were friends but the general had more power. If Haremhab wanted me, he would have me. I would be his conquest and there was nothing I could say about it. He was used to getting what he desired and again I couldn't believe this was happening to me. Like a lot of the things that had happened since my arrival here. I wanted to laugh, it was all so ludicrous.

Ironic, I thought, all these years I'd cherished and saved my virginity, for marriage to my one true love, to perhaps lose it like this...a toss up between two arrogant selfish men? It made little difference what I wanted. To them I was a play thing, not royal by birth, and therefore had little to say. I was at their mercy and I hated it.

"And she has spunk!" My resistance seemed to egg the general on. He grabbed my wrists and yanked me back to his side. "Fire. My kind of a woman. What a bed mate she will be!"

I saw the alarm in Ramose's eyes. So *he really does feel something?* Yet was he worried for me or was he worried for what he might himself lose? I wasn't sure.

Be careful. This time wasn't my time and their ways were not my ways. I was walking a tightrope and beneath me was a bed of lava.

"I am not here for you, my lord," I replied to Haremhab as respectfully but as strongly as I could, blocking his hands from touching places he shouldn't touch. "I know it is a great honor to be asked to your bed, and many women would want to be in my place, but I must graciously refuse it. For now. I am a virtuous woman and….am saving myself for my husband's bed."

He just stared at me uncomprehending, or not wanting to, then grabbed for me again.

I tried to put him off, stay out of his clutches. Wasn't easy. He'd had too much to drink and he was strong. I could barely fight off his advances.

What was it with these men…was sex all they thought about?

I caught Makere smirking at me and had the crazy idea that she'd somehow arranged this misunderstanding between Haremhab and me. I'd seen her whispering to one of her slave girls earlier, her painted eyes on me. Had she sent a message to Haremhab that I was meant for him? I wouldn't have put it past her.

"This has nothing to do with what you want or not, woman, but what I want and will have. I say I want you and, by the gods, I shall have you." Haremhab ignored everything I'd said, ignored Ramose's warning glare, wrapped his bear sized arms around my neck and continued slobbering all over me. I tried to fight but couldn't. He was stronger than me.

Then, he scooped me up into his arms and rose to his feet. I struggled and fought in earnest. Everyone stared. No one helped me. I was on my own. And how often had I seen *this* scene before in a movie? Too many. It never ended well.

I couldn't let this man take what I didn't want to give; what I was saving for the man I would someday love. I couldn't allow him to take that. So I resisted.

For a moment I thought of using the knife, small as it was, hidden at my waist, but something told me that would sign my death warrant for sure— drawing a General's blood in front of all these people—so I didn't.

I remembered my training. My fingers found his eyes, I pushed, and he dropped me.

I'm sorry Nefrure, I tried to behave! It wasn't my fault. What have I done?

As Haremhab yelled, I landed on the table, rolled, and found myself staring up at Ramose. Face to face.

He was frowning at me, but his eyes were laughing. Makere's body was pressed up against his sensuously; her lips near to his and her hands tight on his arm as he came to his feet. Her face was a storm. She felt threatened by me all right.

"Help me!" I cried to Ramose, throwing my hands palm upwards. "Please."

Ramose said nothing.

I couldn't wait for him to make up his mind, so I slid off the table and ran for an exit. If I could run fast enough, perhaps I could run all the way back to my time where I'd be safe. I didn't belong here.

Haremhab was bellowing behind me for his personal guards to fetch and bring me back.

If I had to take my chances out in the desert with the lions and the scorpions, so be it. It would be better than being ravished by a drunken soldier, general or not.

If there was ever a time for you to do your thing and send me back home, I grabbed the amulet around my neck, as I ran down the long hallways towards what I hoped was a way out of the palace, *now is the time. It's been a nice visit but I've had enough of this topsy-turvy world and its people. All right?*

Send me home!

It didn't work. Darn. Why did I know it wouldn't work?

Isn't time yet.

What punishment would there be for spurning Haremhab as I had done? Of laying hands on him? Death probably. I couldn't expect mercy and I couldn't expect Ramose to step in and save me this

Egyptian Heart

time. He didn't have the rank.

Down one hall and up another. I heard heavy boot steps behind me and I knew I was a goner. I fought the tears. I had to keep my wits about me. Had to be able to see.

I ran right into a soldier's arms and was caught. I fought him off, knocked him down with a well-placed foot kick (my karate expertise again), and would have gotten away but too many other soldiers crowded into the corridor and I was surrounded. Even my knife wouldn't have helped me. Would only have made them angrier. Game over.

I was taken to a room and locked in. "What's going to happen to me?" I shouted through the door. No answer. I leaned against the wall and took stock of the room. There were torches that threw soft orbs of flickering light across the walls. No windows, but the room was richly decorated with wall hangings, rugs and carved furniture. A huge plush bed covered in pillows dominated it.

Was this Haremhab's room and was I here to await his pleasure or displeasure? Maybe he would rape me before he had me executed.

Makere must be laughing somewhere. I'd sealed my own fate and taken care of her problem at the same time.

I tried to find a way out of the room. A few walls were all that was keeping me from escaping. Escaping to where? To the desert. I could somehow find my way back to the slaves' village among the sand dunes if I had to. I was pretty sure I recalled the way. I'd always had a good sense of direction. The village was empty but would provide shelter until I could figure out what to do. I still had my knife, small as it was, and I could use it to protect myself from the wild animals if I had to. None of that made any difference, though, if I couldn't get out of this room. There was nothing I could use to get out. No skeleton keys. No battering rams. No dynamite.

So there was no way out. The door was barred from the outside and the walls were thick. The whole weird night caught up with me and I collapsed onto the bed. I could have cried, but I knew it wouldn't do any good.

I lay there brooding instead. There'd been a connection between Ramose and I. I'd felt it. Was he going to allow Haremhab to have me so easily? To maim or kill me? As short a time as I'd known Ramose I'd believed that he was at least my protector.

He was probably with Makere or one of his many other women and had already forgotten me.

So I rested and waited, gathering strength to fight Haremhab, by words, guile or self-defense, whenever he would come.

If the amulet wouldn't send me back home then I'd somehow have to find a way to survive. Anything but yield to Haremhab's lust...or to death. I wouldn't go easily to either.

Chapter Six

I'd been sleeping. Dreaming of home. I was in my apartment feeding Snowball. The cat was so happy to see me, as if I'd been away for a long time. Outside, snow was falling and there was ice glittering along the branches of the swaying trees. The wind sounded like an unhappy wanderer wailing to get in. I was fixing myself a supper of left-over pizza, my favorite food, in the microwave and making a chocolate malt in the blender. Oooh, that malt tasted so good. So creamy. Cold.

My favorite show was coming on television in ten minutes and I'd received the first copies of my new novel in the mail that afternoon. Still I wasn't happy. I was waiting for someone. To call or come, I didn't know. But I was waiting for him.

My heart ached because he was no longer by my side, in my life. I didn't know who or where he was, only that he wasn't with me. The dream dissolved as I looked out the window into the snow, searching for the man I loved to come. I was so lonely.

I woke with a shadowy man looking down at me.

Haremhab?

I scrambled out of bed, my fingers grasping my tiny knife at my waist instead of the amulet, and jumped to my feet. And the man stepped forward into the torchlight.

"Lord Ramose!" I was surprised but then relief flooded in and reality shifted. I thought the necklace was sending me back, but my sight cleared and my body was real again.

"Are you here to punish me for offending your general?"

His face was stern. "Is that what you think? Ah, what a mess you are in. After you left everyone could speak of nothing but you. Your strange looks and beauty. That odd accent you speak with and your peculiar ways.

"Your defiance. How you attacked Pharaoh's most powerful general and then got away like the jinn many already believe you are. There are rumors and stories of you circulating the palace and growing in legend with each hour. By now everyone will have heard of the magical woman who was at the feast and then disappeared into thin air. Some are frightened of you."

How could I have forgotten that ancient Egyptians were even more superstitious than their modern counterparts? They used to stone people to death for dabbling in bad magic. I sat back down on the bed, my body trembling. I knew I should have been standing or bowing. But if I was going to die, I didn't care anymore. "Am I in real trouble, my lord?"

"You were." Then I saw the smile teasing at the edges of his lips. He was laughing at me, my plight.

"I have taken care of it."

"How?"

Ramose sat down beside me. The warmth of his body was a magnet drawing me towards him even as I fought it. I wanted him to wrap his arms around me and tell me everything was going to be all right. I wanted it desperately. What was the matter with me?

"It was *my* soldiers that found you, not the general's. As soon as you fled from the hall I sent my men to find you and bring you to safety. Haremhab does not know you were apprehended. I told him you escaped out through the gates into the desert and after looking for you the night through he has given up. He believes you to be a sorceress as well and that he is well rid of you.

"Then Pharaoh's messenger arrived an hour ago summoning the general back to Amarna immediately and he had to go. So now you are safe. He will never know what became of you and I will never tell him."

"He will forget me that easily?" I couldn't believe that, but I wanted to.

"I know my old friend well. Let me assure you, he is not always as crude as he behaved last night towards you and I apologize for him. It was the beer. It was too many months spent in Lebanon keeping Pharaoh's peace. He was overly drunk last night from celebrating his latest victory with his men.

"When he drinks much he forgets much when he sobers up. I imagine now he barely remembers what happened last night, much less that you were there or what you did. Keeping you from him last night was what was important for your well-being. You are safe now.

"Since the general has many women in Amarna he will be kept busy enough and will not be this way again for many months. The Hittites have begun plundering the cities of our bordering neighbors and Pharaoh is sending him to fight them."

The Hittites. I knew about them. Barbarians that lived up north in Asia Minor and were always threatening to spill into Egypt and plunder. If they were already making war noises then it must be closer to 1340 B.C., which was when the final battles with Egypt and the Hittites took place. These then, were very perilous times. All hell was about to break loose. I was the only one who knew it. Lucky me.

"And you," I asked Ramose, "will you have to go fight the Hittites?" I didn't know why it mattered but it did. The thought of Ramose leaving now before I had time with him made me sad. I could learn so much about Egypt from him. My mummy in the tomb.

"I will soon. Though not today or next week. Haremhab will send for me when he needs me. I have been away from home for a long time—much longer than the general—fighting Pharaoh's wars. I was wounded and this is my reward. To recover and rest, enjoy my peace for a time." He sighed and I could see the exhaustion in his face. I wondered what part of his body he'd wounded. If it pained him still.

Egyptian Heart

He was an enigma. This man. A soldier, a spoiled aristocrat, an alluring hunk of a male specimen...what else was he?

I felt funny sitting so close to him. Alone. On a bed. I worried what I looked like in my wrinkled finery and smeared make-up from last night. Was my eyeliner still there or was it all over my face? I was as nervous as a teenager with her first boyfriend.

It was then I noticed that Ramose no longer had a linen covering on his head. His hair was long, black and wavy and his face without the elaborate makeup looked years younger. His chest was bare with a sprinkling of hair while he was dressed simply in a white kilt wrapped around his lower body and tucked into his waist. Sandals. He was so handsome I couldn't stop staring.

"I want to thank you for saving my life, my lord." And I meant it. This man had saved me twice, had it meant anything to him at all?

His eyebrow lifted and he bent his head to examine me closer. "How could I not save the life of a magical woman?" he teased, but his expression was solemn. "You captivate me. You have from the first moment I saw you fighting the captain of my guard in the courtyard. All teeth and claws. A way of fighting I have never seen. Fearless. You do not behave like any woman I have ever met. You do not look like any woman I have ever met. I sense mysteries and secrets behind those cat's eyes of yours and I want to know what those mysteries are.

"You are not what you seem." Then in a voice so low I wasn't sure I even heard him right. "Then there is another reason I cannot speak of. Yet."

I shivered. He wasn't what he seemed, either.

"I do know that you were meant to come here, Mag-gie." He pronounced my name with his little affected accent on the second syllable. "And I am not going to lose you. Not to one of my soldiers, the desert or my lord Haremhab."

"What about Makere?" I shouldn't have asked but once the question came out I knew I had to have an answer one way or another. I didn't want to make her any angrier than she already was.

Ramose's face changed. A hardness dropped around him. "I will not lie to you. I have been with her for a long time." He looked away into the corner's shadows. Was it daylight outside yet? Hard to tell with no windows.

"I have never loved her. Desired her, yes. Wanted to possess her beauty and her body. Until you she was the most beautiful woman I had ever laid eyes upon. She is also the most vain and selfish. She wants to be my first wife. She thinks she will be. But there is a meanness in her heart that keeps me from truly loving her, from asking her to be one of my wives.

"She has given me no children yet."

I could see that disturbed him.

"Makere thinks you are a demon, a sorceress or, at least, a spy from Pharaoh." Ramose smiled.

"I am none of those things." I tried to sound truthful. It was hard; I wanted to smile at the thought that what I really was, was far worse. A time traveler with a magic amulet. Then my curiosity kicked in. "Why would she be afraid that

Egyptian Heart

Pharaoh was spying on you?"

"Akhenaton has grown paranoid of late. Since his beloved daughter, Meketaten, died, he has turned away from all our gods and embraced his one God, Aton. He wants all of Egypt to do the same. The priests he has put out of business are plotting and he fears his people are against him. He has put down the sword and now spends most of his days alone praying while our enemies, the Hittites, are gathering forces to invade.

"But enough of Akhenaton and our woes," he suddenly announced. "I wanted to come and talk more to you. Just you and I. I could not give you much attention at the banquet."

I needed to know something. "My lord, what do you really want from me?" It was more subtle than asking if he expected me to go to bed with him. Not that that was starting to sound so bad any longer. He'd been kind to me. Had saved my life. Twice. I was attracted to him. I had no lover waiting for me at home and no idea if I was ever going to see Boston again anyway. The loneliness inside of me that had never been assuaged was still there. I had begun to think: Would it be so awful for me to care for someone here and now? What harm would it do, even if I were sent back?

Harm enough, I mused. My good sense warned me I shouldn't get involved with anyone. It could get messy.

He was very close to me. So close I could smell his warm body's scent and the food aromas clinging to him from the night before. Food. I hadn't had time last night to eat much before I'd had to flee. I was starving.

He must have read my thoughts. "Are you hungry?"

"I am *very* hungry. I did not eat much last night. I was too nervous, scared. Too busy being pawed by a drunken general." Being baited and glared at by a jealous woman who would rather have scratched my eyes out than looked at me.

"And," I took a chance because he was being nice to me and smiling at my quick wit, "could I have a basin of water, soap and a towel so I can wash this makeup off my face? I am not used to—"

"Looking like a Kewpie doll, as you put it?"

I nodded. "My lord, you have an excellent memory."

He went to the door and clapped his hands. A crowd of slaves came rushing in and Ramose told them what we wanted. In what felt like seconds, servants were spilling into the room with platters of food and drink and basins of water and cleaning materials. The regal treatment was so different than the night I'd spent jailed in the stone house with the captured slaves that the memory came back to haunt me unbidden. What had happened to those slaves? I'd been thinking of them a lot.

Ramose sat on the bed, his eyes never leaving me, as I got up and went to the other side of the room, turning away from him, and quickly cleaned up as best I could. Rinsed out my mouth and brushed my hair. I'd taken the jewelry and the head ornaments off before I'd fallen asleep. Ramose's attention made me uneasy. What *did* he really want from me?

Egyptian Heart

To keep my mind off that, I said, "My lord, may I ask what has happened to the slaves I was rounded up with in the desert a few days ago?"

"You are worried about them and you are not even one of them?"

"I am worried about them."

"They are locked up awaiting their punishment. I am to decide today."

With no water and no food. No light. I felt so sorry for them. They were only people wanting to be free. Wanting to be treated with human dignity and fairness. I took another chance and told the truth. "My lord, they only ran off because while you were away fighting for Pharaoh your guards brutalized them. Beat them and...." The words were hard to say, but necessary. "Raped the women. They were fearful for their lives. You were not here to protect them and you were gone so long."

There was a heavy hush behind me so I put down the towel I'd used to dry my face and turned around.

Genuine anger was simmering across Ramose's face and not at me. "I did not know that. I thank you for telling me what no one else would." He stood up, walked over and looked down at me. Caressed my cheek softly as I gazed up at him. "Little cat, I am not a brutal heartless man. I do not allow my slaves to be treated thus. I will take care of it. I will question them myself and learn the truth. If it is as you say, they shall not be penalized more than they already have been. I thank you for telling me."

His expression was thoughtful when he said,

"You are a strange woman, Mag-gie, but you have a gentle, good heart. I do not think you are an evil jinn." He sat back down on the bed where the slaves had left the plates of food and gestured at me to join him.

I didn't know what to say, so I remained silent, and did as he bid me. I sat across from him on the bed and we ate our meal together.

We talked about other things. Everyday things.

Eventually he asked, "Tell me of *America*. That land of yours. Where is it?"

I hated deceiving him; pretending not to remember my previous life. I told him that some things I indiscriminately remembered and some not. "Over the water somewhere." I kept it vague and he didn't push. "I do know that the people are free in America. There are no slaves. We govern ourselves. I know I was happy there."

"Your land sounds different. You have no leader like our pharaoh?"

"We do. He is called a President. He does not have as much power as Pharaoh." I had to smile at my little joke on him. He'd never understand about Democracy and that all men are equal, so that was all I said. I asked him about Akhenaton and Nefertiti and he regaled me with fanciful stories of them and their court. Ramose was close to the Pharaoh and went often to his golden city of Amarna on the River Nile to attend court functions and pageantries.

"Pharaoh's queen and I are related by blood," he confided. But that was all he would say.

I looked at Ramose differently. So he wasn't

merely a wealthy warrior, he was a true aristocrat. I couldn't understand why he was bothering with me.

What did he see in me that no other man in my old life had never seen?

He stayed a long time with me. As we talked, mostly me asking questions about his land and his people, he seemed to change more towards me as the hours went by. Sometimes he seemed almost wary of me, but always respectful.

Maybe he thought, no matter what he'd said, as Makere believed, that I was a desert demon sent to test him.

I never forgot for a moment who he was and who I was. I was careful what I said and what I did. Falling often on the excuse of my spotty amnesia if I needed to.

I don't think Ramose always believed me.

After we'd eaten he stood up. "I must leave now. There are duties I must see to before nightfall. But if you agree, will you meet me for supper this evening?"

As if I could say no. "I am your guest. I must agree."

"No." His eyes were serious. "It is your choice."

I smiled. "Then I agree."

"We will not be in a crowd," he went on to say. "Tonight it will be you and I. As today." His face was close to mine and suddenly his arms were around me, strong but gentle, and his lips came down hungrily on my lips. I fought the kiss for only a heartbeat and then the feelings overwhelmed me. It was as if I'd known him a long time. As if I could trust him. I felt safe with him.

The kiss was passionate and when he pulled away I saw something strange in his gaze. Shock. Then a genuine tenderness I'd never seen before in any man's eyes. He laid his hand on the curve of my neck. I couldn't breathe and I didn't know what to say. Was this what falling in love felt like? I didn't know because, in my whole life, I'd never fallen in love before.

He held me in his arms and I could hear his heart beating. "I do not know what I want from you, little cat," he whispered into my hair, answering the question I'd asked when he'd first came in the room that morning. "At first, it was to have you in my bed. Own you. Possess you. Tame you. As I have so many women before. Until last night as I watched you stand up for yourself to lord Haremhab and Makere, when I looked into your eyes, as we spent time together today, I knew forcing you to my bed would not be enough. I want you to come willingly."

And then he said, "When you are ready."

I didn't have to ask if he usually treated his woman like this. I suspected he didn't.

Take it slow, I told myself. *Slow. If you act like a whore, he'll end up treating you as one. It's your purity he's intrigued by.* My old Catholic upbringing returned to torment me. I wanted him so badly I could hardly stand it, but I had to be a lady and I had to remember the promises I'd made to myself.

Was it this time, this place that was bringing out my sensuality so strongly? It had to be. Or I was under a spell. Perhaps, I thought, watching Ramose, we were both under a spell. That would explain a lot. *That damn amulet.*

He came to his feet. "I will send for you after nightfall. Until then consider this room yours. I will leave a guard at the outer door so if you need anything only ask for it."

"Could I have the slave, Nefrure, to keep me company?"

"I will see that she is sent here. Until tonight, Maggie." Then he was gone.

First thing I did after he left was check the door. It was still locked from the outside.

So Ramose didn't trust me totally. He was afraid I'd run off. It made me doubt his overall sincerity.

But when Nefrure arrived a short time later, I was so happy to see her that I forgot about Ramose and his hidden intensions.

"You are still alive, Mistress! Bless the Gods." She was grinning as she threw her arms around me and I hugged her back. It was good to see a friendly face.

"Why would you think otherwise?"

The look she gave me made me laugh. "It is all over the slaves' quarters, your run in with my lord Haremhab last night. Your refusal to do Makere's bidding. We were all sure you were dead. Your body tossed out to decay on the desert. Dead, if not by the general's hands, then by Makere's."

"I am not dead." I caught her up on what had occurred since I'd seen her last. Told her about Ramose's interest in me.

"I knew the first time I saw you that you were different." Nefrure looked sideways at me. "Whether you have caught my lord Ramose's eye or not, I begged you not to cross Makere. For you, she is more dangerous than anyone. She would kill you if she thought the master favored you over her." She grabbed my hands, her eyes feverish. "You must be careful."

"I am being careful. Yet what has happened has happened. I cannot change it now."

Then I got it. "Nefrure, *Makere* was the woman you displeased, the one who shaved your head, was she not?"

"She was. And I was lucky. She could have done worse. I could be dead or missing fingers or toes. She loves to kill slaves. Shows her power and spreads her fame."

With a sigh, I looked past her to the remains of Ramose's and my earlier feast. "Nefrure, enough of unpleasantness, here sit with me and eat some of this food. Or else it will go to waste. There is so much of it."

At first she resisted, but I bullied her into it. She ate as if she were starving and that's when I realized that, no matter what she'd said about the slaves having enough to eat, they didn't. When she was full, I encouraged her, "Gather up the rest and take it to some of the other slaves. Let them eat, too."

"I cannot. If I am caught, I will be punished."

"No. I will say I gave it to you. Go. Then come back. I have so much to ask you."

There were tears in her eyes as she thanked me

and took the food away. She wasn't gone long. "Ahhotpe, Safurat, Negla and the others asked me to thank you. You have made friends today. They will look out for you now as I do."

It made me sad that so little a kindness could be so rare in this place.

Nefrure was to stay with me from now on and was delighted about it. So was I. I requested of the guard outside the door to have someone bring bedding so she would have a place to sleep. Then the slave and I spent the remainder of the day becoming better friends. I wanted to learn everything I could about Ramose and Makere. Wanted to learn more about what was going on in this world from a slave's point of view.

Between what Ramose had divulged and what I gleaned from Nefrure, I roughly calculated that I'd been sent back near the time when Akhenaton's reign had become dangerously shaky. Ramose had said that Akhenaton was already in Amarna and that he, having no male heirs from his queen, had already set Nefertiti aside to marry his second daughter, Meritaton.

Now, knowing Ramose's close ties to Nefertiti, it made me speculate if there was another reason for my being here besides meeting Ramose. My whole career I'd been curious about the ultimate fate of Nefertiti and their children. Akhenaton had died mysteriously around 1334 B.C., but before that Nefertiti and her remaining daughters had simply disappeared. Could I discover what their fate had been? It was a fascinating notion.

I didn't have much time to dwell on it, because

Ramose sent me clothes to wear for the evening and an hour later guards arrived to escort me to where he was. I was so excited going to meet him, I could think of nothing else.

I was falling in love with a man who'd been dead for thousands of years. Heaven help me.

Chapter Seven

The guard, a short and thick man with scraggly long hair and a square jaw who wouldn't look at me, led me down the halls and into a suite of rooms that I took to be Ramose's personal quarters. Ramose was busy writing at a large desk, flanked by scribes and soldiers. They gawked at me as I was led in; some pretended I wasn't there. Ramose appeared tired.

I'd been resting and lollygagging all day and apparently he'd been working.

A smile curved his mouth the moment he saw me. He excused himself and took me by the arm. "Come with me," he said and ushered me through a hall into a series of beautiful rooms and outdoors into an elegant garden, lit with incense lanterns. Under a bright tent there was a table set for supper, the wine poured and the meat sizzling on silver platters.

"My private garden. Sit here, Mag-gie. Eat what you want. I have a few more matters to attend to inside. I will not be long."

He left and as soon as he did, I got up and quietly snuck closer to the room's entrance. Staying out of sight, I eavesdropped on what the men surrounding Ramose were discussing. They conferred in hoarse whispery tones, were clearly upset, and all I could make out was that it had something to do with Pharaoh and the Hittites.

When Ramose rose to his feet with an annoyed flourish of his hands, I fled back to the garden and the tent. I was eating a slice of beef when Ramose rejoined me.

"Is there trouble on our borders?" I pressed innocently. There was no way I wasn't going to ask. Nosiness, under the circumstances, was boiling in my blood.

"You are an odd woman. Asking such a question. None of my other women would care about such things as politics and wars. They only care about what gown they are going to wear that day, what eye color and jewelry. Or pleasing me. Do you really want to know?"

"Yes." I'd taken another bath before I came, had washed and brushed my hair but hadn't worn any of the make-up Nefrure had brought me that afternoon. I'd put on the simplest of the gowns, an indigo colored cotton sheath as soft as spun cloud, that Ramose had sent me, and none of the jewelry. Just my amulet. I'd never been the kind of person to rely on artificial beauty, and I wasn't about to start now. If Ramose were to respect me he'd have to respect the real me. Not the Kewpie Cleopatra doll me.

Ramose sat down. He talked to me as if I could understand. "I received a message from my lord Haremhab this morning. The Hittites have been ravaging Canaan. They are taking city after city. Lord Haremhab has been besieged with letters from

Egyptian Heart

the rulers of Mitanni, Babylon, Syria, Palestine and others, begging him to intercede with Pharaoh and send Egyptian troops to help fight the invaders."

Ramose was dressed as he'd been that morning, without makeup, his hair free and flowing and his face looking so young. How old was he? Around thirty? Younger? Older? I couldn't guess.

"What does Pharaoh say?"

"What he has been saying for a long time. That his one God, Aton, will protect them and us. He prays day and night. There is no need for our armies to attack. No need to fight."

"What does Lord Haremhab say?"

"He is furious at the cowardice of Pharaoh. He thinks Pharaoh is weak."

"And you?"

"I follow my pharaoh." Ramose's eyes were guarded. "Whatever he commands I will obey." There was a struggle going on deep inside him as scorching as the midday desert and I could feel it. Time to back off.

Slaves were fireflies flitting about pouring wine and serving. They made me uncomfortable and somehow Ramose picked up on that. He waved them away and we were alone.

I could hear the twilight creatures singing among the flowers and Acacias trees around us. The fragrances were strong and sweet. The trickle of water flowing through the ponds was background for our thoughts. "Tell me about your day."

"You are truly interested?"

"Yes." We ate our meal as Ramose unfolded the hours since he'd left me earlier. He seemed delighted to discuss it with someone, as if he had no real confidants. He was turning out to be an intelligent, well-informed man for his time.

I believed he was lonely.

We ended up discussing the pyramids and then Ramose spoke of the old gods of Egypt. I devoured every word. He knew so much I'd never read in the pages of a book. "Alas, though, last year Akhenaton outlawed worship of all other gods but Aton," he finished.

"He closed other temples, even the temples of Amon, and sent Amon's powerful priests into hiding. The Egyptian people hate him for this. Rebellion and unrest are growing. I fear for my country these days."

That this pharaoh was not popular, I knew, but it was enthralling to hear it and all the other juicy details I'd never known from an authentic Egyptian who was living through it.

After we'd eaten, Ramose rose and offered his hand to me. "No more religion or history lessons. Walk with me through my gardens, Mag-gie. Let me show you this pretty oasis I have carved out of the desert. Be sweet to me. Laugh with me. Smile at me."

And love me? I mused as I put my hand in his and we meandered the sculpted paths of colored stones among the manmade miniature ponds and water falls. Torches lined the route and lit our way.

There were trees heavy with fruit curving over the path and I couldn't help but wish, after eating the feast we'd had, the fruit could be given to those who were hungry. The slaves.

"Why have you been so nice to me?" He was tall beside me and his hand warm in mine. There was electricity between us tonight. Stronger than ever and almost irresistible.

"Besides the obvious reasons?" A hint of humor in his voice. He halted and pivoted me to face him. A lantern cast a faint glow across his handsome face and his eyes, black diamonds, shone.

"You find me attractive?" I played along. I was no longer afraid of him. We weren't lovers yet but I felt as if we were. I'd come to no harm from him.

"I find you more than beautiful. Unusual. Exciting. Clever. You make me believe that women and men can be friends. You make me believe in love again. Real love. When I had come to believe it did not exist—or not for me."

He pulled me close and kissed me. His lips were hot and demanding and when his arms circled around me, I thought I'd gone to heaven.

I'd never felt the way I was feeling. Every nerve ending was tingling. My body was vibrating. One second I was warm and the next I was hot. I blended into his body, snuggled in as if we belonged together. A perfect fit.

He was gentle and didn't take liberties, but he was attempting to seduce me. Trying to make me fall in love with him.

I gazed up into his face, unable to hide my emotions, which were at war. *How could I fall in love with this man when I didn't belong in his world and could be sent home anytime?*

"Why," I repeated, "are you being so good to me? Is it because I have ivory skin, silver hair and emerald eyes?" I was teasing, but also serious.

He laughed, hugging me as he did. The ancient Egyptian crickets were noisy around us. The night hid us in a gray blanket. I was in a lovely dream and afraid to wake up. "In a way, yes." He stopped talking and kissed me again.

"Tell me."

We resumed walking and I could see his profile in the misty light. He was looking at the skies, which were full of dazzling stars. There was a chill in the air, I shivered and he tucked me in nearer to him to warm me. "I've never confessed this to anyone. You are the first. When I was a child, my mother was told by a seer that one day I would be a great man but I would never find happiness or love until a woman with ivory skin and the eyes of a cat would come into my life. That woman would be my lover, my life's partner in all things, and give me many sons. I was to look for her always, find her no matter the tribulations, or I would never know true happiness."

"Did that seer say anything else about this mysterious woman?" I pretended to be amused, but beneath that I was acutely interested.

"He foresaw that she would be a woman of power and magic. A sorceress. She would come at a time when I, and Egypt, would need her most."

I stopped in my tracks. "Do you think I am that woman?"

"As of yet, that I do not know."

"You suspect it?"

"Since the first moment I laid eyes on you among those runaway slaves, standing up to my guards." Ramose's breath was soft against my cheek. "And in your honor I forgave them. The recaptured slaves will have no further punishment. The soldier who hit you, I disciplined as a warning to the others to never unjustly abuse another slave."

I didn't know what to say. He'd punished one of his men because of me. The guilt settled in and it had sharp teeth. Yet the guard had deserved it, I told myself, and if it made the slaves' lives better I could live with it.

"Do you think I am a sorceress?"

"Are you?"

I chose to shrug it off, play it safe, but if he believed I was the one it would explain the way he'd been treating me. *If he thought I was a sorceress he'd be careful with me.* "As if I would admit it, my lord. They stone women who practice sorcery, do they not?"

"They do in some places. Ah, do not worry, if you were a sorceress I would not tell anyone. I would protect you. Unlike many people, I, as does my mother, do not believe all magic is evil."

Was that the real reason Ramose was interested in me? He thought I possessed magic? Was he, then, afraid of me? I sighed, knowing it was best to protect myself, even from him. Tell him a half-truth. "I am no sorceress. Will you send me away now?"

"No. I will not let you go." Ramose shook his head and tilted my chin up so he could kiss me.

We stood there for a long time kissing and holding each other. I wasn't a child, I was a woman. Ramose wanted me as much as I wanted him but going to bed with him, as he had said, was my decision and something inside cautioned me to wait. He could have any woman, any time. He wouldn't respect me if I gave in to him now.

Anything won too easily was never valued highly, my mother always said. Or was I scared of committing my body and my heart that deeply? Possibly.

Ramose must have sensed my hesitation, for he moaned, and stepped away. "Come, Mag-gie, it is late and I have to ride out early tomorrow morning to see to the fortifications. If war is coming we must be prepared."

Outside the rooms, I was surprised to see Nefrure waiting by the door, her head down, but a shy smile on her face.

Ramose explained, "I took the liberty of sending for your slave woman. From now on, these are your new apartments."

"I am to stay here? With you?" My heart sped up. So, no matter what I'd thought, was occupying his bed something I had no choice in any longer?

"No." He smiled softly, seeing the way my thoughts had gone. "These are *your* rooms. I will not enter them without your permission. You might like more space and access to the gardens, I thought."

"Thank you." It was all I could think of to say. "Are you not afraid I will run away?"

"You have nowhere to run. The desert is merciless. Endless. So I beg you not to try." He pulled me to him, brushed my cheek gently with his lips and whispered in my ear, "And I fear that if you are not hidden safely somewhere that something terrible may befall you. There will be guards posted outside day and night for your protection."

"What do you mean, my lord?"

His sigh was troubled. "I informed Makere this morning after I left you that I would not marry her. Ever. I ended our relationship. She is a vengeful woman and I would not put it past her to try to harm any woman who comes after her."

"Me?"

He nodded. "My quarters, as you saw, are not far from here. So I can keep an eye on you. Be near you. We share the gardens.

"I shall see you tomorrow?"

Now it was my turn to nod. "Tomorrow." I thought of something. "My lord, could I ask one more favor of you?"

"What do you want?" Ramose looked at me and for the first time I heard disappointment in his tone. He probably thought I would ask for gold or jewels.

"May I have writing supplies, paper and something to write with? Paints to draw with? I used to write in a journal, draw and paint. I miss it. I would love to paint a picture of the garden. It is so lovely."

He seemed relieved. "You will have all you ask for in the morning. I will notify one of my scribes to bring what you need. Is there anything else you wish?"

"No. You have already been too kind. Too generous. Thank you." He stared at me with an interesting expression on his face. I couldn't tell what it meant.

He strode out of the room and a soldier standing outside closed the door behind him.

Nefrure ran up to me, her eyes dancing. She'd heard everything Ramose had said to me. "He loves you, Mistress. He *loves* you."

"How can you tell?"

"I know. It is in his eyes. In the way he treats you and you haven't even gone to his bed yet. I have never known Lord Ramose to behave this way. He *pardoned* all the runaway slaves. He is kinder to everyone and was not like that before. He is in love. The news is spreading through the palace.

"It is *you*. The mysterious woman he has been searching for all his life. Thank the gods, Makere has lost favor." I took her hands, she was crying. "If she had become his wife, our lives would have been the worse for it. This is a great and happy day for us slaves. We thank you."

I embraced the small woman. "Do not thank me. I did little." Then it occurred to me. "Nefrure, now you can grow your hair back. If Makere has lost her influence, you need not worry about her any longer."

"I can!" The slave was smiling. I'd never seen her so pleased as she touched her bald head. "No more shaving it every day. I can grow it out again."

Her smile curved down into a frown. "Oh, but there is a bad thing. If Makere finds out it is you Ramose loves, she will try to hurt you in some way. She has done it before. She still has her followers.

"Once," her voice fell, "it was rumored that Makere had a woman *killed* over him. A woman who had caught his attention. She had eyes almost as green as yours. I remember her. One of my friends overheard the planning of it.

"Makere made sure the woman had an *accident.* From this day forward you must be vigilant."

Now I understood why Ramose moved me here. Closer to him. With guards at the door.

"I will help protect you, Mistress. I will watch and listen. Be your eyes and ears. The other slaves will help. No one will hurt you." There was true concern in Nefrure's brown eyes.

"Thank you, my friend. I am safe here. Ramose will not let anything happen to me. I will not let anything happen to me. I will be careful." I walked to the doorway of the gardens and my eyes searched out into the night. A mischievous breeze played with my hair and I thought about Makere and her murderous envy. Thought about Ramose and the intimacy and the kisses we'd shared.

I rubbed my fingers across the cold amulet and wondered how long it would allow me to remain. Was I here for a short time or was I here forever? It was the first time I had thought of it and I wasn't sure if it made me happy or not. Oh, how I wanted to go home...yet I also knew I was falling in love with Ramose. Was it fate, my destiny, or was it a terrible mistake.

Oh, but I was smiling. I'd never been so happy. Nothing, not Makere, not anyone or anything, could change that. I was falling in love and I think Ramose was falling in love with me.

What would tomorrow bring?

I didn't know and, at that moment, I didn't care.

Chapter Eight

The time moved quickly after that and fell into a comfortable pattern. I'd spend the day with Nefrure learning about the world I'd fallen into, writing in a journal where I'd begun to record my adventures; drawing or painting the scenes around me or walking in the garden. Taking the scrolls of writing papyrus I'd been given from one of Ramose's scribes, I'd cut them into manageable squares with a knife and had fashioned the pages together with heavy twine. Made an awkward diary, but it worked. It was tricky using a reed pen to write with but I got used to it. Ha, what I wouldn't have done for a good old ballpoint pen or a number two pencil.

Each evening, after his duties were done, Ramose would join me for supper and we'd spend time together. Talk about our day, ourselves, our feelings and dreams. Everything and anything. We made each other laugh. My convenient amnesia enabled me to play dumb and ask all kinds of questions. He was taking his time getting to know me and, though it was sweet, I had the impression that there was more to it.

He slowly brought me out of myself. We'd debate life or politics as we strolled the gardens beneath the myrrh and palm trees and he'd entertain me with tales of Pharaoh and his queen, their court, their enemies and friends. Soon it was as if I knew all those people.

"One day I would love to see the royals for myself, spying from among the crowd at court. I am not important enough to meet any of them," I admitted to Ramose one night as we sat in my rooms. Outside a desert squall had made it too inhospitable to be in the garden. The storms came up like that. In an instant. They departed just as quickly as well.

Ramose had been teaching me a game, somewhat like chess, with little colored stones you moved around on a painted wooden board. I'd become addicted to it and good at it, though I let Ramose beat me some of the time.

"I would love," I said to him, "to see the great city of Amarna someday."

Amarna, Nefertiti's golden city, *also known as the city of flowers.* I'd read somewhere that Queen Nefertiti had adored flowers.

"Someday you might," Ramose had replied. "Someday." I knew he was bothered about the people's growing antagonism at Akhenaton in the cities, even in Amarna. There was growing rioting. Amarna wasn't a safe city to be in.

The Hittite menace was spreading like a plague, a ground fire of pillaging and killing. Ramose acknowledged they'd invaded into Palestine and Syria and were marching closer to Egypt every day. Fierce warriors and skilled horsemen, they'd had chariots before the Egyptians and were one of the few people the Egyptians feared.

"Still," Ramose told me, "Akhenaton refuses to send troops to aid our allies. General Haremhab has become disillusioned and enraged with Pharaoh. Great trouble is coming."

How well I knew that. Yet Ramose remained loyal. I couldn't tell him that soon the country would despise Akhenaton, but it would make little difference because Pharaoh's days were numbered anyway. Nefertiti's as well. I couldn't bring myself to dash Ramose's hopes. He revered Pharaoh and his queen. He'd fight, kill and die for them. I gathered that listening to him.

During the day, I painted and drew with a vengeance to keep my mind off the reality that I was still here in ancient Egypt. And falling in love with a man I could never have, or thought I could never have.

Who was I? A woman found wandering on the desert. A nameless nobody to these people and Ramose.

Inspired by where I was and the awakening feelings I was having for Ramose, my journal entries, my paintings, of the slaves, Nefrure and Ahhotpe, of my rooms and the gardens were the best work I'd ever done. Ramose studied my paintings and smiled proudly. Good thing I was a realist. Abstract wouldn't have gone over as well. He thought I was as fine an artist as he'd ever seen. "You could paint in the royal tombs, you are so good." That he believed that tickled me.

Every day I remained made me think that perhaps this was the real world and my past had been the dream. Boston and the college were fading. My old lonely life was fading. I missed my mother, my family and Snowball. Dreamed of them often. But I knew they were happy and healthy, living their own lives; knew that my mother would take good care of my cat. Besides, none of them would even live for another three thousand years.

I mentioned to Nefrure that first week, when she'd caught me teary-eyed about an existence I no longer had, how I remembered having a cat in my old life. How I'd loved that cat and missed it. Two days later, Nefrure brought me in a tiny gray kitten hiding in her cupped hands.

"Her name is Min. One of eight kittens that Ahhotpe's cat, Bastet, had weeks ago. Ahhotpe wants you to have her in thanks for the food you keep sending her."

"Min is the god of sensuality and Bastet is the Egyptian cat goddess, right?"

"True." Nefrure grinned at her little joke. She'd told me that I reminded her of a sensuous cat goddess and that was why Ramose was so attracted to me. Imagine, me sensuous. If my stuffy professor colleagues could see me now.

I was thrilled and fell in love with Min when she scrambled into my arms and clawed her way up to snuggle at my neck. She had a cute little saucer shaped face and big gray eyes. She took to and followed me everywhere like a tiny shadow. Slept with me in my bed at night. It was almost as good as having Snowball back.

It wasn't all easy times. Some of the household had come to believe I was a jinn or a sorceress who'd bewitched their master. That's what Nefrure informed me. Some thought I possessed white magic and therefore I was good, not evil, but many weren't sure and were afraid of me.

Nefrure reported that Makere was responsible for most of the malicious gossip. Makere, exiled to distant rooms beyond the palace somewhere and losing more power with every day, hated me. Can't say I blamed her. I'd ousted her and ruined her life. Not on purpose, but I'd done it just the same. Bet she was hopping mad.

I hid my journal from Ramose. From everyone. It wouldn't do to have anyone see my English scribbling. See anything that made me spookier than I was already perceived as being. I didn't need to give my enemies anything else to condemn me. Though it did surprise me that I could still write in my own language. I didn't seem able to speak it out loud any longer. Just write and read in it.

Nefrure saw me writing in my diary and, after I'd closed it so she wouldn't see the writing, asked me one morning, "In your land, Mistress, you said that everyone has the right to learn how to read and write. Do you think you could teach me to read and write?"

I thought for a moment. Nefrure was intelligent and wanted to learn. Slaves who could read and write were held in higher esteem by their masters than field or house slaves. Some were put to work on the master's correspondence, family history or recording the household's expenses. But I had a problem. I wasn't as good at reading and writing *their* language as I was at mine. No one in my position, being zipped into the long dead past, would be. I knew some hieroglyphs, but not enough to write fluently.

"Please teach me," Nefrure begged. "I am not getting any younger and if I had those skills I could earn my keep without being sent into the fields. A hard life." Her hair, a short shining cap of black, had begun to grow out. Each day I saw her security and happiness growing along with it. She was no longer afraid of Makere hurting her.

I had to find a way to teach Nefrure. Then it came to me. I'd become friends with Khnumbaf, scribe to Ramose's second high scribe, Thuty—as Khnumbaf always described his household position—when my writing materials had been delivered. At first he'd been suspicious of me, a grim-faced gnome of a man, bald with small eyes that blinked a lot. A short man, I was inches taller. He, too, was a slave, but had risen in the ranks because of his knowledge and devoted loyalty to Ramose.

After our second meeting, I'd started talking to him. Asking questions about the hieroglyphs and the writing styles he was so expert at. Stoked his ego a little. He would do anything for me now if I asked. Maybe I could ask him to help me brush up on his language. Then I could teach what I learned from him to Nefrure. I already had the basics. It could work.

"I will teach you to read and write," I promised Nefrure and her rare smile was my reward.

The next morning Khnumbaf began teaching me how to better read and write his language and two mornings later, Nefrure's lessons began. She picked it up much quicker than I would have thought. She was a natural.

This all kept me busy and the time passing.

Then there was my food relief program. I'd started something that first time I'd sent the extra food with Nefrure to her hungry slave friends I couldn't stop. I'd talked to Ramose about giving his slaves more rations every day but could not get any concrete promises out of him. I guess my ideas were too liberal for him. For now. I didn't give up and continued to sweet-talk him as often as I could get away with it.

I found that I could ask the guard at the door anytime day or night for food and it would be brought. Platters and bowls of it. Far more than Nefrure and I could ever eat. When I was having a meal with Ramose five times as much food as we could eat was prepared and brought. There were always leftovers. So, late each evening, after Ramose would leave me, Nefrure would gather it up in baskets and take it out to the main gates. Under cover of darkness she would divvy out the meat, fruit, bread, wine or barley beer and whatever else we had to the slaves of the household. Every night there were more and more slaves waiting at the gates. Silent. Hungry. Grateful.

"I tell everyone the food is from you, Mistress."

"No, tell them it is from Ramose." Because it was.

I wanted to interview some of the slaves at the gate for my journal, get to know them and what their lives were like, in case I ever did write that book I'd have real stories to tell, so one night I snuck out through the garden with Nefrure. I'd discovered a place in the high walls that, with help of a tree, was easy to climb over. I was tired of my pretty prison. I needed to connect with people. At home I'd had my colleagues, my family and my students. If I never went home, I needed a life here, too. That meant friends. People.

The slaves and their lives interested me. What stories they had to tell. And I wrote some of them down in my secret diaries at night when I was alone. I got to know the slaves and saw that, though the random brutality had ceased, not much else had gotten better for them. I was determined to sway Ramose into treating his slaves with more fairness. It would take time. My ways, my world, weren't his ways or his world. Yet. I wouldn't give up.

So when Nefrure pleaded, "Can you teach other slaves who want to learn to read and write? When they have learned they will go and teach others, as I will do."

I agreed. "I will teach every slave you bring to me if they want to learn."

"They will." Nefrure and I had become friends. I would have been lost without her.

So that was how the slaves' classes began. Early in the morning I'd go out into the garden by the tree against the wall, my pupils would stealthily climb over and I would teach them what I'd learned the day before from Khnumbaf.

And more time passed.

Ramose and I grew closer. We behaved as lovers, snuggling and kissing, but we hadn't slept together yet. I knew he was impatient, but withholding that final act was my trump card. If I wasn't what he expected, would he toss me aside as he'd done to Makere and countless other women before me? Possibly. Unless he knew me well and loved me completely and that would take time. Then there was my Catholic upbringing. Guilt was built in. And my personal promise that I'd only give myself to a man I truly and completely loved. The man I was to marry. I needed time. Love was more than just sex.

Or maybe I was just afraid. Ramose scared the hell out of me.

I explained most of my inhibitions to him and he said he understood. He would wait. But how long?

I'd been in Ramose's time about a month when a message from him was delivered at suppertime.

"What does it say, Mistress?" Nefrure glanced up from setting the table out in the garden. Twilight was seeping in and the scent of eucalyptus was a perfume around us. We'd been expecting Ramose any moment. I couldn't wait to hear the news of the outside world and see the man I was beginning to respect and care for more each day. I'd gotten prettied up and had a new drawing to show him. One of him done by memory.

I frowned, standing under the darkening trees, the message heavy between my fingers. Soon Nefrure would be lighting the lanterns. "Lord Ramose will not be coming tonight."

There was apprehension on Nefrure's face.

She wouldn't ask, so I told her. "He has been

summoned by Haremhab. Prince Aziru the Amorite has allied himself with the Hittites and has betrayed Pharaoh. Others are following. Haremhab needs all his commanders to fight."

The message didn't say where he'd gone or how long he'd be away. I felt abandoned and lonely. Worried for Ramose's safety.

Thank goodness I had Nefrure and Min. Since I'd gotten the kitten she'd doubled in size. She was bouncing around my feet and I reached down to pick her up and snuggled her against my chest. She meowed and nuzzled me.

"Well, we will just eat supper by ourselves," I said to my friend. When Ramose wasn't around I insisted Nefrure and I eat together. That night we ate in silence. Nefrure took the food to the gate by herself. Min and I went to bed early.

I was lost without Ramose and how much I missed him shook me.

The days that came afterward were emptier without his voice, his smile or his touch. I threw myself into teaching the slaves, my journals and my painting. Kept as busy as I could.

Each day I waited for news from Ramose. Nothing came. A week went by. There were rumors that Akhenaton had lost control of Egypt. He'd secluded himself away from his family. His followers believed he'd gone insane. Two weeks passed. There were rumors that the Hittites were amassing their armies to invade Egypt.

History was trundling along right on track.

I began to wonder if Ramose was all right. Was he fighting somewhere? Was he even alive?

And what would I do if he never returned? I was in a precarious position here. Ramose was my protector. Who would protect me if not him?

Then there was another part of me that at times thought he was back and was with Makere. Though I was sure Nefrure would have told me if that had been true.

At the end of the third week, despondent and anxious over the man I loved and my future, I resolved one night to resume helping Nefrure take the food out to the gate after dark. It'd get my mind off Ramose, off my own problems. I was lonely. Nefrure wasn't always with me. She had chores to do and spent a lot of time practicing her writing and reading. I didn't mind because she was learning so quickly and I was proud of her. She was way ahead of the other slaves I was teaching.

And I needed more fodder for my journals. If I went back to the twenty-first century they'd be priceless. Never mind that I didn't ask myself *how* I'd get them back, when and if I was ever *sent* back. My writing, as my other activities, was just as much to fill my time as anything. I wanted to get out among the people and mingle. Go to the markets. Shop and reconnoiter human stories.

Ramose had forbidden it.

So sneaking out to the gate was my only option.

The night had no moon and the air was building to a windstorm out on the edges of the desert. It felt good to be doing something else besides sitting in my rooms. The people we gave the food to were so thankful and so talkative.

This night there were more than usual,

according to Nefrure, as we came to the gates. They were surprised to see me with her and at first were ill at ease.

I smiled and helped Nefrure hand out the food. "Can you tell me what your name is?" I requested softly, touching hands. "What position do you hold in Ramose's household? What is your day like? Is there something you want me to ask of the Master? A grievance or a need?"

At first they didn't respond, held back, unsure. Then a teenage boy spoke to me and then a woman not much older than I. In minutes, as we gave out the food from the baskets, some of them had warmed up to me. Some even answered my questions or humbly asked me to speak to Ramose. One wanted me to inquire on a sister sold away and another asked about a sick child who needed a physician because the boy was having trouble walking. I promised I would help if I could.

One timid woman confessed that a soldier was pressuring her to sleep with him and had her child beaten because she wouldn't. Next time, the soldier had threatened, the child would be taken away.

Slavery and poverty seemed to be companions in this time. When I'd first met Nefrure she'd said that being a slave here wasn't bad. I was beginning to think she'd lied. Probably to keep herself out of trouble. Saddened by the simple, yet unfulfilled needs of these people I kept thinking that if I could get closer to Ramose, I might persuade him to be a better master, a better man. Was I fooling myself? It was too early to tell.

At least I was doing something.

"Be aware of the soldiers tonight," a woman with a baby in her arms and a little girl tugging at her skirt warned. "They are everywhere watching and they are in a foul mood. They are up to no good."

"Has something happened?" I questioned the woman. Terrified she'd say that the final civil war had come or that Ramose had been hurt or killed. The slaves were the first ones to learn some things.

"I think they are looking for someone."

"Who?" Nefrure wanted to know, but suddenly there were noises around us and the slaves scattered like dust before a broom. Disappearing into the night.

Soldiers. There were soldiers in the shadows around Nefrure and I. Closing in.

"Run!" Nefrure hissed at me under her breath and gave me a shove. "They are Makere's men. They are here to kill you! Run! I will try to keep them from you." Then she stepped in the path of the man coming at me.

A hand grabbed my arm before I could move and there I was, fighting some soldier in the dark. Instinct and my defense training took over and my leg came up and slammed the hulking shape in his stomach and down he went in the dirt with a grunt. His knife went flying. I saw the glint of its blade and heard it clatter against the stone before the gates.

Nefrure had been right, he'd been trying to kill me. He scrambled away on all fours, shrieking something about me having evil powers.

I was glad night's darkness hid my fighting

prowess from other prying eyes.

Nefrure was fighting as well, scratching and kicking. I heard her scream and tried to get to her but I was busy sparring with a third man. How many were there and how had they known I was out here by the gates tonight?

We must have been followed. They'd been watching us, perhaps for days or weeks and I obliged them by coming out tonight where they could get to me. No one would have tried to hurt us if we'd been in our rooms or the garden. Ramose's guards protected us there. I'd been foolish, I reflected fearfully, as I kicked and hit the man attacking me. I knocked his knife out of his hands, too. Another lucky shot.

A well placed chop to my second attacker's face and a hard kick to his lower body and he ran away as well. I rushed to help Nefrure. She was on the ground with a soldier looming over her. But he peered up at me with terror in his shadowed face as I stood above him. All I could think of was that he'd hurt Nefrure and I was so angry I couldn't think straight. It showed in my stance, my reactions.

I kicked him until he stopped moving.

Then knelt down beside Nefrure. "Are you all right?"

"I am bleeding." Her voice was feeble and I knew she'd been badly hurt. She grabbed and clung to me and fainted. There was something warm and sticky on my hands after I'd touched her. Blood.

Out of the shadows slaves crept and encircled us. Hiding, they'd been waiting until the soldiers had left and they helped me get Nefrure back to my rooms. I asked the guards at the doors to bring me a physician without delay.

A man who announced himself as Safurat el-Sherif arrived at the door a short time later and said he was one of Ramose's physicians who'd been ordered to be available if I had need of him. Dressed in a striped red and white kilt, a square of linen wrapped around his ample body and fastened at his waist, he had an askew wig on and a bag at his side. Looked like he'd dressed in a hurry. He seemed offended when I told him Nefrure was the one who needed his services, not me.

"You drug me from my bed at this hour for a slave?" His pudgy bearded face crinkled and his eyes held disdain.

"She is really hurt," I told him, tears in my eyes. "A knife wound she received trying to protect me. She has lost much blood. You must help her. I would be so grateful. Lord Ramose would be so grateful."

He sighed. I'd gotten to him, either with my tears or by reminding him I was Ramose's favorite these days.

Nefrure hadn't come to. I hovered fretfully as the doctor examined her.

"She is dying," Safurat el-Sherif announced to me afterwards. "The wound came too close to her heart and, by the scent around the cut, the knife had poison on it. There is little I can do. Little you can do. Make her comfortable. Stay with her. She will pass into the afterlife soon."

"There is no hope?"

"None. I am sorry."

Egyptian Heart

I thought I caught sympathy in his gaze, but I turned away to keep from sobbing in front of him. I couldn't believe that my first and only true friend in this place was going to die. That knife had been meant for *me*. Nefrure had taken it instead.

If Makere had been in front of me at that moment I would have wrung her throat myself.

I never should have gone with Nefrure tonight. Me being with her had put a target on her back. My fault.

As she'd cared for me that first day I'd been brought to her months ago now I tried to care for her that night and into the next day.

Min, as if the cat knew what was happening, lay besides the slave woman quietly and waited, too. Not even purring.

I would have done anything to have just taken Nefrure to a modern hospital with modern nurses and doctors. Electricity and machines. It wasn't to be. I'd never missed my time more than I did as I watched my friend die.

By late morning Nefrure was gone. I held her hand until it was stiff and cold, and prayed for her. She never woke up once. Better that way. It kept her from suffering any more than she already had.

I cried when the body was taken away. Curled up in my own bed with Min, I finally fell into a restless sleep.

My dreams were full of me, lost, looking for first Nefrure and then Ramose. They were both on their way to the afterworld and I wasn't allowed to follow. They waved and smiled to me, next to their ba, their spirit selves, as they sailed away on the boat. Where Anubis, god of the underworld necropolis, with the head of a jackal, waited for them along with all the other dead Egyptians that had gone before.

Leaving me alone back here in my rooms.

Hunger pains forced me to finally get up, and I had to feed Min. I felt as if I'd had nightmares all the time I'd been asleep. There was a drawing of Nefrure leaning against the wall. One I'd done just a few days ago and seeing it, I began to cry again.

What was I going to do without her?

I asked about Nefrure's body and if there'd be a memorial service for her. The guard at the door reacted as if I were simple minded.

For a slave? No. Their bodies are buried unprepared in the tombs of their master. The slave woman is already there.

In Ramose's tomb. It seemed like a century ago that I'd discovered his tomb and his sarcophagus. Strange, if I were back there today, would I find Nefrure's body buried there, too?

I spent the next couple of days writing furiously in my journal. Tried to put everything down I'd learned from Nefrure. I kept thinking of her hair. It would never grow out now.

In the beginning the slaves stayed away. No Nefrure. No classes. Ramose still hadn't contacted me and I couldn't get any news from the guards. Ramose could be dead on a battlefield somewhere and how would I know?

Then one morning when I was walking in the gardens, Ahhotpe showed up. I hugged her. "I am so glad to see you! How have you been? How are the others?"

"They are sad over Nefrure's death. We miss her." The sunlight shone off her long hair. She was growing up and she was so pretty, I thought. What would happen to her if some soldier or some wealthy aristocrat took a fancy to her?

"I miss Nefrure, too, Ahhotpe. She was my ears and my eyes beyond these walls. Please, come and sit with me. There is food left over from breakfast. Eat with me, please? Keep me company, I've been so lonely." The girl tagged along behind me into my rooms and sat at the table. She was hungry and ate everything I put in front of her.

The girl's amber eyes, so like Nefrure's, met mine. "Everyone knows that Makere's soldiers tried to kill you and Nefrure died defending you. Makere will try again, be careful. Stay here where she cannot harm you."

"Has anyone heard anything about Lord Ramose?" I asked.

She caught me up on what was happening or as much as she knew. "No, Mistress, none of us slaves have heard anything, except there has been fighting along our borders not far from here and Pharaoh's armies are still not marching. They say the Hittites enslave, torture or kill all slaves they come across. Terrible times are coming and most of us are sorely afraid."

She hung her head and when she lifted it, she muttered, "Mistress, I know Nefrure was the one that brought the food to the gates most nights and now that she is gone some of us were wondering if—"

Kathryn Meyer Griffith

"You could continue the tradition?" I'd been waiting for that by the way she'd greedily consumed the food. The girl bobbed her head, eyes pleading. "Return after nightfall and I will have it ready for you." I'd order extra food for lunch and supper. It wouldn't be hard to fill a basket or two.

Ahhotpe stood up. "And will you keep teaching some of us to read and write? The others begged me to ask you."

I was relieved they still wanted to learn. I'd missed the classes, too. "I will. Tell them to come tomorrow morning, usual time, and I will be at the tree by the wall.

"When Lord Ramose returns, or if you or your friends hear anything of him, would you come and tell me?"

The girl said she would.

"When he returns if I ask him for a new woman to keep me company when he is not here, would you like to be that woman?"

Her smile was like the sun. "I would greatly like to be that woman." I could see that I'd pleased her by asking.

When she was gone I was lonelier than ever.

Thank goodness for Min. The cat and I had lunch together and she observed me as I painted a picture of her in the garden. At the last minute I brushed in an image of Nefrure standing in the shadows smiling. I cried softly the whole time I painted.

That night I sent the food to the gates with Ahhotpe. Later I couldn't sleep. Finally as the dawn's soft light began to seep into the night's blackness, I put a cover around me and roamed out into the garden. In the shimmering twilight of morning it was soothing to my soul and senses to sit among the flowers and sighing trees. To breathe in the aromatic air. These scents were so different than the modern scents of Boston mornings I'd been used to most of my life. No car fumes or factory smoke. No traffic noises or airplanes.

But I missed other things about Boston and I let my mind dwell on them.

I missed the quaint waterside restaurants with their ocean views and their delicious seafood. The salty air. Stopping by the bagel store to buy fresh bagels and flavored cream cheeses. The bookstores and the people milling around the college, debating politics and academia and taking all their modern luxuries for granted. I missed the autumn with the tangy scent of winter drifting through the air and the brightly colored leaves falling from the stately trees. If I stayed here any longer, I'd miss Halloween's jack-o-lanterns glowing on the porches and the Christmas lights twinkling in the snow.

I missed hot fudge sundaes with whipped cream and nuts and cherries on top. I missed chocolate. Right now I'd almost kill for a fat piece of milk chocolate, like I used to get at the neighborhood candy store. I missed my mother and my sisters and brothers. Snowball, even though I had a substitute. If time passing there was the same as here, then I'd been missing from the dig for months. Had they searched for me? Were they still searching? How was my family taking it and did they miss me as much as I did them? I wondered.

I sat on the bench in Ramose's garden in Egypt around 1340 B.C. and longed for the things I'd left behind in the future. Sitting vigil as the sun came up, I let my thoughts wander between the past—my past—and the future.

What was going to happen to me now? Perhaps someday I would go home, perhaps not. Maybe Ramose will return, maybe not. All I could do was take one day at a time. Keep living. I had no other choice.

That morning, I went back to teaching the slaves. There were more of them this time. By the end of the week there were even more. It felt good to be teaching again. It felt good to be among friends. To talk, teach and laugh.

After that Ahhotpe visited often, helped me in my day to day needs, after I sent a note requesting her to the slave who controlled her time. I still had power in the household. Slowly she took Nefrure's place and I was grateful. With someone to talk to I wasn't so lonely.

Another month passed without word or sign of Ramose and just when I'd given up hope and had started to think about what I would do if he never came home, where I would go and how I might survive, he returned.

Chapter Nine

Ramose came back in the middle of the night. He woke me gently, sitting beside me on the bed and smiling down at me. Reached out a hand to caress my face, push my hair back so he could see me better. I was so happy to see him I cried and threw my arms around him. There was the smell of sweat, leather and horses about him, but I didn't care.

"Are those happy tears, my love, that I have returned?"

I nodded against his shoulder. "I was afraid for you. There is unrest everywhere." All the worry and dread of the last weeks had caught up with me and shaking it off my shoulders gave me such sweet relief. Ramose was back. He hadn't died or abandoned me.

"I have been gone too long, Mag-gie. I have missed you so much. I never knew what missing someone meant until these last months. I never knew what loving someone meant."

As I came fully awake, my eyes took Ramose in. Dusty and road weary, he looked ten years older. There was a fresh scar along the side of his face and there were cuts and bruises below his left eye.

He looked like a man beaten in body and soul. But he held me in a tight embrace and I thought he was never going to let me go. He kissed me over and over on the cheeks, the lips. It was all I needed to know. He still loved me. He was still mine.

"My lord, I had no word all this time."

"I sent you messages. Many of them."

"I never received one."

"They must have been intercepted."

"Who would do such a thing?" I asked, but the name Makere echoed in my head.

"I have enemies, it could have been any of them, but I have no doubt it was Makere. The letters were to you and she wants you to disappear. She will not let me go easily."

Wait, I thought, until he hears what else Makere has been up to. She killed Nefrure; tried to kill me. Though at that moment I was only interested in what was wrong and why Ramose looked so defeated and haunted. There was a desperate look in his eyes I'd never seen before.

"What happened to you, my lord?"

"I have been fighting the Hittites and we are losing while they are gaining ground. Pharaoh never sent the reinforcements we needed so we had to retreat. General Haremhab and I had a falling out over Pharaoh and I have spent the last few weeks getting here. I could not let anyone know I was coming, for there are spies everywhere.

"My men and I returned on the run and most likely barely ahead of Haremhab's men. In Haremhab's eyes I am a traitor to him and to Egypt." He ceased talking, as if he'd said too much already and a groan escaped him.

"I had to check on my home. I had to see you again," he whispered in my ear. "Even before I washed the travel dirt from my body. To be sure you were still here…alive."

He released me and stood up, preparing to leave the room.

"I knew you would come back, if you were able." I smiled up at him.

I couldn't believe how happy knowing he was okay made me. There was this air about him of the fugitive. "Cannot you stay awhile with me?"

"I cannot. It is nearly dawn and I have matters, some grave, I must attend to. Yet I will return tonight for supper. We will talk. About everything."

He leaned down and kissed me one more time and petted Min, who was half-awake, snuggled beside me in bed. "I see you still have your little friend. She has grown."

"She has."

His eyes all of a sudden were serious in the lantern's faint light. "I heard your slave woman was killed. You were fond of her, I know. I am sorry.

"You must promise never to leave these apartments again without guards or me. Promise!"

"I promise." The tears were welling up and I was afraid of what I might say about Makere. That I loathed her for murdering my friend. That I wished she would vanish into another time…preferably the ice age.

So I said nothing. If he knew about the murder attempt, he probably knew who'd been behind it. Home just a short while and he knew everything. Of course, he'd have his own spies in the household. Someone had been watching me all along.

"I will find a new slave to replace the one you lost."

As if Nefrure could be replaced that easily, but he wouldn't understand that. "There is one, a young girl about twelve or so, they call her Ahhotpe. Can she take Nefrure's place?"

"As you wish. I will see you tonight," a whisper and Ramose was no longer at my side.

I fell asleep hugging Min and smiling.

When I woke a short time later, for confused moments I thought I'd dreamed Rarnose's coming back. Then I heard the ruckus outside and heard someone yelling that the Master was home. Get working. Look quick.

I jumped out of bed. On the table there was a small cloth wrapped package for me. A present from Ramose. I opened it.

It was an exquisite golden cat pin for my gown. The eyes were emeralds and there were other stones, carnelian, turquoise and lapis lazuli, on the tail. Tiny and delicate, it was the prettiest thing anyone had ever given me and probably, in my time, worth a small fortune.

Ramose. Again I asked, how had it happened that I'd fallen in love with this amazing man from another time? Was it fate or accident? Was I meant to love him? I didn't know. The amulet at my neck was cold and dark and silent. But I was still here in ancient Egypt. And Nefrure was dead. Ramose had turned away his lover Makere and loved me.

I'd changed history already. Hope it didn't mess

up the future.

Ahhotpe brought in my breakfast. "I was sent for, Mistress. I am to take care of you every day, all the time. No more waiting on petty women or Ramose's visitors in the palace."

She made an ugly grimace. She'd confided in me that she detested Makere and her women friends, who she sometimes had to attend to. They were vain and spiteful.

"I am to stay here with you from now on." She was clearly thrilled about it and hugged me in welcome. "Now you can teach me how to read and write whenever you wish. I can learn so much faster."

Having Ahhotpe around eased my heart. Nefrure had loved the girl as a daughter so I felt as if by helping her I was repaying Nefrure back in part for the life she'd given up for me.

And it was nice to have a friend again.

The day seemed fifty hours long because I wanted to see Ramose so badly. I had a hundred questions to ask him.

Since Ramose's night visit I couldn't stop brooding over his betrayal of Haremhab and what that might mean for us all. Haremhab was second in power in Egypt behind the pharaoh. If Ramose was Haremhab's enemy now, we all were.

I remembered from history that Haremhab was considered a sadistic and vengeful man, who, once he turned against the pharaoh and went after the crown of Egypt, disposed of anyone in his way.

"There are black days coming, Mistress," Ahhotpe predicted later after I'd asked why so many soldiers were marching past the windows. "There are reports that war with the barbarians is at our doorstep. That Tunip, Simyra and even Babylon have fallen under their swords.

"We are preparing to fight while Pharaoh cowers in his great palace and does nothing. We are all fearful for our very lives and even for Egypt's future."

"Ramose will protect you," I said, sure of it and not overly concerned.

Ahhotpe's eyes widened. "They say Ramose has fallen out of favor with my lord Haremhab. Soon *his* soldiers will come for us. We are all doomed." She had her long ebony hair braided and coiled at the base of her neck. Her sheath was so thin I could see every line of her frail body. Sweat gleamed on her skin.

Sometime in the last few months she'd grown up. She had the figure of a woman now, no longer a skinny girl. Food had helped. She was very pretty.

Summertime in Egypt. The days were so sweltering it was like living in a steam bath. Every day I was thankful for the coolness of the garden and its ponds. Grateful I wasn't one of the slaves toiling in the fields or in the kitchens.

"What do you mean?" I couldn't comprehend what the slave girl was talking about. She showed no emotion, no alarm. Just resignation. Would Haremhab come here? Attack us?

She never got to answer because Ramose stalked in, his face grim until he saw me and smiled, held out the arms that I flew into. His kiss was fire and I melted against him. In his arms I felt safe.

Egyptian Heart

Nothing bad could happen to me.

I pulled away and saw that his wounds had been attended to, he'd bathed and was wearing a clean kilt of green and white stripes. No jewelry, no makeup, no head covering. We had become that comfortable with each other, we could be natural.

I was in a gown of white that left one shoulder bare. The cat pin he'd given me was attached to the other shoulder of the gown. Sandals. No other jewelry except my scarab necklace. I'd pulled my hair back and had flowers in it. I'd spent a long time preparing for tonight. More than anything I'd wanted to be attractive for Ramose.

His eyes told me I'd succeeded.

"Thank you for the present." I touched the pin on my gown.

"I had it made for you, my little cat. It was waiting when I returned. Do you like it?"

"I love it."

The next thing he said wasn't what I expected. "We do not have a lot of time, my love." He took my hands tenderly, led me towards the doors that opened on the garden, and looked at the feast waiting for us outside on the patio. "We can eat, and I will tell you what is happening. There are decisions to be made." His tone was solemn.

We sat down. He didn't send Ahhotpe away. She lingered in the other room by the door, listening.

"Why do we not have much time?" My eyes drank in every contour of his face, the way he moved his hands as he spoke, the set of his jaw, and my heart was full. I had the feeling our time together was drawing to a close and it terrified me. Was he dumping me for Makere? She was so beautiful. Much more so than me. Had he seen her, succumbed to her charms, and changed his mind about me?

Makere would give him what I was not giving him. Sex. Or had he heard about my fighting with the soldiers; heard the surreptitious gossip about me being evil?

"I must take a long journey." There was food around us on the table, food on his plate. He hadn't eaten a thing. "A long dangerous journey and I will be gone for longer than before. Perhaps forever."

Forever? That could mean death. His death. My misery was overpowering my good sense. I was wallowing in sorrow already and he hadn't even left. "Where are you going?"

"There are forces lining up against me, Mag-gie. I have broken a sacred trust to an old friend. Openly defied him. Now I must do what my heart, not my head, tells me to do."

Ramose leaned over and took my hand. "I must leave tomorrow at dawn and I do not want to leave you."

"Then take me with you!" I pleaded. "Do not leave me here at Makere's mercy again. I can ride a horse. Live out on the desert. Sleep in a tent. Take me with you."

Ramose grinned slyly at me. "You at Makere's mercy? I think not. I heard about your run in with her soldiers. I heard what they are saying you did. You fought like a tiger and used magical powers to beat them. It is all over the palace what you did."

Egyptian Heart

He drew me closer across the table so our faces were nearly touching over the plates and goblets. "As I also know about you teaching the slaves to read and write and handing out food at night at the front gates." But there wasn't any anger in his voice. There was admiration. Awe.

"In a short time you have managed to become beloved by a large portion of my household. There are those who would already do anything for you. The guards outside your door love you. For your beauty, your intelligence and your kindness. Even for your strange ways."

"You are not upset with me?" I moaned, trying not to smile. I could see he was proud in some peculiar fashion. He looked at me as if I was an angel. Do these people believe in angels? I wasn't sure. Spirits, surely. Jinns and minor gods. Good and bad. Not angels, though. They'd never heard of angels, I'd bet.

"Why should I be? The slaves are happier, are working twice as hard and you told them it was me who sends the food each night. Now they smile at me when I pass instead of hang their heads and pout.

"I find I like being adored as much as being feared. Perhaps more. You have done me a favor.

"And you have made me more sure than ever that you are the woman that the seer foretold would come someday and change my life. Come someday to be my wife and the mother of my many sons. You are that great love I was promised."

He kissed me. I slid back into my chair. I didn't know what to say. I knew I loved him; had known it almost from the first moment I saw him sitting on that white horse of his in the courtyard. But how could this be? How could I stay here and become what he wanted me to become. Didn't that mess with history or the future or something?

God, the thought hit me as it had so many times in the last few months, perhaps I was really dreaming all this or maybe I was just nuts, locked up in some asylum back in the twenty-first century. My scholarly ambition and hard work having driven me over the edge somehow. Oh, my.

"And you will no longer have to worry about your rival, Makere." Ramose was still speaking, and finally eating as he gave me the rest of his news. "I have banished her for trying to harm you."

No further mention of Nefrure's murder. But then to Ramose, Nefrure had just been a slave.

"I sent her away. I gave her enough gold to set up her own household far from here. From me. She is a vindictive, malicious woman. I cannot bear to look at her these days. I do not see now how I ever put up with her." He shook his head and released a sighing breath. "It is me that has changed.

"Makere is nothing like you. You are good. Kind. You remind me of my queen." I saw the adoration, the love, he tried to hide for Pharaoh's wife, Nefertiti. I didn't begrudge him that, either. Many people had loved and adored Nefertiti, the lovely queen who'd stood faithfully beside a misunderstood, ugly little misshapen Pharaoh.

I skimmed over most of what he'd said, except the part about him leaving. "If you're leaving, fleeing, then take me with you. If you love me, do

Egyptian Heart

not leave me here alone again." I had another reason for wanting to go with him. We'd wasted so much time already and what if the amulet did have me on a timetable? What if I only had so much time with Ramose and no more? I couldn't stand to think of wasting what was left of it by being apart. "We have been separated too much. I want to go with you."

I could see the mind working behind the eyes. Weighing the possibility. Unmovable. Then unsure. Then hopeful. "It will be dangerous. There could be assassins behind us the whole journey. Lord Haremhab will guess soon enough what I am up to and will try to stop us."

I knew I'd won. "So where are we going and why...and when do we leave?"

Ramose actually laughed. "You have courage, I will give you that. We leave at dawn tomorrow. We ride for Pharaoh's city of Amarna on the banks of the Nile far from here. It will take weeks if we are favored by the gods or longer if we are not. We cannot be seen.

"And the *why* we are going?"

He lowered his voice because Ahhotpe was eavesdropping, "To beg our Pharaoh to *fight*. To convince him to send his armies against the Hittites and protect his allies that are crying for his help before all their cities fall before the sword. *To save Egypt and the pharaoh his throne. His very life.* If Pharaoh doesn't get off his knees and lead his armies into battle then General Haremhab and his army will find some way to rid Egypt of him and his family. The children. Their children's children.

They could all disappear or die."

The queen and her children, I thought, seeing the despair in Ramose's face. Pharaoh was considered a god and you didn't kill a god, but Haremhab doesn't kill him, I thought, Akhenaton dies first. Of natural causes, or unnatural? Yet Haremhab must be desperate enough to consider such an act. Is that, then, what actually happened to Nefertiti and her daughters in 1340 B.C? Haremhab slaughtered them?

Could we stop that? Is that also why I was here?

"We leave at dawn. Pack light, yes?"

I was excited. To be able to see Amarna and Pharaoh and his queen, that and being with Ramose. I was ready for the next adventure.

I heard Ahhotpe moving about inside. I knew she couldn't come along. I couldn't endanger her. She would have to remain here. I'd see if she could stay in my rooms and not go back to what she'd been doing before. That would please her. And eventually if the household was overrun with Haremhab's men, I'd see to it that she'd escape somehow to safety.

"We will be traveling hard," Ramose remarked. "Can you keep up?"

"I was born on a horse." I had only been on a horse once in my life. A trail horse that plodded along at five miles an hour and stumbled twice. I amazed myself and didn't tumble off. "I will not slow you down."

We finished our meal and Ramose and I sat for a time in the garden. He told me of the battles with the barbarians, his falling out with Haremhab and his flight from camp. I told him of being assaulted by Makere's soldiers and losing Nefrure. Explained as best I could why I was helping the slaves. We talked, holding hands or I leaned against his shoulder. I kept waiting for him to make a move, an attempt at seduction, but he didn't.

I wasn't insecure. I believed he loved me. I could feel it with every look and touch he gave me. They were promises of what we'd have someday. There was just a lot on his mind.

"I will leave you now," he said, as the night birds made their mournful calls up in the shadowed trees. "Dawn comes quickly and I have last minute duties to take care of before we ride out. I am sure you do as well. I will be here at dawn. Pack. Be ready."

After he left I went inside and with Ahhotpe's help, I packed for the journey. It didn't take long. I took my simplest gowns, one or two nice ones for court, if we made it that far, and their accessories, including the cat pin, and some slave's clothing that Ahhotpe had found somewhere for me. She'd brought me simple robes and headdresses in case I wanted or needed to dress as a common desert person or as a slave. Which I realized was a good idea. Hidden behind a baggy robe with my hair tucked beneath a simple cloth head covering, I wouldn't attract unnecessary attention. On a horse in the desert beneath a hot sun, keeping my skin covered also seemed like a wise idea. No skimpy see through sheaths for me.

I'd been surprised at how little I really needed. Being at the dig had taught me to live out on the desert and I was a camper from way back. My family used to camp up in the hills every summer. I was used to roughing it. Ahhotpe stuffed food, dried dates, figs, hard bread and cheese in a separate bag, and put water in a flask, to put on my saddle to eat and drink along the way. Three canvas bags of clothing and necessities.

"I hate leaving you, Ahhotpe," I admitted.

"With Makere and her women gone I will be safe. Do not worry, Mistress, I will keep your rooms, your things," she glanced at my paintings and my art supplies, at the cat sleeping on my bed, "safe."

"Do not give Min too much to eat or she will become fat," I kidded the girl, picked up the cat and snuggled with her. Min ate more than any cat I'd ever seen. She'd eat herself sick if I let her. She already had a tummy. I would miss her furry little face and her crazy antics. I'd take her along but Min loved her home. The gardens. Loved Ahhotpe and the other slave children. Her cat brothers and sisters. I let the cat lick my face and laughed.

"I will make sure she does not eat too much." Ahhotpe looked at me. "Would it be acceptable with you if my friends and I kept working on our letters at the wall as usual?" Ahhotpe, as Nefrure before, had learned so quickly from me she was far ahead of the others and had begun to teach them. She was a clever girl.

"It would be. Feel free to use anything here for the classes. And Khnumbaf, if you use my name, will bring you whatever supplies you need. Tell the others I will think of them. Ask them not to forget me." I smiled at the girl and thought how I would miss her, too, when I left. It seemed that every friendship I made here in the past held such emotion for me. Every feeling seemed heightened. Would I ever see Ahhotpe again? Would I ever see Min? I didn't have the answers.

Ramose had warned our journey could be dangerous. If Haremhab's soldiers caught us but I refused to think about that.

"Ahhotpe, if something should happen to me and I do not return, I want you to have everything here. My clothes, paintings, and jewelry." Ramose had sent me gowns of fine cloths and many expensive baubles. Ahhotpe could sell them or trade them. My journal I was taking with me. I didn't want it to fall into the wrong hands. "I will leave a written letter saying that they belong to you."

The girl was astonished, and her eyes were wet as she thanked me. "But you will return, Mistress. You must!"

"I will try. Yet if I do not, remember what I have said."

After Ahhotpe went to bed in her corner of the room, I was so wound up I couldn't sleep. It was only hours before we would ride out. Hours. I got up and wandered around the room and into the garden remembering the times I had spent there. It had been months and, yet, in some ways it felt like years. Other times it seemed like hours.

I had the feeling that I was never coming back.

I forced myself to lie down and rest. I slept for a few hours and then rose to dress for my journey in a cotton robe with a hood that could hide all of me, if need be. I drew back my hair in a braid and put a cloth over it tied in the back. On my face, arms and legs I rubbed a lotion that would protect my skin from the sun that Ahhotpe had given me. No make-up. No jewelry besides my amulet, which I tucked inside the neckline of the robe.

I'd said my final goodbyes to Ahhotpe and Min and was ready when Ramose came for me. He admired my disguise.

"You look like a pretty boy," he said. Then gathered me to him and kissed me. "You don't feel or kiss like a boy." He smiled, but I could see it was forced. He was nervous, tense. Every sound outside made him stop and listen. Whatever had happened when he'd been away had changed him. He was a man on the run.

This morning he was dressed in soldier's garb. Plain and efficient. Hues all in drab brown or beige so he would not stand out against the desert sands. A square of cloth protected his hair. Leather vest and short kilt left his legs bare except for tall leather riding boots.

"We will stop and eat lunch once we have put miles between us and Lord Haremhab's men. I—we—have stayed too long already."

I produced the pouch of food and the flask of water to tie around the pommel of my saddle. I'd eaten some dates while waiting and now gave Ramose a handful, which he chewed and swallowed as we were leaving. He seemed to get a kick out of me being prepared enough to bring along food.

Out in the sunlight the horses and men were waiting for us. I counted ten men and two enclosed

Egyptian Heart

carts being pulled by horses. The carts must hold our food and supplies, tents for sleeping. The desert, with its cold night temperatures and sandstorms, could be a hostile place without shelter. A soldier brought out my bags and loaded them into the rear of one of the carts. No slaves were coming with us.

"His name is Geb," Ramose said as he helped me into the saddle of a huge gray horse with mean eyes. Geb was the Egyptian earth god. Geb. I'd never seen such a big beast. The minute I was on top of him he started prancing in place as if he couldn't wait to go. I only hoped that I could handle him. Now I wished I wouldn't have lied to Ramose about being an experienced rider. But how hard could it be?

As we rode through the gates and I glanced back, there were slaves everywhere waving to us, to me. I recognized Ahhotpe and some of the slaves I'd been teaching. I waved back quickly with one hand and caught Ramose staring at me. Then I concentrated on what I was doing.

We galloped out into the desert and rode for what seemed like a long time. Of course I was bouncing around on the saddle like a ball until I thought my head was going to explode and my butt fall off. It wasn't hard steering the creature because he seemed to naturally follow the others ahead of him, who were all going at a brisk pace.

It was exciting, riding in a posse, escaping from danger as if I was in some storybook tale. For the first hour or so, then I wanted to stop and stretch my legs. Rest my butt. We kept riding. Whenever we slowed down I'd sneak my hand in the food pouch and eat something. Twice I rode close to Ramose and offered him some. Once he took it.

Ramose finally gestured and the horses trotted down and came to a halt behind an outcropping of rocks and scraggly trees. The desert wasn't all sand and dunes yet. There were sparse patches of green and brown here and there.

Ramose helped me from my horse. "You are not an experienced rider, are you?"

"No," I mumbled, stretching and hobbling in front of the horse. I avoided Ramose's eyes as I got my land feet back.

"You will learn quickly," he assured me and gave orders to some of his men to take away the horses, feed and water them, make a fire and prepare the food.

Ramose and I sat on soft cushions and ate roasted pig, drank a little wine and much water. We still had a long way to ride, he told me, before we could set up camp for the night.

"We would keep riding day and night if I could manage it, but it would be hard on you," he smiled, "and kill the horses and then we would never get to the river that will take us to Amarna."

I could see the wisdom of that, besides I'd be lucky to get through another half a day on that horse without my butt going numb and falling off. And sleep…I already wanted a long nap. The riding, excitement, air and sun had exhausted me. By evening it would be a miracle if I could stay on the horse much less keep riding it.

The lunch break was short. We ate, spoke a little, mostly trivial stuff because soldiers were around us attending to their duties. Ramose had a reputation of fierce warrior to uphold. He didn't fawn over me around his men. I found I respected him for that. I'd catch him glancing at me and he'd smile that secret smile of his that reassured me he loved me and everything was all right.

The day was hot and getting hotter, but off to the east there was a threatening blackness crawling along the edge of the sky.

"That is a desert storm approaching." Ramose squinted his eyes and searched the horizon. "It will be a bad one and it will be here by dark. So now we had better ride."

I'd been in Egypt weeks and ancient Egypt for months and had only seen rain once in either place. Here. A light drizzle. Never seen a bad storm. I wrongly thought: Well, how bad could it be?

We packed up and rode away.

Chapter Ten

The rest of the day the storm shadowed us, a horde of dark ghosts creeping closer. I don't know what came first, the storm night or the real night. When the wind turned chilly and howled around us and there was the smell of water heavy in the air, Ramose ordered we should make camp. We found a copse of shrubs and bowed trees by a group of towering stones and set up camp. The stone formations would give us sanctuary from the winds.

The soldiers pitched a tent for Ramose and I and secured it firmly to the ground with deep wooden stakes behind the largest rock. I rested inside, as the men finished setting up camp, and listened to the horses neighing on the rising wind and the soldier's distorted shouts. The noises swirled, lost, about the camp.

It was a steel gray outside. Examining the tent as I laid out our sleeping rolls and placed my belongings in a corner, I hoped it would withstand the coming storm. A strong tent, it was fashioned with thick canvas and well-sewed seams. A portable house.

Later, when the storm hit and Ramose joined me in it we had a meal, mostly bread, fruit and leftover meat from lunch that the men brought us before they retired to their own shelters for the night.

As the rain and sand outside pelted against the tent and the wind tried to knock it over, Ramose and I huddled beside each other, wrapped in blankets to keep warm. He could hardly keep his eyes open, but it'd been a long time since we'd been together and he didn't want to sleep yet.

"Are we safe?" I heard the sounds of the storm, a monster rummaging around beyond the walls of the tent. Here inside we were protected and comfortable. For now.

"We will be safe. I have prayed to Aton, the one true god, to protect us until we can get to Pharaoh's city. That is a small enough favor to grant, unlike saving a country."

I was caught off guard. "You believe in Akhenaton's one god?" Many times he'd spoken of other Egyptian deities so I'd thought he believed in the old ways. In the old gods.

Sitting so near him, I could feel his shrug. "It is time I proclaim that I do. Having broken ties with Lord Haremhab, and condemned his plans, I can finally speak of my true belief openly."

"That belief is very unpopular these days."

Giving me a tortured look, he said, "That belief has torn Egypt apart. Most still worship the many gods and goddesses of Egypt and have not forgiven Akhenaton for moving the capital city from Thebes to Amarna, much less for outlawing the Priests of Amon from worshiping their Gods. The Priests are beloved and very powerful. Do you believe in just one god, Mag-gie?"

I smiled in the lantern light. "Yes, I do. One god."

"What do you call your god?"

I decided not to go too deeply into details. I gave him the simplified version. "He has no name. He just is. But he is a good and kind god. Forgiving. All knowing."

"So," Ramose kissed my cheek, "you have remembered more of your old life?"

I wanted to tell him the truth, yet I couldn't. Not yet. We knew each other well enough that I sensed he knew when I was lying.

Someday, I would have to tell him, if I stayed. Not tonight. In his exhausted state he'd think I was either demented, mad, or he was. "Bits and pieces only. The memory comes and goes."

"You have such a strange way of speaking at times." I felt his lips, against my cheek in the gloom, curved in a smile. "Yet you speak our language expertly. There are many strange things about you. I discover more each day.

"How *did* you fight off Makere's men when they attacked you? I was told you fought like a demon, all hands and feet, in a way no one has ever seen."

This could be tricky. "It was something I must have learned somewhere, sometime. I do not remember much more than that. I just know how to defend myself."

"And I am grateful for it."

"So am I."

"And do all slaves read and write in your land?" he wanted to know, still trying to get me to tell him

Egyptian Heart

what I wasn't.

"We do not have slaves."

He turned my face to his and in the dark I could feel his eyes on me. "What are you really, Mag-gie? Are you truly human or are you a jinn as so many say you are? *Who are you? Where did you come from?"* There was a plea in his voice that hurt me.

"I am Maggie Owen. The woman who loves you," I breathed, and tried not to sound too guilty for continuing to keep the truth from him. He just wouldn't understand, no matter how I put it. He just wouldn't. "And I come from a faraway land—"

"America? I have never heard of such a land and no one I ask has heard of such a land. What lands is it near?"

"I do not remember what lands surround it. Water, I think."

"An island?" He chuckled and hugged me tighter. He knew I wasn't going to answer. It had become a sort of game with us. He asked questions and I evaded them.

"Now it is my turn to ask a question," I said. "Why did you let me come with you?"

He was silent for such a long time I thought he wasn't going to answer. Then, "I might not be able to go home after this and I cannot live without you. If you are a warrior jinn, you may be of use if Lord Haremhab's soldiers catch up to us. You can use your powers to help us fight them."

I didn't know if he was teasing or if he meant it. I didn't need to. *I cannot live without you* was all I had heard.

"I want my queen to meet you. You are special

and she will be delighted with you. She appreciates uniqueness and beauty."

"I am not beautiful."

"In that you are wrong. You are very beautiful. Too beautiful. I keep asking myself if it is a smart move to parade you through the royal court."

"Afraid you will lose me to another more powerful man?"

"You might say that."

"You have nothing to worry about," I responded softly. "I will not leave you." If only I could be sure of that. I had heeded Sayed's warning to never take my amulet off. I'd wanted to so many times, especially in the beginning, thinking it might then automatically send me home, but I'd been afraid to. What if I took it off and it did nothing? Or if taking it off destroyed the magic and left me stranded here forever?

"I am not worried about you leaving me yet more that someone will take you from me."

"Of that you have nothing to worry about, either."

"Ah, you will beat them up until they give you back?" Humor in his suggestion.

"Something like that." I nestled closer to him and let him kiss me.

Outside the storm screamed and pounded like a banshee at the tent. Ramose held me firmly as I shivered. Though outside the world was in turmoil, I felt content with him. All alone in our own little world, I didn't want it to end. No slaves or servants or generals tearing us apart. I was happily cozy with the man I loved.

Egyptian Heart

We held each other, kissed, and laughed; he didn't attempt any other liberties with me.

Perhaps because he hadn't slept in days and was bone weary, he was holding himself back, and since I wasn't ready to go any further myself, I was glad not to have to say no again. I kept asking myself: How long will that last? How long can I keep out of his bed? After all, he was only a flesh and blood man. They had their needs. As I did. It was getting more difficult by the hour, not letting him make love to me. I wanted him so badly in every way. But a nagging voice in my head kept warning me not to succumb. For now. I knew I had to listen. I always did.

We fell asleep in each other's arms as the storm raged outside and when dawn came we climbed out to see if the rest of the camp was still there. It was.

The day was clear and sunny. No remnants of rain, as if miles of sand had soaked it in like a dry sponge. That was the way the desert was when you were on it. Thirsty and endless.

Two of the soldiers, a prickly headed, gravelly voiced man and another one with many battle scars on his body, cooked up breakfast over a campfire as the others got us ready to move out, fed and readied the horses and took down the tents. I noticed that wherever I was, the soldiers weren't. I came around a tent and I saw them striding away. I walked towards them and they scattered.

They were afraid of me.

Before we saddled up Ramose gave me pointers on how to ride. It helped. When we cantered off into the desert I wasn't bouncing in the saddle as much as before. Ramose slowed our pace down. Not just for me, he said, but to spare the horses. "We have a long journey ahead of us and if we kill our mounts we will have to walk to the banks of the Nile."

"A long walk?"

"A very long walk."

The next day was pretty much like the first. Ride, rest, eat, ride some more in the hot sun then, after a meal of roasted meat or dried fruit, collapse into our tent for the night. We rode through sand and rugged terrain with few trees, many rocks, and no sign of people. Ramose had told me that morning that we would ride for many days through sand but that ultimately we'd meet up with the Nile River.

He hadn't seemed as worried about being followed the second day, yet he still left scouts behind our path to check if anyone was trailing us. They reported no one.

By the third day I was so sore from riding I could barely move at the end of it. I hid it well. Didn't want Ramose to think I was a hindrance. I slept like the dead every night.

Yet I loved every second of it. I was with Ramose, riding through a time I had once only read and dreamed about. Slowly, as we drew closer to the river, we began to see more palm and fig trees and other vegetation. We came across settlements, nomads and desert dwellers. Common Egyptians living their lives in their huts of reed mixed with mud, working in the fields that had begun to clot the land; eating their bread soaked in barley beer at the end of their long days. Most of them ignored us. Some, frightened, ran away or hid in their houses.

Egyptian Heart

If you were a poor Egyptian, any soldier or rich man was someone to be distrustful of. Fearful of.

We traveled for days and days. I lost count. I got to know Geb better and soon I had him eating out of my hand. Ramose said I was spoiling him with all the treats I gave him. I didn't care. I'd grown to love that horse. He'd come when I called him; followed me around when I dismounted, if he wasn't tied up. The horse had so much spunk, but had a huge heart as well. I became a fairly decent horsewoman. I grew to depend on and love Geb. He was a really smart horse, avoided snake holes almost supernaturally and became very protective of me. Heaven help anyone who looked menacingly at me or got too close. Geb was right there, snorting and eyes afire.

I'm sure the men thought I'd bewitched him as well.

Getting closer to the river, sometimes we'd find wells, ponds or streams where we could wash up and replenish our water supply. As the days passed into weeks the soldiers riding with us became less wary of me. Some even smiled or chatted when they had to, but they all treated me with deference just as they saw Ramose treat me.

Most nights Ramose and I would talk late over the campfire and go to sleep in each other's arms in the tent. He told me he loved me though he didn't attempt to make love to me. He said he was waiting. Waiting for what he wouldn't tell me, just that he was waiting.

Perhaps waiting for me to tell him the truth.

And I also think it had something to do with our

visit to Amarna. I wasn't sure. Some nights when our snuggling would almost go too far, Ramose would kiss me gently, get up, and go sleep right outside the tent. I knew he desired me. Loved me. He'd more restraint than any man I'd ever met. I thought it amazing that he would wait for me. That was the way I was raised so I didn't think it was unusual to wait, to save sex for a true love and a commitment. I loved Ramose more for caring how I felt.

One morning, I woke before dawn, slipped into my clothes, and went out into the scrub trees and bushes behind the tent on a call of nature. It was dark but the air glowed the way it does right before the sun comes up. Afterwards, I trekked a ways from the camp, exploring and enjoying the pristine morning. It was nice to have a few moments alone. Being a woman in a camp full of warriors wasn't easy.

Finding a stone ledge that jutted out enough to sit on about six feet off the ground, I climbed up and sat. Thinking about the last few months, the last few days.

Slowly the sun began to come up. It was beautiful. I drank it all in.

I heard the horses in camp neighing and whinnying in nervousness and then fear and it brought me out of my reverie. There below me, about fifteen feet away was a lion.

A real lion. Lounging lazily in the sun. I had a crazy image of tiny Min the first day I'd gotten her, sleepy-eyed and bored as a cat can look, don't know why. This cat in front of me was no pet. He wouldn't purr if I tried to pet him.

I'd never seen a flesh and blood lion except in a zoo. Behind iron bars. Lions were extinct in modern Egypt but thousands of years ago, in Ramose's time—this time—lions had been plentiful. They'd roamed the deserts in prides and the Egyptian people had worshipped them as gods when the royals hadn't been hunting them for sport. Many a traveler had feared wild lions.

I never should have left the camp alone, without a weapon. Too late now.

I knew I should get down and run. But my legs were jello. Not my mind. It was going so fast I couldn't keep up with my own thoughts. I was freezing but the air was heating up from the rising sun. A misty vapor hung in the air around me.

My lion was a huge shaggy beast with a massively maned head and feral eyes. Three times my size. Its tawny-hued hide, as the sun's light shone on it, looked deceptively soft to the touch. Steel muscles rippled beneath the fur. It lifted its head and scrutinized me as its mouth yawned open to show rows and rows of yellowed razor-sharp fangs as big around as my fingers. It looked like a furry Jaws.

What would it feel like to be eaten alive? I didn't want to find out. Fight or flight?

I could pretend to be part of the rock and maybe the beast will just go away.

The lion roared and my body shook. It swatted a huge paw in the air at me.

Tried it. Didn't work. The lion was staring hungrily right at me and started to pad my way, its tail thumping back and forth, and its muscles getting ready to spring. It was so *big*.

Definitely flight.

The lion growled loudly, showing its teeth, and someone screamed. I think it was me.

I frantically looked around. I could climb higher up the rocks. Did lions climb? I think they did. Scratch that idea.

I could run. Lions could run, too. Really fast. I remember that from the nature channel. Scratch that. I looked for a stick or a big rock on the ledge. Wasn't any.

I began to scream and shout. The lion was advancing on me anyway. Maybe I could scare it off or someone would hear me and come to help.

That's when I saw the loose rocks up above me. I climbed like a monkey, yelling for help the whole time.

When Ramose and his men arrived I was throwing head-sized rocks at the creature. Hit him a few times, too. Between the eyes and on the nose. It hadn't stopped it. Just made it really, really mad.

Without hesitation and without uttering a word, Ramose swiftly took aim and threw a spear that embedded itself deeply into the chest of the beast. The lion roared in pain as it clawed at the wooden shaft. It forgot me and tried to lunge at Ramose. The second spear, handed to Ramose from one of his soldiers, hit the lion between the eyes in midair.

Ramose jumped aside at the last moment and the beast missed its mark, collapsing to the ground without a whimper.

Ramose had killed the lion. The danger was

over. I was safe. I closed my eyes in relief and crumpled against the rocky ledge.

When Ramose stood below me and spread his arms, I didn't waver. I threw myself from the rock into his strong embrace. He caught me easily and clasped me passionately to his chest. "I love you, Mag-gie. Do not ever leave me," he murmured and kissed me.

"How did you find me so quickly?"

"I heard your voice asking for help in the tent as clear as if you were beside me. You said there was a lion. I roused the men, got our weapons, and we came searching for you. Then I heard your screams."

If he hadn't been looking for me he wouldn't have made it in time. I'd have been mauled or dead. How had he heard me while still in the tent? I didn't know and I didn't question it. I was merely grateful to be alive.

"I love you," I said. "And thank you for saving my life."

Ramose wanted a souvenir of the day so his men took the lion away to skin. But I heard them muttering about my magic and how it had brought Ramose to my side in time to save me.

The rest of the day I saw them eyeing me from a distance, their faces full of awed respect and a touch of that old fear again. My reputation as a sorceress was growing.

That night before the campfire Ramose teased me about the rocks. "You were doing pretty well before I got there. That lion was ready to run."

I only smiled. We both knew that wasn't true.

That lion had been ready to eat me.

I was happy that night. The man I loved had slain a wild beast for me. He'd saved my life. What more could a heroine in a story want? What more could a woman want?

That was the last time I wandered off alone from camp. Not that I could have. Ramose wouldn't let me out of his sight as our journey continued. More desert. More heat. More riding. Sand in my teeth, my hair, and hiding in my clothes.

We were lucky and the weather held. No more storms. About a week later the air began to cool and the desert began to gradually turn green. We began to see more water. Streams and ponds here and there. We began to see more people and small villages.

One evening, almost two weeks after the lion incident, as twilight was settling in and the world was a haze of rosy light, Ramose led my horse and I to the top of a large hill.

"Look, Mag-gie, the Nile. She goes on forever. Is she not breathtaking?"

Geb quivered beneath me as I pulled him to a full halt and gazed down at the miles and miles of glistening water. "Breathtaking," I echoed. I'd seen the Nile in my time. Muddy and full of boats and barges but not that impressive as it curled through the Egyptian lands. It'd reminded me of a ghost river with ghost people. Its glory days long over.

This Nile was different. The water clearer and the colors, more vibrant, were bluer, greener and grayer. The sky seemed more vivid. There was no smog. No lights in the distance.

Egyptian Heart

Now the ghost people were alive and floating on their menechous and bairs, quaint wooden boats I'd only seen in drawings, their voices hovering over the flowing currents. The river was truly alive now.

The hazy tangerine light lit the boats and the water up so it looked like a picture postcard. So distant, so unreal and so incredibly breath stealing. The skies were a pure azure-blue, darkened by the setting of the sun. It was that time of day my mother had called magic time. The enchanted hour of twilight.

"I would love to paint this. It is so lovely." I soaked in every detail to remember for some later date when I could recreate it. The people on the boats were tiny bodies moving or lolling around on deck and their voices were whispers on the breezes. It was a miniature world creeping down an endless river of sublime beauty. Tiny villages lined the shores with tiny buildings stark against the horizon.

I couldn't stop looking at the river world. Ramose eased his white mount, who he called Khons after the moon god, up against Geb and clasped my hand.

"We will spend tonight at my father's house," he said.

"Your father?" Had I heard right?

"Chnum and his wife Tiye live a few miles down the river. I sent a messenger ahead to let them know we are coming. We will board our horses there and take a boat for the remainder of our journey. The boat will be faster and will allow the horses to rest."

"Chnum and Tiye are your father and mother?"

Ramose had never mentioned either one. I was beginning to believe he was an orphan.

"Chnum is my father and Tiye is his wife. My true mother died at childbirth. She was the queen's sister."

I twisted in the saddle to stare at him. His mother had been *Nefertiti's sister*. That explained so much. Nefertiti was Ramose's *aunt*. Now I knew why he loved her. Nefertiti had not been of royal blood, so neither had her sister. It had probably changed Ramose's life. He couldn't become Pharaoh because of his bloodline so he hadn't been important enough to keep from being brought up by his real father. If he'd been a son of one of Pharaoh's true sisters, he'd have never left the palace. I'd never have met him.

"Tiye raised me. She has always been a mother to me. She is the one who was told by the seer about you. I owe her much and my father adores her. He has no other wife but her."

I knew how rare that was.

"And I get to meet her and your father?"

"Soon." Ramose heeled his horse back the way we'd come and I followed. My mind was mulling over what he'd revealed.

Ramose was related by blood to Nefertiti and that meant I was probably going to meet her. It was an Egyptologist's dream come true. One of *my* dreams come true.

I watched Ramose ride ahead of me. He sat so strong and tall in the saddle and I had come to love him so much. But there were many secrets he was keeping from me, as I was keeping secrets from him. I thought I'd known him and realized I didn't know him well at all.

Nefertiti was his aunt by birth. My, my.

Chapter Eleven

Chnum's house was a palace much like his son's. The basic layout was similar, large and rambling; same sort of gleaming white buildings and extravagant courtyard. They had the same taste. It had gardens, man-made ponds, stables and slave quarters in the back far away from the main house. There was much wealth there. Pharaoh had been good to Chnum Nakh-Min.

Yet where Ramose's was a desert palace, Chnum's was a river palace. Hardly any sand. There were lush grass, tall trees, shrubs and bright flowers everywhere because we were near water. Lots of shade. It was a gorgeous place.

Ramose gave me a little background on his parents before I met them. "My father was Public Administrator under the last pharaoh and for a while under Akhenaton when he first came to the throne. He served faithfully for many years until he disagreed with Akhenaton on some court policy or other—it was so long ago I cannot recall what it was over—and Akhenaton bade him retire. My father was ready to come back home and tend to his people and lands and did not fight Pharaoh's decision. My father is content here away from court and its endless conspiracies.

"My mother, Tiye, is happy my father is home, as well. You will like her, Mag-gie. She has a warm heart and she believes in signs and omens and—"

Egyptian Heart

"Seers?" I'd laughed.

"Yes, soothsayers she finds in food markets." Ramose had even grinned at me when he'd said that.

We rode in and a couple, perhaps in their fifties, which was old for ancient Egyptians, greeted us at the gate. The man, a shorter, stockier version of Ramose stepped forward and embraced his son after he dismounted. The older man's hair was gray, thinning on top, and he had a mustache. Eyes with a tinge of brown in the black took me in as he welcomed me without a smile.

The woman, dressed in a one-shouldered gown of pale green and a collar necklace of silver and colored stones around her regal neck, was still lovely, her figure trim and lithe. Her dark hair was gray streaked and her honey-brown eyes were sharp as she watched me sitting up in the saddle.

Ramose squeezed her, kissed her on the cheek and called her mother. It was easy to see he loved both of these people and they loved him.

Ramose turned, put a hand up to help me dismount and gave me a kiss in front of them. "This is Mag-gie 0-wen," he introduced me with pride.

"The woman who came to me from a faraway land without a memory. A remarkable woman. The woman I love."

I heard Ramose say the words but that he'd actually told his parents he loved me didn't sink in until later. I was too worn out and hungry for much of anything to register except that we could rest and get something to eat and drink. Get out of the relentless sun. The last few weeks it seemed I'd always been either thirsty, hungry or hot.

I caught the expression of surprise on his father's face and the startled look cross his stepmother's. She was looking at my hair and my face. Did she remember the seer's prophecy?

"Mag-gie, this is my father, Chnum Nakh-Min, and my mother, Tiye Nakh-Min."

"We are honored to have you stay with us." Chnum's voice was a huskier copy of his son's. He was smiling. While his wife kept looking between Ramose and me as if she was searching for answers in our faces. To what, I didn't know.

She seemed distracted at first but then a smile also warmed her face as she looked at me.

I was wearing one of the mud-colored slave robes I'd gotten from Ahhotpe, my face was sunburned and dirty. I've looked better, but gave her a weak smile as I took the linen covering off my head and tried to wipe the grime from my face with dirty fingers.

It was cooler than it'd been in weeks and it felt good to be standing on my feet again. I'd grown to love Geb, but my butt was almost as numb as the first day I'd ridden him.

We'd been on the road a long time and the thought of a real bath and a night's sleep in a real bed sounded like heaven to me.

Ramose's mother took over. She marched up and put an arm around me. "My child, you look exhausted. Come with me inside. I imagine you would enjoy a bath and a meal, yes?" She smelled of oranges and eucalyptus and her kindness was sincere.

Egyptian Heart

"Yes." I nodded and flashed a look at Ramose over my shoulder as the older woman led me away.

"I will see you at dinner," Ramose mouthed and threw me a kiss. The last glimpse I had was of him walking away, deep in discussion with his father. Their laughter and conversation accompanied me into the cool hallways of the palace.

It was as splendid inside as it had been on the outside. It put me in mind of Ramose's palace the first night I walked the corridors with Nefrure, gazing at the wall art and sculptures.

Thinking of my dead friend made me melancholy. She would not have cared much for this place, saying it was a rich person's world. One she didn't belong in. I smiled, reminiscing.

The Egyptian life scenes painted along the passageways were so realistic it was as if I was moving through a crowd of real people. Hieroglyphs filled panel after panel and Tiye caught me studying them.

"They are the story of our family, Ramose's family. Our history, past, present and our dreams and hopes for the future. Ramose says you can read and write?"

"I can."

"He also says that you are a woman of much intelligence and kindness to those beneath you and that you are a woman of great magic?"

I wondered how she could know so much about me.

"The great magic, no. That is only malicious gossip that has been spread about me." There was no way I was going to admit to being a sorceress when I wasn't one, even to Ramose's stepmother, as nice as she was being towards me.

We reached the end of the hallway and started down another. The floors beneath my worn leather boots were marble. Slick and cool. There were renderings of the pyramids in the sunlight, twilight and moonlight all around us. It seemed as if I'd stepped into another land.

"My son writes to me all the time," she said in explanation. "He has told me about you, including the malicious gossip." So she could read and write, she was an educated woman, too. I should have known.

She turned to me. "Meeting you, I do not believe it. I can see my son loves you. I am happy he is with you and no longer with Makere. A truly *evil* woman." She chuckled and caught my eye. There was acceptance there. It made me feel good, for here was an ally.

"I am happy he is with me as well."

Tiye embraced me, as she would have a daughter. It warmed my heart that she was so willing to accept me. I liked her already.

She showed me to a suite of comfortable rooms and said they would be mine for as long as I stayed. I didn't tell her that wouldn't be long. One night. Ramose was anxious to get to Amarna. She called out and slaves came running. A few words later and I had a tub full of hot water, soaps and perfumes. Food on the way.

"I will go and attend to the night's menu," she declared and swept out of the room as I was beginning to disrobe for my bath. I'd become less ashamed of showing my naked body since I'd been in ancient Egypt. I'd become more Egyptian I guess. I wasn't about to dance around buck-naked, especially in front of men, but I didn't feel as uncomfortable undressing in front of other women as I once had. I was adapting. I'd seen children in Ramose's house running around unclothed during the hottest parts of the day, which was common, so I'd lost some of my shyness.

I lounged in my tub for a long while. Washed my hair thoroughly. It felt good to be clean. Then I took some time and caught up my journal. I'd been writing in it the whole trip, whenever I could steal a few minutes alone from Ramose and his soldiers. Not often enough.

The day was ending and I'd finished washing, had eaten some of the food and drink the slaves had brought me, and was half-asleep on the bed when Tiye returned.

"I have brought you clothes for tonight, Maggie." She pronounced my name exactly like Ramose did; making it sound exotic. I was beginning to like it said that way. In her arms was the loveliest gown I'd ever seen. A long flowing sheer-linen robe of white, with purple vertical stripes that were lined with silver thread that strapped under the breast and fell into pleats. There were bright colored ribbons tied into the skirt. She placed the gown in my arms and I stroked the fabric with my fingers. It was cotton but it felt like silk.

"It is lovely." I met her golden eyes. She was staring at me again. Probably because of my hair which now was clean and looked even lighter, or my ivory skin and strange colored eyes. But she said nothing about them.

"Ramose has asked if you would wear the jewelry he has sent as presents for you." She handed me a beautifully engraved box. Inside was a lovely pair of silver and purple stoned dangling earrings, an arm bracelet and ring to match, and a tiara, made of dangling delicate twists of silver to hang from my hair. Another fortune in baubles, I mused, as I lifted an earring to the light from the windows and watched it sparkle. There was make-up in the box, too. Not a lot, just enough for me. Ramose knew I didn't care for it. This was his way of asking me to wear at least a little. He wanted me to impress his parents.

"If you see Ramose before I do, thank him for these gifts." I knew better than to protest or not accept them. That's when I remembered Ramose's comment about me becoming his wife. I looked up at Tiye and we both smiled at the same time.

"I have never seen my son so in love," she remarked. "You must be a very special woman."

"Not so special." I hung my head. I didn't belong here. Not really. It was something I had let myself forget too often the last weeks, riding besides Ramose and his men in the desert or sleeping in Ramose's tent by his side each night. At the campfire, under the night sky, chatting and laughing, sharing the day with Ramose and his men. Being saved from the lion. All so exhilarating. I thought it would never end. This dream had become way too real.

But, as everyone else I'd met here, I could not

tell any of this to Tiye.

"He loves you," she said. "He believes you are the one he has waited all his life for."

I glanced up. "The one the seer foretold you of?"

She sat down on the edge of the bed and laid a hand over mine. "I believe you are the one also. Yet it is more than that. I see something in you I have never seen in another. Your eyes are far away, Maggie. There is a look about you that says you are not one of us. Not of our...world."

I was flabbergasted by her intuition. Was she guessing? Fishing? Had she meant not one of us as in their class, or something else? Not of their world, as meaning from another world or another time? There was a difference about her, too, something deeper than her outer beauty and generous ways, something so spiritual.

It was in her amber gaze. *An old soul,* as my mother called it, and it recognized mine. Then I had it. Tiye reminded me of my mother.

And I couldn't stop my tears. Suddenly I missed my family so much. My time. My old life. I never thought I could have, but I did. I loved Ramose, but I missed all that.

"I am so sorry! I did not mean to make you cry." Tiye was beside herself. "Please. My son would never forgive me if I made you sad."

"It is not what you said, it is a memory I had of something I loved and have lost." I wiped the tears away and got up from the bed, the gifts still in my hands.

She sat there looking up at me, her face

perplexed but calm. "Ramose told us about your forgetting." She said the word as if it clarified my whole problem. Which, in a way, it did. My *forgetting*. I almost laughed, but covered it with my hand and laid the gown and the box on the bed.

"I am sorry for your troubles." Tiye stood up and smiled at me once more. "While you are here you are one of us. Our family. Do not feel lonely or unwanted. I welcome you, *daughter*. I hope we can become friends." She held her arms out and I fell into them. It felt right and somehow so familiar, as if my own mother were hugging me through her.

Mom would have a field day with this. Seeing as she believed in reincarnation and all. She'd probably say that Tiye was her in an earlier life.

Afterwards hearing the woman go on about the dinner and the festivities they had planned for Ramose and I, the way she chuckled when something tickled her, I could almost believe in it myself.

My mother also believed that in every new life a person met the same souls that had been close to them in other lives. In a way this was like a new life for me. Would I meet my sisters and brothers here as well? My friends? Was Snowball the reincarnation of Min? Gave me something to think about.

That evening, dressed and prettied up, I sat next to Ramose, who was lovingly attentive and held my hand most of the night or begged for kisses, in an informal eating hall with his family around me. His mother and father, his father's grandmother, Sitamun, who was so ancient she was nearly a walking mummy, and a younger sister he clearly doted on called Hegt were also at the table.

Sitamun barely said anything the whole evening, barely ate anything, but her old eyes were alive and watched Ramose and I like a hawk. Every once and a while, she'd grab my arm with her claw hand and squeezing, croak something like, "You sure are a tall one, child." Or, "You look like the goddess Isis, do you know that?" Or, "Eyes of a cat. Bet you can see good in the dark, ey?" The grandmother I'd never had. Mine had both died young.

Hegt was a quiet girl—at first. Once she got over her shyness of me, she jabbered constantly. Pretty. About fifteen. The only true child of Chnum and Tiye together. Her doe-brown eyes were tender, her long cinnamon hair shiny and her skin tawnier than Tiye or Chnum's. She had a true Egyptian nose: long, sharply chiseled and narrow. She adored her older brother and hung on him all night, as if he would leave again if she let him go.

She asked me a hundred questions about our journey. About me. Was as curious as a normal teenager from my time and wanted to know if Ramose and I were lovers yet. She confessed to me by the end of the evening that she had three admirers that her parents approved of and had to choose which one she would marry.

"If I do not marry soon, I will be an old hag. I am way past marrying age," she complained.

Made me wonder what she thought of me. Heck, I was way past marrying age by her standards. She giggled too much and tossed her hair a lot. She made Ramose smile. I felt a fondness for her right away.

There were other people there as well. Friends of Ramose that lived close enough to make it there for our visit and an aunt and uncle on his stepmother's side. They were all nice people. But they gawked at me when I wasn't looking, like most people had since I'd gotten to Egypt. They covered it well, though, I had to acknowledge that. They were polite.

They didn't talk behind my back.

There was entertainment, but family style. Nothing like the almost naked dancers and provocative singers from my first banquet. Which now seemed so long ago. There were young slaves softly playing flutes and singers singing love ballads. Some of them very young and very good. I really enjoyed the music. All of it. It soothed and made me forget my…troubles.

Tiye insisted I tell her about the lion and sat there with wide eyes as I did.

"You were so brave. I would have fainted."

"I almost did. Then your son," I flashed a grin at Ramose, "arrived to save me. I have never seen a large beast killed before. Your son was so brave."

Tiye leaned over, completely serious. "You would have dealt with the creature one way or another with your magic if you would have needed to, my son says."

I was shocked. What had Ramose been telling these people? "I told you before, I have no magic." My smile was unsteady. "I know how to defend myself. My looks and my ways are strange, I grant that. I have many talents. I can read and write. I use my head. I am lucky. That is all. Those are my magics."

She looked at me, falling silent, as if she didn't believe me, her eyes twinkling knowingly.

To change the subject, I asked Tiye to tell me about Ramose as a child and a young man. She didn't stop talking until she overheard Ramose say to his father that we were sorry we couldn't stay longer than one night.

"So you must leave us tomorrow morning?" Tiye switched her attention to Ramose.

"At dawn, Mother. I am sorry, for time is short. I must have audience with Pharaoh and the queen before it is too late. I have important information for them."

Chnum's expression was distraught. "It will not be an easy meeting you will have once you get there, my son. The court is in chaos. These are terrible times for Egypt. You know firsthand of the battles we have been losing, but have you heard that Akhenaton had a child, another girl unfortunately, with his eldest daughter, Meritaton, and he is much displeased?

"He had already set Nefertiti aside for her, saying that Nefertiti has given him six daughters, one of which, his favorite, his god took back as punishment, and that Nefertiti could not give him a son so he had no choice but to take another wife. Now Meritaton is as much in disfavor as her mother." Chnum had been away from court a long time but he still had his spies, and Nefertiti, there to keep him informed of what was going on.

"He desires a male heir so badly," stated Chnum. "There is talk that if Meritaton cannot provide a son for Pharaoh that Pharaoh will take his third daughter, Ankhesenpaaten, for wife as well.

"Queen Nefertiti is so livid she will not speak to Pharaoh. It makes no difference, he does not summon her any longer anyway. He only cares for his prayers and trying to get a male heir."

"Seems as if Pharaoh does not care for Egypt any longer, either," Ramose's voice was troubled. "I have honored and loved him and Nefertiti all my life, but what he is doing to Egypt and Nefertiti is not right."

His voice fell, "I fear Pharaoh is mad."

"Some say that. Others say he is an aging man who sees death coming for him." Chnum shook his head. No one else was listening to their conversation but me. I found it extremely interesting. "You believe speaking to Pharaoh will change anything, my son?"

"I can only try, Father. I cannot sit back and watch Egypt fall to the barbarians or be destroyed by a civil war from within."

"Or watch Akhenaton die at the hands of the Priests of Amon? There are many plots to kill Pharaoh, you know." Chnum looked right at Ramose and there was admonition in his words. *Be careful.*

"His enemies are gaining support. The people want their old gods back. They don't want this war to continue. They believe it and all the disasters have been brought on us like a plague because we have set the old gods aside for Akhenaton's one god."

"I know," Ramose sighed, "what the people believe." He'd heard it many times before.

He caught me listening, my eyes heavy from need of sleep, and taking my hand in his, he kissed it.

"You are tired, my love. Go to your rooms and to bed, get some rest, and I will see you in the morning. There is much I need to discuss with my father. He gives good council and I need that now."

The night had become late and the truth was I was exhausted. But I forced myself to stay awake. I didn't want to miss a moment of all the secrets that the night had uncovered. Didn't want to leave the party early. Good food, wine—which I'd had too much of—and haunting music. Visiting Ramose's family had been enlightening. I understood Ramose a lot better now.

"I can stay longer. I am not tired." So I remained and learned more for a little longer.

I'd known from my studies about Akhenaton's dalliances with his daughters. To these people, a pharaoh marrying his daughters wasn't shocking, it kept the bloodline pure, but it was fascinating to hear them speaking of it so matter-of-factly. Since I was going to see some of them—Akhenaton, Nefertiti and their daughters—soon, I drank in all the gossip I could.

Then again I couldn't get enough of Tiye's stories of Ramose growing up. His first horse, the day he went off to join Pharaoh's army, his first promotion and commission.

The day he brought Lord Haremhab home with

the whole army behind them.

When he went off to build his own palace out in the desert.

I found out that Ramose loved to read. Loved to sail. Was a self-made man, no matter that his aunt was a queen. That he'd had many lovers but had never loved any of them enough to take one for a wife. On and on. I could have listened forever.

Eventually, the need for sleep won out, that, and knowing we were leaving at dawn. We were to take a menechou down the river for the rest of our journey. I'd eaten so much, and eavesdropped so much I couldn't stay awake. Tiye led me back to my rooms herself and wished me goodnight, which I thought was sweet of her.

"You were kind to me today. I want to thank you," I told her before she left. "I hope I get to see you and Chnum again."

"You will. Of that I am sure." Then she went away so I could undress and sleep.

Of that I am not so sure, I brooded, getting into bed. Ramose hadn't confided everything to me about our mission and it bothered me. What wasn't he telling me? All I knew was that we were going into an unstable city and a touchy situation. Anything could happen.

I could even be sent back to the future. But I'd never forget this day, this night, these good-hearted people. It'd been a memorable experience. One of many since I'd first come down through the rabbit hole.

When I fell asleep, I dreamt I was in Boston, drifting through the shops on the wharf by the water's edge. It was a sunny Saturday morning and my colleagues from the University were on the streets and in the shops with me, browsing, bargain hunting and visiting in their T-shirts, blue jeans and casual jackets or coats.

It was very cold. Had to be late October, or November. I could see my breath puffing from my mouth. There was ice trimming some of the outside trees and patches of fresh snow on the ground. A winter wonderland New England style.

Except I was dressed as I had been that first night at Ramose's banquet in honor of Lord Haremhab, in a very sexy and provocative gown, with jewelry and full Egyptian regalia. I could feel all the eyeliner caked around my eyes. Feel the eye shadow. I peered into a mirror in one of the shops and saw the iridescent green above my eyes. I either looked like Cleopatra or a surprised raccoon.

I didn't think anything of my strange apparel as I sauntered into a fudge shop and stood at the counter waiting for service. I was going to buy the biggest box of chocolates and heavenly hash fudge I could get and was going to pay for it when I discovered I didn't have my credit card or my purse with me. How odd.

I looked down and saw what I was wearing. Felt the gold jewelry dangling from my head and my ears. Saw the arm bracelets glittering in the store's lights. Rings on every finger. Feet bare. I could see *right through* the fabric of my gown. *Oh, my.*

This was not Egypt, nor ancient Egypt, where near nudity was accepted. Boston was pretty uptight all in all. It was so embarrassing. How would I explain this to my coworkers or the dean? Would I lose my job because I was parading around the downtown district practically naked?

I glanced up and there were my fellow professors around me, gaping at my skimpy attire. Some people on the streets were pointing at me through the glass and snickering. Laughing. At me. Published Egyptologist, artist and esteemed college professor.

Then it hit me. I was home. *Home!* I started to laugh and cry at the same time. My fingers reached for and found the amulet around my neck and—*poof*—I was waking up in my rooms at Ramose's parents.

Boston had been a dream, but I could still smell the chocolate from the candy shop. Smell the salt tang in the sea air. I missed the sea. Missed Boston. My old safe life.

The melancholia that followed me around like a cloud found me. I loved Ramose, but there were obstacles to our love. It would have been easier if I would just poof back home.

The sun was rising and I could hear people in the courtyard below. Horses pawed and neighed. I heard Ramose's voice and grinned, got up and dressed in the desert robe, now clean, I'd arrived in, and joined him.

It was difficult leaving Ramose's family, they'd made me feel I belonged somewhere again, but I was going on a river cruise and was going to finally see Amarna, the great heretic Pharaoh and his court. Nefertiti and her daughters.

Those were worth leaving for.

Egyptian Heart

Chapter Twelve

We galloped our horses down to the river and, after our supplies were loaded onto the boat, Chnum's men returned the animals and carts to the stables where they'd stay until and if we came back.

I said goodbye to Geb, petting and hugging his neck, hating to leave him.

Ramose had made a gift of him to me after he'd seen how much I loved him. I'd never had a horse before and couldn't believe how much I'd grown to care for him. He'd carried me over miles of desert as I'd murmured confidences to him about my life and my dilemma.

Geb had listened and had never condemned me for being from another time and another place. He'd nickered as if he'd understood every word. Pawed the ground and shook his beautiful head when he'd disagreed with something I'd proposed. He'd been a good friend.

I was so excited boarding the boat, an immense wooden planked menechou that had been common in Akhenaton's day. I'd never seen one up this close, never been on one.

It had to be seventy-five feet long, twenty-five feet wide, had a narrow carved prow and a deck cabin where Ramose and I would sleep.

Ramose's men would bunk out on the open deck under canvas shelters provided by the crew.

The boat's thick wooden planks were lashed together by rope fed through mortises and the seams between the planks were filled with bundles of reeds, while more reeds carpeted the floor of the boat. The sail was a lopsided square of finely woven ivory linen and the outer sides of the boat were painted mustard yellow.

They'd see us coming all right.

The men who owned the boat were merchants who dressed in cotton robes not much different than mine. The sun had darkened their skin to a terra cotta brown and their heads were wrapped with cloth to protect them from its rays. They became oarsmen when there was no wind or when we wanted to navigate the river faster and they didn't lift their eyes as they bowed when Ramose and I breezed by them.

The soldiers, who were setting up camp in the stern of the boat, visited among themselves and one or two of them smiled at me as we began our voyage. They'd come to accept, even like me, and to be accepted by the very men who'd once avoided me meant a lot.

I stood at the prow with Ramose's arm around me, wind in my face, and admired the scenery as we glided swiftly over the water. The riverbanks swept past. The sails snapped behind us in time to some song I couldn't hear. The sky was a sizzling blue with a few wispy clouds and a sun so big and bright I could have reached out and touched it.

Some of Ramose's men behind us were cooking fish they'd caught from the river, preparing lunch. The air, fragrant with the essence of river water, fish, waterfowl and native flora, was a sweet perfume I couldn't get enough of. The perfume of an ancient time.

I could smell, see, and feel the differences. I wasn't in Boston any more. Yet I was happy to be near water again.

"See the hippopotamus there to your right?" Ramose pointed.

"I see it."

"Look, there's more."

A herd of the ugly beasts were swimming towards us, and our boat gave them a wide berth. They'd been known to tip a vessel if riled.

"Are there crocodiles in the water as well?" I asked, knowing well there were. In this time they were plentiful along the Nile. And they were deadly.

"Below the water. They stay out of sight most of the time, as the snakes do. If you take a stroll along the banks you would see crocodiles sunning themselves in the hundreds. They hide among the reeds waiting for unsuspecting prey."

"Then I won't be traipsing along the banks much." I'd slipped and used a contraction, but I didn't think Ramose had noticed.

"No, you will not." He pulled me closer and gave me a passionate long kiss.

My blood raced and I was glad there was a cool breeze. Lately, Ramose never wanted to be parted from me, not for a minute. I'd never been treated as he treated me. With such tenderness and love. Tender appreciation. As if I were a priceless jewel.

We enjoyed the scenery together as the menechou traveled down the river and talked as lovers talked.

I stood there for a long time, even after Ramose went to the stern of the boat to see to his men, their voices wafting on the air around me.

I would never get tired of this, never, I thought, sitting precariously on the rim of the boat. Cruising along on this river. Contemplating the wispy foam churning on the waters, the interesting shoreline that sailed by. And daydreaming.

Though it'd occurred to me more than once on our long journey, that in my time, an airplane, a train, a bus or a car would have gotten us to Amarna a lot faster.

I studied the other boats around me. A smaller vessel was skimming in close and would pass by shortly. It was painted cobalt blue and was crammed full of people and endless rows of pottery jars.

I could hear the passengers grumbling amongst themselves, their voices ghosting across the space between us. They didn't look like tourists. Didn't look like crew. They didn't look happy.

Ramose, food on a reed plate in his hands, appeared beside me as the other boat pulled past us. It was keeping a safe distance. There were so many people, men, women and children on board I couldn't believe the craft could stay afloat.

"What is that boat transporting in those jars on deck?" I shaded my eyes from the sun and looked at the passing boat. The water made the glare worse, made the sunshine hotter, but the nice breeze balanced it out.

"Honey or Barley beer, most likely. Or incense from Nubia."

Egyptian Heart

"And all the people?"

"Slaves. They are transporting them to market to sell."

I shivered remembering that first night, locked in that windowless stone prison with the slaves at Ramose's. The hopelessness and fear I'd felt, along with the thirst and hunger.

Then my mind brought up Nefrure and how she'd been terrorized and punished by Makere. Now that I was under Ramose's wing and being treated as someone important, sometimes I nearly forgot the bad things about this time. Forgot how the rich abused the poor.

"Why do you look so unhappy, my love?" Ramose was beginning to sense my moods.

I cocked my head at the boat of slaves and beer. "I feel sad for them, my lord. They are human beings just as you or I. They have feelings, wants, needs and dreams. Pride. Their bodies get hungry and tired as ours do. They feel pain. They long for happiness.

"By an accident of birth they are the slaves and you," I glanced at him, "are the master. It is not fair."

His look was puzzled but thoughtful. It was hard for him to change the beliefs of a lifetime. He was not a heartless man, yet to him, slaves were there to serve him and he'd never thought of them in any other way until I'd come along.

"You care for everyone, no matter how insignificant they are? Is that what your God preaches?"

"That is what my heart preaches." I touched my

chest. "No one is insignificant. We are all equal, remember?" Someday perhaps I would make him understand.

"Ah, I remember. In your America, there are no slaves and all are equal." He smiled and handed me a hunk of steaming fish and a cup of wine. "Here, eat. There is more if you want more. Fruit and dates as well."

"Thank you." I took the food and the drink gratefully. We'd been on deck for hours and the fresh air had made me hungry and the soft movements of the river had made me sleepy. I'd gone to bed late the night before and gotten up too early.

So by the time I finished eating, I could have laid down and taken a nap. I didn't. I didn't want Ramose to think I was a weak woman who needed to be coddled all the time. He'd had less sleep than I.

After our meal, I explored the menechou as Ramose conferred with the Captain on our route. As I passed one of Ramose's soldiers, he reported that a storm was coming and that's why the crewmen were busy lashing things down.

By the end of the day the wind had picked up; unhealthy looking clouds covered the sky in an eerie swirling pattern that would have been pretty if it wouldn't have been so threatening. I'd never seen clouds look like that, but they were beautiful.

The sails were taut against the wind and the menechou was flying down the river like a water bird. I had to fight to stand straight. It was invigorating.

Egyptian Heart

A cry of a river creature disturbed the twilight and my eyes scanned the lovely Nile, the shadows of evening softly kissing the water. The sails of the boats were catching the last of the day's sun in a rainbow of muted shades.

Most of the other boats belonged to peasant fishermen or merchants, all trying to make a living. It was like a city on the water. No war boats that I could see yet. The fishermen's boats were weathered and the sails were patched. They were quaint, though, bobbing past us like children's water toys.

Standing at the bow of the boat, my hair and robe flapping wildly around me, I stared at the clouds until Ramose came up behind me and slipped his arms about me.

"The storm, a swift one, will be here soon. I have seen clouds like these before. It will be mostly rain and will pass quickly. Go into the cabin now or you will get drenched."

"If it is only rain, then I would like to stay out for a while. The shower will feel good." It'd been a hot day and I didn't want to leave the cool winds and go into a stuffy dark cabin.

"I do not care if I get wet. I have other clothes."

He gave me a funny look as I tilted my face up to the falling rain. "As you wish." He chuckled. "I have never known a woman less interested in her looks than you. My other women ran from the rain as if it would melt them. Afraid their make-up and clothes would be ruined. You are nothing like *any* woman I have ever met." He'd told me that many times before but it still made me smile. I couldn't believe I was that different. People weren't that different all in all, through the ages, were they?

"I am just me. I love the fresh air and I love rain." Laughing, I grabbed Ramose's hand and we enjoyed the rain together. "Does not the rain feel good on your skin?" I asked him.

"It does." He hugged me tighter, we kissed and cuddled, as the falling water soaked us. The rain, at first hard driving, slowly dissipated into a gentle drizzle. The clouds melted into a normal dusk sky of muted colors and shadows. I could see the stars as the light fled.

By nightfall the rain had stopped and Ramose and I lingered in the front of the boat as our clothes dried out. Moonlight glinted off the rippling water like sprinkled diamonds.

Somewhere, someone on the river was playing a flute and the music filled the night. Across the water a sleepy child was crying for his mother and muffled voices wafted on the breeze. The moon, a glowing disc of luminous white, began to rise higher and night creatures chattered amongst themselves in animal tongues. Ramose and I spoke of the trip so far and then Ramose talked of the future.

"I meant what I said yesterday to my parents," he reminded me. "I love you, Mag-gie."

I hadn't forgotten what he'd said. Just hadn't wanted to think about it. I'd put it out of my mind.

"I want to make you my wife."

His direct proposal took me by surprise, filled me with unbelievable joy for a moment before my heart sunk. How could I marry him when I could be

Egyptian Heart

dragged back to the future at any second? How could I promise anyone anything when I didn't belong here? My fingers found the amulet. It was cold as a piece of ice around my neck.

"Where I come from each man only has one wife, not many. It is the only way I know." I said what I thought would put him off from wanting to marry me. It was the only excuse I could think of. Besides the truth; which I couldn't tell him. "I could never be married to a man unless I was his only wife, his only woman. Forever."

Ramose didn't say anything for a long time. His face profiled against the moon and the night. He let go of my hand. I was afraid I'd gone too far. Ramose was a powerful man desired by many women. Who was I to give ultimatums?

Maybe I'd hurt his pride by not falling at his feet in gratitude for the offer. Maybe I'd broken some kind of weird unspoken Egyptian law, or had offended him in some other way I had no idea of. I was sick at heart but I had said what I needed to say.

I couldn't marry him, could I? Could I?

At that moment I had to face the truth. *I loved this man.* For the first time in my life, I truly loved someone enough to want to marry them. It was a revelation that changed everything for me.

I swung around and looked at his face in the moonlight and I knew. *He was the one I was meant to love.* Ramose, a man not even of my time, impossible as it was, was my *destiny*. Until that moment I had been ambivalent about our bond. Now I was sure and it rocked my whole world.

I loved Ramose.

I wanted to stay here and be his wife. Live in his world the rest of my days. Oh, no. When I knew that wasn't possible. Wasn't to be. Any minute I was going to wake up. Going to find myself back in that dank tomb. Fate couldn't allow me to actually stay here, could it?

I wanted to weep. I'd never felt so lost, so lonely.

My one true love was a mummy in a sarcophagus over three thousand years old. I could never *marry* him.

It was a whisper and at first, I wasn't sure I'd heard him right.

"What?" I asked him to repeat it.

"I agree," he said again a little louder. "You will be my *only* wife. I will never take another if you marry me." Then he turned and I could see his eyes gleaming in the faint radiance of the orb above us. He was smiling as he gathered me to him and held me so tightly I could barely breathe.

"You will be my greater wife and I will have no other as long as you live. I promise," he moaned into my hair, his arms caressing my waist. His body against mine was strong, warm. "Marry me! As soon as we get to Amarna. It is why I wanted you to meet Pharaoh and my queen. Now, with the way things are going, I am not sure I will be allowed to ask their permission to take you as my wife. Nefertiti is out of favor. Pharaoh is unwell.

"Yet I can introduce you to the queen, my aunt, and get her blessing. I want you and her to meet. I have written to her of you. You are so like her in many ways."

I didn't know what to say. Ramose's eyes were pleading with me, his lips on the verge of a celebratory smile as he faced me, my hands in his. Then he fell to his knees.

"I love you, Mag-gie. I have never loved before until you. *Marry me. Please?"*

Hadn't expected this. Not this soon. Well, not ever.

I began to shiver, but Ramose must have thought it was the chilly wind that was playing around us now that the night had come. The temperature had fallen quickly. I was shaking, but not because I was cold. I didn't know what to do, didn't know what to say to Ramose.

I'd been living a lie. A big fat deceptive lie. And, I realized sadly, it wasn't right of me to keep lying to this man. He'd been nothing but good to me. Fair. Generous. He loved me.

I had to tell him the truth. Now. Throw the dice and let them fall as they might. Send the e-mail and hope for the best. Confess my big secret and pray.

My lord, there is something you must know about me first. I have not been telling you the truth."

He was quiet a moment then said, "About what?" I couldn't help but hear the caution in his voice. This was a man people never lied to. His pride wouldn't allow him to be deceived without consequences. I almost decided to forget it and then I recognized the expression on his face. Fear. He loved me enough to be afraid of hearing what I had to say.

In the background, I could hear Ramose's soldiers singing some campaign song, their voices husky and blending in with the music of the night creatures in the air and along the darkened banks of the river.

The sailors had lit lanterns along the boat's length and were traveling the river by their light and their memories. They knew the waterway well.

The storm and the rain had passed and the night was crisp and clear.

The moon, virtually full, was shining like a lighthouse beacon. It lit up the Nile almost like day.

Sighing, I plunged in. I owed him the truth. "I am not who I said I was. My memory is not gone. I remember exactly who I am and was. Where I came from. Everything."

"Why did you lie to me? Say you had forgotten?" His body had stiffened and his words were already pulling his trust away from me.

But I'd gone too far now to stop. I couldn't take the words back. I couldn't lie to the man I loved any longer.

I was glad it was nighttime. It hid the devastation I was feeling. *This is not going to work. He isn't going to believe me. Why am I doing this?* I couldn't stop.

In an unsteady voice I told him everything. Who I really was and where I came from. That I'd been a teacher in my time, an artist and a writer. A twenty-first century woman living in Boston, U.S.A. Told him about my grant to come to Egypt and how I found this tomb—but I didn't tell him it'd been *his* tomb—and how I had suddenly found myself wandering in the desert on a night three thousand years in the past. My past. His present. How I thought I got here. Holding the necklace up for him to touch.

I confessed everything that mattered and he didn't interrupt me once. He was strangely reserved, yet I could feel his eyes on my face from the first words.

When I was finished there was dead silence between us. He'd moved away from me and was staring at the moon as if he'd never seen it before.

"Talk to me, my lord. Do you believe me?" I whispered, a dread growing in the pit of my stomach. The longer he ignored me the more I feared I'd made a terrible mistake by revealing my secret.

Did he think I was insane…or worse, that I was an evil sorceress sent to harm him?

I had no idea. But something was wrong. The man who'd been my friend, my love, and companion was no longer standing beside me. This man was a stranger. A powerful stranger who held my very life in his hands.

"It is getting chilly out here on deck," he said coldly. "It would be best if you went into the cabin and got some sleep. It has been a long day."

I didn't know what else to do. Was he dismissing me? Was he telling me that he no longer wanted me for his wife? No longer could love me? I didn't know. Did he hate me now?

Or did he just need some time to think about and accept all I had confessed?

"My lord, are you mad at me? It's the truth, I

swear, all of it. I just couldn't lie to you anymore. Please, don't be mad at me. I never meant to mislead you."

He wouldn't answer. Wouldn't touch me, even when I reached out and laid my hand on his. He pulled away and refused to look at me.

"My lord—"

"*Go to the cabin...now,*" he snarled through his teeth and stalked away towards his men. He disappeared into the recesses of the boat and for me the night was empty.

I had no choice but to retreat into the cabin. Hide. Inside it was damp and lonely. There was a narrow bed, chairs and an incense lamp on the table throwing a feeble light about the room. A creeping sadness coursed through my tired body.

Everything had caught up to me. The days of endless riding, the sun, the voyage, and the trauma of telling Ramose who I really was. I felt unreal as if I was dreaming *now*. My fingers found my amulet at my neck and pressed at it.

Send me back, please. Send me back. Send me back. Send me back....

I was still in the cabin on the boat. In the past. Where I didn't belong. Damn.

But I loved Ramose. How could I leave now?

I crawled into the bed, soggy clothes and all, my mind shutting down as the tears came. All I wanted to do was sleep. Forget everything.

Forget this crazy dream or whatever it was. Forget the way my heart was breaking. I was sure I'd lost Ramose forever and I'd come to love him so much. Too much.

Egyptian Heart

He hadn't believed me; hadn't believed any of it. Was I surprised? Would I have believed such a story if I'd been him. Probably not. Egyptians, present and past, are such a superstitious lot.

I'd been so stupid.

What would happen now? Was I in danger? Would Ramose send me away…have me imprisoned…have me stoned to death for being an evil sorceress? I didn't know and that was the worst of it.

I lay there in the tiny cabin and all I wanted was for Ramose to come find me, take me in his arms and make everything the way it had been. I wanted Ramose to still love me.

You fool. You shouldn't have told him. You fool. So naïve. Too late now.

When sleep claimed me I welcomed it like death. And I dreamed of my mother and my family, of Snowball and my apartment. Except this time my two worlds merged.

First Nefrure stopped by for a visit complaining about the deep snow she had to drive her car through to get there. Her hair was really long and she'd had a curly perm, she told me, grinning. How did I like it?

"I love it," I replied, making her a cup of hot tea in the microwave. I'd been baking all day for my guests. "The brownies, your favorite, will be done in ten minutes. I hope Ramose likes them, too."

"Oh, he will," Nefrure said. "He loves everything you make him."

"When is Ahhotpe coming by?" Somehow in the dream Ahhotpe was Nefrure's actual daughter and she was going to Boston College to be an archaeologist like me. Making straight 'A's. We were so proud of her.

"Be here in about an hour. She had finals today." There was another knock on the door and there was Ramose.

He looked so different. He had on a long heavy wool coat and his hair, still long and flowing, was covered by an expensive suede hat with a brim that matched his coat. His face was clean-shaven except for a mustache he'd begun wearing. No eyeliner. No jewelry but a diamond earring. He looked so handsome.

He smiled at me and as I peeked outside past him I could see his horse, Khons, tied to the porch in front of my apartment beside Geb. The white horse blended in almost invisibly with the snow. Only his black eyes stood out. Geb was whinnying for me to come out and give him a treat. I didn't think Boston permitted horses to be tied up in front of city apartment buildings. Wasn't there some kind of law against it?

"Didn't bring your new Cadillac, eh?" I teased.

"No," Ramose answered as he swept me into his arms. "Khons is better in the snow."

"Oh, okay," I said, as we hugged and then kissed passionately.

We'd finally become lovers and what I'd hoped had been true…he was a great lover. He knew every way to please me and I was learning to please him. We couldn't get enough of each other. I hadn't forsaken my promise to myself, either. I'd saved myself for the man I would spend my life with. We

Egyptian Heart

were getting married in three days. Big, big ceremony at St. Paul's Church. Relatives were flying in from all over the world. I'd never been so happy.

Ramose had forgiven me for lying to him and had even come back with me to my time. Well, not before we'd gone to Amarna and I'd met Akhenaton and Nefertiti and their daughters, had attended their court. It'd been a real experience.

But I couldn't remember anything about it. Strange, that. Ramose told me I'd talked Nefertiti into claiming her independence from Pharaoh and standing up for herself.

She'd taken her girls and had divorced the religious fanatic, kicked him out of Egypt. Been queen by herself. *You go girl.*

I was writing a book on it and was sure that it would be a best seller. While Ramose was making the college lecture circuit talking about his life and all the famous people he'd once known. Pharaohs and generals and other mummies. Making a bundle.

I'd hired Nefrure as my secretary and she'd caught on to computers so quickly. She was so smart.

I had everything. I had Ramose. Nefrure. Ahhotpe. My family, job and friends. The best of both worlds.

The dream finished with the four of us eating a gourmet meal I'd made in my new double oven, talking and laughing at old memories of Egypt as the snow fell outside and Snowball purred in my lap. Min sat at my feet cleaning herself. All of us were so happy. I was so happy.

I woke up in the shadowy cabin to the swaying of the menechou. I wasn't sure how much time had passed, but the lamp's wick had gone out. There was darkness everywhere. Must still be night.

Ramose hadn't joined me. I was alone.

I went back to sleep. I couldn't get enough. I couldn't get enough of the dreams which transported me to a familiar, happy world, that I desperately wanted to return to. Was I mistaken.

When sleep took me this time I dreamed I was wandering in Ramose's desert and his soldiers caught me and threw me into a dungeon for lying to him and for being an evil jinn. I was there for a long time. Years.

My only friend, a tiny white mouse who only spoke Egyptian. I taught him to play checkers, but couldn't understand anything he said because I'd lost the amulet.

When I awoke the next time, daylight flooded into the cracks of the cabin door. Someone had visited me in the night and left bowls of fresh water, for cleaning and drinking, towels, soap, and a plate of food.

I scrubbed up as best I could and put on a clean robe that Tiye had given me for traveling and ate my breakfast alone in silence.

I kept listening for Ramose's footsteps coming to see me. Nothing. I was heartsick remembering the way we'd left things. I was scared.

I finished my meal and went out on deck.

But for that day and the days that came after that we spent on the boat, Ramose avoided me, stayed with his men and didn't utter a word. The cabin was mine. Alone.

I hid and slept there alone each night. Spent my days brooding on deck by myself and gazing out at the river. The time went slow.

I kept waiting for Ramose to approach me and tell me why he was so upset.

The nights I went to bed by myself and grew uneasier each day. Was Ramose ever going to forgive me? Did he still want to marry me or would he send me away?

I'd told him the truth and I didn't know if he'd believed me or not, but I think I'd scared him. Talking about being from the future. Of magic amulets. I saw the look in his eyes. I hadn't said much about my time, the technology and the medical advancements, realizing that it would have only confused him more.

I wondered what was going to happen to me when we got to Amarna. I didn't know. All I knew was that I loved Ramose and wasn't sure he still loved me. Being without him forced me to accept how much I'd come to love and need him.

I tried to catch his eye so many times, but he'd never look my way. It was as if I no longer existed and it hurt more than I could have imagined.

I missed him so much.

One morning I came on deck and saw we were coming into a city. A great city. There were barges and ships of various sizes crowding in around us and the noise was deafening. Merchants selling their wares from deck and people shouting to each other across the spaces.

People and animals were crawling along the

riverbank, going towards or from buildings that were growing denser with each mile as we floated towards the city.

The town must be Amarna or the outskirts of it, I thought, with my first smile in days. It was beautiful. The structures were glossy in the sun and made of mud, reeds or wood and painted white. The smells of cooking and animals and people packed closely together flowed out onto the water.

Amarna. Akhenaton's golden City of the Horizon of the Sun. Nefertiti's City of Flowers. I'd waited my whole life, in a way, to see this metropolis.

And nothing, not even Ramose's indifferent face when we docked could change the excitement I was feeling at soon being able to ride into that city.

Amarna, the capital of Egypt and home of Pharaoh, his court, and his great queen.

Egyptian Heart

Chapter Thirteen

We were ready to leave the boat. Nefertiti was awaiting us in her palace and Haremhab's men could be right behind us, coming in by land, so Ramose was in a hurry. He paid the boat's captain and gathered his men. Then he found me.

He wouldn't look at me directly but I'd caught him staring earlier when he didn't know I was watching. I'd dressed as attractively as I could that morning. Clean gown. The cat pin Ramose had given me on it. I'd washed my hair and put on make-up, which wasn't easy with the boat swaying and having a limited amount of water. Tired of the way Ramose was treating me, I was going to show him what he was missing.

How long would he punish me for lying to him? Or for telling him the truth?

If our relationship was over, the least he could do was say so, because I had to know. Had to figure out what I was going to do next.

Ramose's men were leaving the boat and mounting the horses that the Palace had sent for them. Ramose, holding back until his men had disembarked, hadn't moved away when I'd walked over to stand by him. Days of the silent treatment had begun to make me angry.

I couldn't help what had happened to me. I couldn't help that I was from the future. Sure, I kept the truth from Ramose about all that, but I felt I had to, for our safety. I would have it out with him here and now. What did I have to lose?

"My lord," I said softly and with enough humor to disguise my heartache, "are you ever going to speak to me again? Have I scared you so much that I must go away?" I hesitated. Ramose was listening, but still hadn't looked at me.

I took a chance. "If you no longer want me, I'll leave you here. When we get off the boat I'll disappear into the city crowds and you'll never be bothered with me again."

I didn't care if I used contractions or not, spoke my own English, now. "I'm sure I'll be able to make my way. I can take care of myself." A bluff.

I had no idea what I'd do alone in Amarna. Where I'd go or how I'd live. I'd have a hard time finding a job of any kind or even begging. My unusual looks were even more of a disadvantage in a congested city. Maybe I could pretend to be sick, hide my face and body, and beg. If I had to. Good thing I had Ahhotpe's slave clothes and Tiye's traveling robes with the hoods as camouflage.

Thinking of Tiye only depressed me. I'd had such a good time with Ramose's family and perhaps now I'd never see any of them again. I was sick of losing people.

Ramose spun around to glare at me and in a swift unexpected gesture he captured both my hands and yanked me to him. "I am not *afraid* of you and you will not leave me, Mag-gie...you belong to me! I did not rescue you from my guards or save you from the lion only to toss you away now. I do not give up what I want that easily. I—" He stopped talking, frustrated as if he couldn't find the words

Egyptian Heart

he needed to explain.

But I heard the passion behind the rage and had the answers I needed. *Ramose still loved me.* I must give him more time—and wondered how much would be enough—to accept who I was and the rest of what I'd confided. It wouldn't be easy for a man like Ramose to admit there were realities other than his own world. He was after all a superstitious Egyptian from the distant past.

Ha, but he loved me and he wasn't going to send me away!

"You want me after all you know about me?" I was fighting a smile. Relieved, I knew now somehow everything would be okay.

"I want you. This does not change anything." Was his pride keeping him from saying more? He pulled me into his arms and kissed me hard and held me tightly before he released me. Still wouldn't meet my eyes. Perhaps he thought I would turn him into a fish or something.

"We are going to the North Palace, the queen's main residence, where she is expecting us," Ramose declared.

"I'm going to meet Queen Nefertiti?"

He was standing beside me, expression disgruntled, but I knew it was an act. "If you promise not to witch her away to another time."

I laughed. He'd made a joke. He didn't laugh.

"I didn't *witch* myself here, I told you that. It just *happened.*" I'd thought I'd been so clear, apparently I hadn't. What other misconceptions was he harboring? I could only guess. I couldn't stay mad at him. Couldn't blame him for reacting the way he was. It had taken me a while to acknowledge that I'd traveled through time and space and I'd fought it for a long time. I'd merely gotten used to it, Ramose hadn't. Yet.

"Do not speak of any of *this* to the queen, or to anyone. It would be dangerous for you. For both of us." Then his demeanor softened. I expected an apology, yet all he added was, "I cannot help myself, no matter what you claim to be or not to be. What you are or are not. I love you. You are the woman I've been waiting for. My destiny. It is my curse."

The day was sunny and the temperatures below ninety, a respite from the usual heat, and the breezes played with our hair and clothes. It was a beautiful day for being happy. Ramose put his hand out to me and when our flesh touched the world was right again. If he'd had doubts about me he was slowly coming to terms with them. "Now we must go. My aunt, the queen, does not like to be kept waiting."

He escorted me to a chariot and ordered me to get in behind him. I had the feeling that he'd forgiven me, but was still miffed, frightened of me. He was polite and distant. I missed my friend and sweetheart but understood. *Give him time.*

We left the docks and the boat behind and rode through the narrow city streets. Ramose's men were on horses behind us. I'd never ridden in a chariot and was taking pleasure in it.

Of course, since Ramose was speaking to me again, everything made me happy. The world was suddenly a beautiful place again.

The horses pulling us were matched dappled

creatures that were not only handsome but cavorted and snorted as if they were in a parade. So like Geb, I felt the pang of missing him.

I got to stand near Ramose and when the chariot began to clatter faster he slid his arm around me and I snuggled into him. I was home. I found myself daydreaming about meeting the queen. I'd done a lot of things as an Egyptologist that had thrilled me in my other life, but none of them could hold a candle to meeting the infamous Nefertiti. I was afraid to ask Ramose if I'd be allowed to actually speak to her.

Noticing Ramose's stern face, I thought, better not push my luck.

Amarna was everything I hoped it would be. A light-filled city of living ghosts in authentic ancient dress and whitewashed buildings snuggled to the ground. The streets, lined by Date Palms and Tamarisks trees, were a mosaic of flat stones that would lead us to Nefertiti's private palace. Flowers were everywhere. The city was colorful. Noisy. Alive. I had to keep telling myself I wasn't dreaming.

People crowded the streets but grumblingly made way for us. They didn't like the rich and they didn't like soldiers. The eyes that swung towards us were insolent and sometimes irate. I was grateful to have armed guards around us because the mood of the crowd unnerved me. The people obviously hated us and I'd revised my idea of what year this must be by the unrest in the city. It had to be closer to 1338 B.C., for whatever that was worth. Give or take a couple years. I'd asked Nefrure once what the year was but their counting system was different than ours in the future. She'd given me a real off the wall number that hadn't made much sense to me.

The city was around me and I wished I could explore it on foot by myself. Interact with the inhabitants and experience what their lives were like; what they did for relaxation and recreation. Visit in their homes and businesses. Touch and see their art up close because this was a city of merchants, artisans and free men as well as servants and slaves.

I'd love to watch the artists at work in their shops, throwing pots or carving stone. I could learn so much. And, truth be told, I missed my drawing and painting. Missed teaching the slaves. I'd always spent my life working. Doing something. These days I felt as if I were on a permanent vacation. Not that I didn't like being on vacation, I was just feeling a little aimless lately.

I could have ridden through the streets of Amarna forever. There was so much to see. So much to soak in. We worked our way through the market section and the bountiful displays of wares, art and food made my mouth water. I wanted to jump off the chariot and go shopping. Ramose didn't stop, didn't slow down. Oh well, maybe some other time.

We arrived at Nefertiti's North Palace, Ramose helped me from the chariot, and there was a woman waiting to lead us to Nefertiti.

"This is Sesehat," Ramose introduced the old woman to me but never told her who I was. "She has been my aunt's personal slave for many years.

Egyptian Heart

She can be trusted."

I muttered the proper greetings and smiled. The old woman bowed her head, acknowledging me.

I was staring at the Palace with the towering pillars. Giant realistically painted images in brilliant colors of Akhenaton, Nefertiti and their daughters were god-size along the front panels. So lifelike I expected them to step from the walls and walk away.

When Akhenaton decreed that there would be one god, Aton, in Egypt it had also ushered in a new form of art unlike the stilted figures of what had come before. These illustrations were prime examples of that new art and they were so real. So perfect. I couldn't wait to get inside the palace and see what else was painted inside. I would have done anything for a camera and a video cam. Even a phone that took pictures.

Though I thought the representation of Akhenaton wasn't as true to life as it could have been. Akhenaton hadn't been handsome. Unlike the painting, he'd been short, a little deformed, with drooping shoulders, spindly shanks, a potbelly and thick thighs. His face had held the hooded eyes of a fanatic set wide apart, his jaw elongated and his neck scrawny. He'd been no prize. Yet his image made him look pretty good. More or less attractive and godlike.

We left the chariot and followed Sesehat through a courtyard and into long cool alabaster hallways. Ramose ahead of me so he could hear what the slave had to say. She was jabbering away like an old magpie. The woman slid her eyes sideward at me a couple of times—I'd put my hood down on my robe—but she'd said nothing to me. I walked quickly to keep up and kept quiet.

I had thought Ramose's and his parents' dwellings were splendid, but they were nothing to Nefertiti's Palace. The building was like a museum with unlimited riches and antiquities. Shiny and new. Everywhere there were treasures. Handmade and carved vases and pedestals, paintings and frescoes. Golden and silver statues alight with shining jewels. Along the walls were pastoral scenes of animals and nature made from tiny mosaic stones in all different hues and shapes. The beauty of Nefertiti's home mesmerized me and I dawdled behind to admire the sculptures and run my hands over their smoothness while Ramose and Sesehat carried on their conversation. Then I had to hurry to catch up.

Sesehat had known Ramose since he was a child and he seemed to listen to what she said. It made me feel good to know there was one slave Ramose treated as a person. Further enlightenment couldn't be far behind.

I overheard Sesehat say, "The queen is not herself these days, Lord Nakh-Min, so do not be shaken at the changes you see in her. She is unhappy. Pharaoh has taken Meritaton for his new wife, and even now Ankhesenpaaten is with Pharaoh in his quarters and she, they say, will be his next bride if Meritaton, who has miscarried for the second time since she gave Pharaoh a girl child, does not give him a male heir soon."

Meritaton was Akhenaton and Nefertiti's oldest

daughter and Ankhesenpaaten was their third daughter. Meketaten, their second girl, had died as a child.

Sesehat kept talking as we trailed her deeper into the palace. "Pharaoh has set my mistress aside and she is no longer called to court except for great occasions of state. She is worried for her daughters. Mistress thinks evil spirits have possessed her husband, but it is said that Pharaoh is very ill. He grows weaker. Months have passed and still he does not send for the queen.

"I am afraid for her. The people have always adored her and that has made her many enemies at court. Without Pharaoh's love and protection she is in danger. More each day."

Ramose seemed distressed at the news Sesehat was giving him.

Then we were being escorted by unsmiling guards through two great doors into a luxurious chamber, with floors of glassy granite and painted columns lined up on either side. Animal skins, leopard and lion, were scattered about on the floor and the walls were decorated with hand woven wall hangings. It looked right out of a movie set. At the end of the large room was a woman surrounded by other women. She lifted her head when we entered and waved a few fingers at Ramose to come forward after he'd bowed to her.

She was lovely. This woman. Classic bones. Glowing skin. Her hair, and I didn't know it until we were a few feet away, was a long shiny black wig elaborately braided and intertwined with tiny strings of gems that gleamed when the woman moved her head and the light caught them. Her skin was the color of ripe apricots and her face was expertly made up with kohl, green eye shadow and lips a vivid crimson. Her features were perfect and her eyes, when she looked up at us, were a cocoa brown, shrewd and disarming all at once.

She was dressed in a sheer flowing sheath, layers of veiling the colors of a new sky that fell to her sandaled feet and was belted with a girdle of precious stones that matched her hair adornments. She glittered like a Christmas tree.

The woman in the black wig was so charismatic that at first I didn't see the other women with her. When I finally looked at them I saw the three weren't women at all. They were children. One looked about eight, one ten and the other no older than twelve and all were miniatures of the woman before us. All delicately lovely with their mother's beauty and poise.

The woman was Nefertiti. Queen and high priestess of all Egypt. She stood up and leisurely moved towards Ramose. As she came closer I could see she wasn't young. Near thirty or so; middle aged for her time, but strikingly beautiful. Her eyes passed over me, lingered, and then returned to Ramose's face.

She held out her arms and Ramose stepped into them. I could tell she cared for him.

"My nephew, it has been so long since I have seen you." Nefertiti's lips formed a full smile. "I have been praying that you would come."

"Your Highness, you should have sent for me sooner." Ramose gave his aunt a hug and then the

Egyptian Heart

girls, giggling, ran at him and embraced him in turns.

"I did send for you, Nephew. Many times."

"I never received your messages."

Nefertiti shrugged. "As I feared. My husband, or General Haremhab, had them intercepted. You are here now. That is all that matters. It was what I prayed for. To have a friend by my side among all my many enemies."

She inquired of our journey and how Ramose's parents were doing. The girls, happy to see their cousin, hung on his every word of the outside world they were imprisoned from.

They noticed me at the same time and then there were four sets of eyes on me.

I stood there and stared back. I couldn't take my eyes off them. The woman was a queen and her daughters were royal princesses of Egypt. I'd read about them and studied them all my life. Wondered what had happened to them because history hadn't known. Only that Nefertiti and her three youngest daughters had disappeared around 1338 B.C. after Akhenaton had taken his daughter, Ankhesenpaaten, for a wife and then had himself mysteriously died.

I was seeing living history and my brain couldn't take it in. Nefertiti and her daughters! Here. Looking at me. Waiting for me to say something.

Ramose had taken my hand and moved me in front of him. "This is Mag-gie Owen, my Queen."

"Who is this Mag-gie Owen to you, Nephew?" Nefertiti was examining me, my hair, my eyes, my skin, as if I were a thief who had stolen into her palace.

"She is someone I have brought to meet you. She is a special woman and a...seer."

I couldn't believe he'd said that. Why hadn't he said I was the woman he loved or the woman he was going to marry? Or was that something that would never happen now that I'd told him the truth?

"A seer?" Nefertiti suddenly had more interest in me. "Come, Mag-gie, sit with us, eat with us, and afterwards we will have a talk. You can tell me my future." And her eyes were so sad as she signaled at Sesehat waiting in the shadows.

"Bring us food. Wine," she demanded.

Sesehat scurried away, the rest of us sat down on pillows and settled in, and soon an army of slaves scampered in with sustenance. Ramose sat beside his aunt and I sat on the other side. The girls sprawled around us. The queen didn't insist on formalities. I'd expected her to sit on a jeweled throne and have us at her feet, but she was behaving like a normal woman. Happy to have family around her.

The girls, busy throwing questions at their cousin about what was happening in the outside world, hogged the conversation as we ate. I was content to sit and watch them. Listen. They were so carefree and lively. So curious and innocent. They had no idea of the trouble brewing in the land outside their palace walls.

After we ate and the girls got to visit with their cousin, Ramose asked if Nefertiti would send them away so that we could converse about important matters he didn't want them to overhear. The girls left, begging to return later, but their mother reminded them that they were to attend a special assembly of foreign dignitaries that evening at the Great Palace. "Go prepare yourselves and I will send for you soon."

"And her?" Nefertiti cocked her head at me after the girls had left. "Is she to stay?"

"I trust her. She will not let anything she hears from us go further." Ramose took my hand and for the first time Nefertiti smiled at me.

"You came, Nephew," Nefertiti said, getting right to the point, "to see if the rumors were true. That my husband has set me aside for our daughter and that the rest of the court is shunning me. It is true. He has taken Meritaton for wife. She has given him only a daughter so far and has miscarried twice. I spoke against the marriage and have been banished from the court. Meritaton sits in my place. For now. I pity my daughter. She is not as strong willed or experienced in the way of court intrigue as I am. Her life will not be easy.

"Though for tonight, as Pharaoh commands it, I and our daughters will all sit in attendance and will pretend to be a perfect family for the dignitaries he wishes to impress. He cannot change the power I have or that I am still a high priestess of Egypt. He needs me still, if only for appearances."

I could see the fire that had once lived in Nefertiti's soul spark in her eyes for a second and then as quickly fade. Too much had happened to her. Most of her power had been stripped away and now her future was precarious.

"Ramose," the queen spoke, "I would like you to accompany me tonight. Stand behind me in the shadows so no one sees you. They say Lord Haremhab is looking for you so I do not want to endanger you, but I cannot face the court alone. Not tonight." She nodded at me. "She may come as well. It is wise if you value her that you keep her in your sight. The court has become an unruly place now that Pharaoh's lifestyle is so wicked. The court has followed suit, I am afraid. A young pretty woman is not safe."

"We will accompany you, your Highness," Ramose agreed as I nodded my head. He knew how much I wanted to see Pharaoh and his court. "And I will keep Mag-gie in sight."

"Good. A staunch protector by my side will lift my spirits." Nefertiti's eyes went hard. "I have not seen my husband in months but tonight I must sit in his presence and pretend that everything is well. If I do not he will do worse to me than he already has.

"He would take the rest of my children from me." A groan as she momentarily shut her eyes. "Those I have left. I cannot let that happen. He cannot have them for his bed and then toss them away when he is done with them. They are our children, not brood mares."

She looked past us, her eyes distant, as if she were remembering a better time and when she spoke next there was misery in her voice. "I never thought to see the day that Akhenaton would no longer love me or want me for his queen. That he would bed our daughters and have children with them. He has broken my heart.

Egyptian Heart

"I never thought to see the day, either, that the country would be rising against him. Our reign began in such hope and laughter and now there is only unrest and strife. Pharaoh sees none of it. He is destroying our Egypt and we are all in peril."

"Your Highness, you and your girls must leave Amarna." Rarnose's expression was grave. "I came to escort you to a safe place outside of Egypt until the troubles are over. Is there somewhere—someone—who would take in you and the princesses?"

"Are times so treacherous we need to flee Egypt altogether?" She seemed stunned. "What do you know, Nephew, that I do not?"

I could tell that Ramose didn't want to tell her, but he must have believed he had no other alternative.

"General Haremhab is plotting to take Pharaoh's place. I am not sure when, but I fear there is a civil war coming. The country is enraged with Pharaoh because he keeps them from their ancient gods; he will not lead his armies against the Hittites. And because he has set you aside. The people still love you."

Nefertiti took in a deep breath and came to her feet. She wasn't very tall, about nine inches over four feet. I stood inches above her. "You want me to abandon Egypt and run away? I do not see myself as a coward."

"You are not, your Highness. Yet you must protect yourself and your children."

"To do that I must flee?"

"I believe you must." Ramose met my eyes. *Is*

she in danger?

I nodded.

I had to admire the queen. She was brave, but she was no fool. She had too many enemies here in Amarna and she knew it.

"You are not safe here, your Highness," I said in a timid voice. She had to know what I knew but I hated telling her. "You are not safe from Pharaoh; you are not safe from Lord Haremhab if he gains control of the throne. He will make sure that you and your blood line end. You and the girls will mysteriously disappear. He would want no one to contest his crown or his heirs someday."

"How can Haremhab take Egypt's crown? He has no claim. He is not of royal blood."

As if she'd forgotten that neither was she, I thought. Though I wouldn't be the one to say it out loud.

I went on. "Haremhab is to be offered Beketaton's hand in marriage by Akhenaton to keep the general from raising the armies of Egypt up against him. It is what I have learned and came here to tell you, warn you of, at great risk to me."

That got through to her and she released a gentle sigh. "Beketaton is to marry Haremhab. Ah, so that is the great proclamation that Pharaoh will give tonight. Sesehat overheard from other palace slaves that something important was to be announced. That must be it."

She looked at me then. "Seer, what do you think I should do? Stay or leave? What does your gift tell you?"

Ramose flashed me a smile. Go *ahead,* it said.

Tell her. We'd talked only briefly about me being able to *know* the future because of me *being* from the future. But only briefly. In his own way he was asking what was going to happen to Nefertiti. He *had* believed me.

"Leave or else you and your girls will...vanish. I see no future for you here, your Highness. Only danger and death." I told the truth, there was nothing else I could do.

Ramose had informed me on the boat, before we'd had our little misunderstanding, that he'd discovered Haremhab was planning to have Nefertiti and her children done away with once he was married to Pharaoh's sister. It's what had precipitated the violent disagreement between the two old friends.

Ramose had also told me that he wouldn't let his aunt and his cousins be slaughtered so Haremhab could steal Pharaoh's crown. He would fight him.

The queen looked into my face for a long time and slowly lowered her eyes and head. "Then I will do as you ask, Nephew, for love of the sister who bore you and died for you. I and my children will go with you. Leave Egypt. Until times are better.

"I have friends in Nubia who will take us in without question and hide us even from Pharaoh. We will go there."

"Tonight," Ramose urged.

"No," Nefertiti replied. "We must be present at the grand assembly tonight. I cannot openly defy Akhenaton without immediate retaliation. Our flight would be uncovered too soon and we would not have a chance to get far before we were captured and brought back. We must attend tonight, act as if all is forgiven and accepted, and then afterwards we will sneak out of the palace. By the time our absence is discovered we will have a fair start."

Nefertiti was clever. Leaving afterwards would be wiser and night would hide our escape. And for selfish reasons, I was glad that we weren't going right away. After all I'd gone through and endured, I desperately wanted to see Akhenaton and his court. More fodder for my journal and my memories when I got old.

Ramose nodded his head. "Then we will escape after. I will go now to see to the arrangements."

Nefertiti took me off guard when she said, "Nephew, leave your seer here with us. She can help us prepare and pack. I want to spend some time with her."

A quick frown was the only tip off that Ramose was worried, so I reassured him, "My lord, I can help. I will be here when you return. I promise."

He looked at me and at the queen and took my promise. After our recent estrangement perhaps he was unsure of leaving me. Thought I'd run off. I wouldn't and the kiss he gave me before he left sealed it. He loved me and he had to trust me.

When Ramose was gone Nefertiti and I got to know each other. She treated me as an equal and then slowly as a friend, but I never forgot for a second that she was the royal queen of Egypt. I had the impression that she'd once been haughty and proud, but no longer. A tumble from Pharaoh's grace and changing times had humbled her.

Egyptian Heart

I caught her staring at me thoughtfully. A shiver rippled through me. This woman had a strangeness about her, too. I felt as if we knew each other, but we couldn't. Felt as if she knew things she shouldn't know. She made me think she wasn't what she seemed to be.

Perhaps Nefertiti was a woman out of her time as well. Now that was a creepy thought. That there were others wandering the ages like me. Lost in time.

I wanted to know about her life and her relationship with Pharaoh. As she called for Sesehat, the only one she would trust to help us, and we began packing for the flight, I didn't have to ask her. She unfolded her story as if she'd been waiting for me to tell it to.

About marrying Akhenaton when she was fifteen and he sixteen and how they'd ruled Egypt together as equals. How happy they'd been at the births of their daughters and devastated when their child, Meketaten, had died years ago of an unknown illness. "Her death was the turning point. He loved her more than our other children. After that, my husband turned more to his God and less to me. He cared not about Egypt."

Nefertiti seemed relieved to talk about such things, as if she'd been burdened too long with the memories, and the time went quickly as we prepared to travel.

I'd never seen so many clothes and jewels. It was like being in a treasure chamber. The queen, though, had little trouble sorting out what to take and what to leave behind. She didn't seem to care for her riches. I felt sorry for her.

The most expensive jewels she took, to sell if she needed to she said, and left the rest. She took the simplest clothes. Still it filled trunks and trunks. I wondered how Ramose and his men would be able to cart it all away.

She kept asking herself if she was doing the right thing by running away. I listened and said nothing. It was her decision after all. I was afraid that if I swayed her choice too much one way or another I would be directly tampering with history. I'd already said too much. My being there might have changed too much.

When everything she'd need for herself was packed I followed her to her children's rooms. They were ready for the royal assembly that night. Dressed in striking gowns and their finest jewels, I thought they were so adorable. The youngest seemed so full of life while the other two were trying so hard to be tiny women. Nefertiti bade them to go into the gardens with their servants and though they questioned why, she was firm, and they went.

While they were gone we packed up trunks of their clothes and possessions and Sesehat dragged them into another chamber so the girls wouldn't see them.

"It is best if they do not know we are leaving tonight," Nefertiti commented. "They love their father and will not go willingly. We cannot risk them saying anything to anyone."

She was probably right. I could hear them laughing in the gardens because they were going to see their father and other sisters that night. Nefertiti had told me that she never spoke badly of their father to them, it was not in her nature to destroy her children's illusions.

"Let them keep believing Akhenaton is a good loving father and a great Pharaoh for as long as they are able. He was not always like this." Nefertiti was confiding in me, her arms full of clothes she was taking with us. "Once he loved us all so much. Spent time with us." She smiled remembering. "We used to go for picnics. Take the royal barge and travel down the Nile to this special place we had with trees and lush green water grass…the place where Akhenaton asked me to marry him so long ago. Akhenaton and I used to laugh, love and do everything together. He loved me. He loves me still, I know it. Why has he forsaken me?"

I had no answer for her.

Her eyes haunted with memories of times past, she turned to me. She must have truly loved her husband at one time. "Seer, tell me. Is this then the end of my reign? Am I to depart into the Nubian Desert and never return to my throne again? Or am I to die? What is to become of my remaining children? Of poor Meritaton and Ankhesenpaaten? Tell me," she begged, grabbing my hand and forcing me to meet her gaze.

What could I say? Enough to save her and her children's' lives. And would telling her what I knew to be true in the future really change hers? I walked a very thin line and knew it. "I do not see everything, your Highness. Only some things. You and your three children will live if you leave this place now. You may never sit on the throne of Egypt again, but in your heart you will be a queen for all your life. Of Meritaton and Ankhesenpaaten? I do not know what will become of them. I see that they will continue and will have other husbands."

"And Pharaoh?"

I told her what I thought would serve her best at that moment. "He will not live much longer and he will not ever have the male child he has destroyed your and your daughter's lives to have. It is the end of his male bloodline, I am sorry.

"But you, your Highness, and your three girls must leave here *tonight.*"

Nefertiti thanked me but seemed dazed by my predictions, then resigned. I hadn't told her anything she hadn't already known on some level.

When the queen had collected what she wanted to take, she had her other servants come in to prepare the two of us for the evening's festivities. In my own room, I had a bath and was given clothes and ornaments to wear. A gown of green and white with silver threads running through it. Jade jewels to highlight my eyes and coloring. A girdle of shells and flowers to hang from my waist. Nefertiti lent me one of her simpler black wigs so my blond hair would not cause undue attention and, if Haremhab were there, wouldn't expose me to him. I'm sure he'd remember me if I looked like myself.

I refused to let them put many cosmetics on my face. I didn't need it and I would blend in better if I were plain. I should hide in a corner and just watch the goings on and the people. If Ramose was smart, that's what he'd do as well. We were only going to keep an eye on Nefertiti not to show ourselves.

When I was ready I sat and waited, alone, wishing I had my journal with me so I could have written down the day's events and my thoughts. But my swatches of papyrus and reed pen were with my other clothes in a cart somewhere in the stables. I'd have to ask Ramose to get me a leather pouch or a saddlebag so I could take my journal with me everywhere. I'd had it on the boat and had spent a lot of time writing during the lonely hours without Ramose. I reviewed all I'd learned that day and made mental notes of what I needed to write down when I got the chance.

Suddenly it was late and Ramose was there again. He'd reported to Nefertiti what he'd accomplished and had come to fetch me for the evening's affair so we could join her and the children. We were all going together.

Ramose had taken time to clean and shave and dress in fine clothes. I couldn't take my eyes off him. He was the image of a prince.

He couldn't stop looking at me. "You grow more lovely each day, Mag-gie." He took me into his arms and kissed me, murmuring, "I am sorry for the way I treated you on the boat. I was afraid when you told me your story. Afraid you were not who I thought you were. For a time, I feared you were an evil jinn as Makere swore you were. Then I thought of all the good things you have done and the way you have been with me and I knew you could not be evil.

"Forgive me for doubting you? Being fearful of you? I love you and whatever comes I will deal with it as long as I have you by my side."

"You don't need my forgiveness, my lord. I understand why you behaved the way you did. It was a shock, that's all. Let's forget it and go from here?"

"As you say, we will go from here." He smiled. "A dangerous enough place as it is. Lord Haremhab arrived today and, I am sure, will be at the gathering tonight. Though we must go to support the queen, I cannot let him see me—or you."

"We'll stay out of sight?"

"As much as we can. There will be many people there. It will not be hard to lose ourselves in the great crowd."

As we waited for Sesehat to come bid us to join Nefertiti we talked softly of a future, our future that Ramose hoped we would have in a distant place. He claimed it would be too risky to return to his lands after we fled with Nefertiti.

"We may never be able to return," he decided. "I am not sure where we will go but we shall be together."

I didn't say anything, but I wasn't sure we would be together.

I didn't know if fate would let me stay with him in ancient Egypt much longer. I'd begun having this sensation of disorientation. Growing stronger each day. Sometimes I looked at what was around me, or at Ramose, and everything seemed to blur and fade for a few moments. Just a few moments. It scared me. I didn't want to leave this time, yet, even though we were in danger. Leave Ramose? I loved him too much.

Egyptian Heart

And I couldn't tell him what was happening to me.

I had to enjoy what we had now. Enjoy the night's celebrations and bask in Ramose's love. All I had, all we had was now.

It would have to be enough.

Kathryn Meyer Griffith

Chapter Fourteen

Pharaoh's court with its ceremony and pageantry was everything I'd ever imagined and more. There were hundreds of people, lords and their women from across the city, as well as foreign diplomats sitting on benches or at tables as slaves wound through the hall with huge platters of food and drink. The women showed a lot of skin and the men were dressed like vibrant birds, but most seemed unusually subdued in the presence of Pharaoh.

It was one thing to read about such a gathering, or see the make believe on a movie screen, but to be there in person for the occasion was like visiting heaven, with the people, the costumes and jewels, the endless and fabulous food as eye candy. For so many people talking and eating, I was amazed that the noise level wasn't any higher than it was. I could actually hear what Ramose said to me when he brought me a plate of food, which we shared and ate of quickly.

The spectacle. The power of the royalty in that room, especially Akhenaton and Nefertiti, as they sat silent upon their gem-encrusted thrones, surrounded by their daughters, filled me with wonder. The children's thrones, five of them, were only a little smaller, a little less grand than the Queen's and Pharaoh's. One throne was empty.

"Meritaton is not here tonight," Ramose breathed to me after we'd slunk into the room,

Egyptian Heart

poised as close to the thrones as we could get and remain partially invisible. Standing by pillars on each side of the throne dais, we could watch the assemblage and keep an eye on Nefertiti and her daughters. "They say she is recovering from her latest miscarriage and has already fallen into disfavor with Pharaoh.

"The woman on the left of Nefertiti is her daughter Ankhesenpaaten."

Nefertiti was unrecognizable as the woman I'd spent the day with. Her slaves had dressed her as befitted her status as queen of Lower and Upper Egypt. Gold and silver dazzled on her arms, fingers and ears. She wore a magnificent collar of precious stones from distant Arabia and a diadem of the same. On her lap she held the symbols of supreme power, the crook and flail and sat at the right hand of Akhenaton.

She was a magnificent stone woman. There was no joy on her face, no emotion in her eyes when she looked at her husband or out over the congregation of their subjects. Only a glimmer of sad pity when she glanced at her daughter Ankhesenpaaten on her husband's left.

Ankhesenpaaten couldn't have been any older than thirteen, a child dressed up as a woman with appealing face and doleful eyes. With her glossy obsidian wig that hung in a fall of braids to her bare shoulders, her snow white gown against her pale brown skin and the showy crown she wore on her proud head, she could have been a younger version of her mother. The girl kept peering sideways at her father and smiling. Trying to please him. She never met her mother's or any of her sister's eyes once. So this was Pharaoh's favorite now?

I felt sorry for all of them.

Neferneferuaton, Setepenaton and Baqtaton were dressed in their finest, bejeweled and made up to look like miniature goddesses, and like their mother they were all beautiful stone statues that did not move or speak unless spoken to by Pharaoh.

Pharaoh Akhenaton wasn't exactly an ugly man, with his droopy shoulders and petulant face, but he looked old for his age. Looked much older than Nefertiti, though they were but a year apart. He looked unwell, even I could see that. He kept hiding his mouth behind his hand and coughing and his eyes were glazed. He never said a word to his wife or his daughters. His whole manner was distracted, as if he didn't know where he was. His advisers clustered around him like monkeys muttering and gesturing while his guards stood sentry beyond the dais to protect him from harm.

I'd seen men look like Pharaoh before. When I'd been a teenager, one summer I'd volunteered to work at a nursing home. Had my first taste of death. The old ones would get this emptiness in their eyes right before they passed away. I saw that same look in Akhenaton's eyes. Not much longer for this earth.

Nefertiti and her children would be smart to desert the palace and get as far away as they could. Once Akhenaton was dead, their lives wouldn't be worth much—if Haremhab had any say in it. They'd be in the way.

I watched as dignitaries from Palestine and

Egyptian Heart

Babylon paraded in to see Pharaoh. All of them petitioning for aid and troops to fight off the barbarians who were overrunning their countries; begging for Akhenaton to lead those troops and save them. Surely the invaders would flee if Pharaoh came himself. He listened, agreed brusquely to consider their requests, but would give them no decisions. "I will pray to our great god, Aton, for guidance. You should do the same," was all he'd say in a flat voice.

Nefertiti wouldn't look at her husband.

When the supplicants were gone, Haremhab swept into the hall and strode up to the thrones, bowed and groveled as if he was Pharaoh's most loyal servant. He appeared as I remembered him, as I crept further behind the pillar and peeked out, though his sturdy frame was clothed in fine linen and he was decked out almost as richly as Pharaoh himself. His dark skin was cleaner and his heavy beard trimmed closer, but there was still that brutish meanness lurking in his eyes and that predatory smile.

Ramose silently signaled to me from some feet away as he fell back into the shadows. I knew he was watching Haremhab as closely as I was. I could see Nefertiti's eyes harden when she looked at the general. Her sworn enemy.

Haremhab had once made romantic overtures to Nefertiti, I'd learned from Ramose. Had wanted to be her lover. "She spurned him. As far as I know, she has never been unfaithful to Akhenaton and never will be, and never with a man as untrustworthy and ambitious as Haremhab. Not a man to trust, much less take as a lover. Lord Haremhab has never forgotten or forgiven her for that slight. It would give him great pleasure to see her brought down."

Pharaoh welcomed the general with open arms and an exaggerated cheerfulness. The sick monarch lifted his hand and called out, "Send in Beketaton!"

Pharaoh's sister was ushered into the room, head down. A glossy short pageboy wig and enough trinkets and face paint pretty well hid her features and disguised what she really looked like. She had lovely skin the color of light chocolate and was very tiny. Her nose was large and her face thin like her brother's, but she was younger and healthier than him. Wasn't as pretty as Nefertiti. She trudged along as if her feet didn't want to take her to her arranged fate. The expression on her face aloft and arrogant. It was easy to see that she didn't want this marriage; that she was being coerced into it.

Akhenaton grew impatient and snapped at her to hurry her steps. She didn't. Yet soon enough she was frozen beside Haremhab, and Akhenaton, who clasped their hands together and raised them high, announced their betrothal in a trembling voice.

"I here today give my sister, Beketaton, to the general of my armies and Chief Administrator, Lord Haremhab, as wife. I join them with the power given me by the one and true god, Aton. From this day forward they will be man and wife. We celebrate their union tonight. Rejoice with them.

Beketaton didn't look happy, didn't raise her eyes, but Haremhab was ecstatic. He was getting what he'd always wanted. A royal and wealthy wife. An engraved invitation into the royal family and his ticket to winning the royal sweepstakes.

Once he rid himself of those in his way.

Ramose was probably furious now. I didn't have to see him to know that. There were people between us but I could feel his anger sulking in the gloom behind me.

Haremhab claimed his prize and escorted her to the right side of Pharaoh's throne.

Something else was about to happen, I thought. I was right.

"My subjects," Pharaoh said in a voice growing weaker with every word as he twisted towards his young daughter, Ankhesenpaaten, "tonight I also take another bride, my beloved Ankhesenpaaten." He grabbed the girl's hand and she rose from her chair to stand by her father's side. I could see her quivering, but whether from joy or dread I didn't know.

I could see the anguish in Nefertiti's face before it morphed into hardness again.

Ankhesenpaaten was given a crown as fine as Nefertiti's, her small head could barely hold it up, and she was given the symbols of power similar to the ones Nefertiti held.

I glanced at Nefertiti, my face flushing, but her eyes were closed. There were tears sliding down her face. In the short time I'd known her, we'd formed a bond and it was hard for me to stand there and watch her suffer humiliation. Why was Akhenaton taking her daughter as his new wife in front of her? Anyone could see that Nefertiti still loved her husband.

To show the people that Nefertiti sanctioned this new marriage, that's why and that she was behind Pharaoh in all he did.

Cruel is what it was. Just plain cruel. But this was the way of the ancient pharaohs. They were gods and could do anything they wanted. Taking sisters or daughters as wives to keep the bloodline pure was customary and expected. It couldn't have been easy on the hearts of the women involved, but it had to be borne.

I remembered Nefertiti saying that once they'd been a happy family. Pharaoh had been a loving husband to her and a good father to his daughters. He'd changed. Egypt had changed. I grieved for her.

A short time later Akhenaton sent his three younger daughters to their quarters. All yawning, and their made up eyes full of weariness from the revelations and revelry of the long night, they seemed relieved to go.

Soon after that, Akhenaton took his new wife Ankhesenpaaten's hand, rose, and they exited the hall together leaving their guests to celebrate and feast on without them. Pharaoh shuffled when he walked and his young bride let him lean on her. The room was quiet until they were out of earshot and then slowly the partying continued.

Haremhab mingled with the guests, busy showing off his trophy bride and scheming with the foreign diplomats.

Nefertiti had been left alone on her throne. The court seemed to ignore her now that Pharaoh was gone. He hadn't given her a glance the whole night.

Egyptian Heart

I've never seen anyone look more abandoned. The merriment continued on around her, muffled near her throne, and louder in the far reaches of the room. She was no longer Pharaoh's beloved. She was no longer the great queen. She was redundant. I saw her eyes dull and finally her chin drop. The night had taken its toll. She'd done her part and now she could be herself again.

Ramose moved towards the queen and put out his hand. She stood and without a look back or around her, took it gratefully. He led her towards the rear doors and I followed behind, trying not to look anyone in the eyes or be noticed. I had nothing to worry about. Everyone's eyes were on the queen and Ramose, or so I thought.

They were through the doors and suddenly there was someone blocking my way. I looked up. It was Haremhab. Too late. He'd seen me.

Beketaton was no longer by his side. I looked around quickly but didn't see her. Maybe she'd left already.

"I know you, do I not?" he demanded in that gruff voice of his as his large hand grabbed my arm. The wig hid my hair and I kept my eyes down. But I couldn't hide my height. Even slouching could only do so much. Haremhab would have to be blind not to recognize me if he looked hard enough. Ramose had been ahead of me and I hoped he'd seen Haremhab waylay me. If he hadn't I could be in trouble.

"No, my lord," I mumbled, slurring my words, trying to conceal my voice as well.

"Look at me!" he commanded, grabbing my

chin and forcing my face upwards. I wanted to kick him but I knew it'd make him a little angry.

I looked at him, squinting my eyes as if it was a natural state.

"Green eyes like those of a jinn."

He yanked my wig off and my blond hair tumbled down around my shoulders.

"You! I thought it was you. So you didn't die out in the desert as Ramose claimed?" He wasn't mad, but seemed pleased. Maybe having won Pharaoh's sister had made him a new man. That or he wasn't as drunk as the last time I'd met him.

The noise had died down in the room and I could feel eyes on us, so I spoke softly. I didn't want anyone overhearing us. "No, my lord. I walked out onto the desert and met up with a caravan. It brought me here to the city." I made up a quick lie so he wouldn't have time to make a connection between Ramose and me. No sense in leading him to Ramose, seeing as they weren't on friendly terms lately.

"You weren't lost out in the desert?"

What could I say? I was frantically trying to figure out something to tell him that would get me off the hook and leave Ramose out of it. "No, my lord. Never. I merely traveled to the city."

He released my chin and captured my wrist, looking around us and again to me. "Who are you here with?"

"No one," I lied, my eyes searching for Ramose. Hadn't he noticed I was not with him yet? Wasn't he coming back for me and what would I do if he didn't?

Egyptian Heart

"You might have escaped from me that time, but you are still a runaway slave."

I tried not to show my anger. Tried to stay respectful. "No, my lord, I am not a slave. I never was. I tried to tell you that that night, but you did not hear me." *Because you were too drunk.* Of course I couldn't say that. Not to Haremhab. He could have me killed simply for looking at him wrong.

Then it came to me. "I serve Queen Nefertiti. I have always served the queen. I am her seer." A justification for why I was at Ramose's house before. Nefertiti was his aunt and I was her fortune-teller. It worked for me.

He let go of my wrist as if I'd been a leper. His eyes suspicious and nervous as he inspected me. I wasn't sure if he believed me or if he disliked seers. He didn't ask what I'd been doing at Ramose's palace months ago or anything else. I had him stumped. He couldn't think of what to say. I gently took the wig back. "This wig is not mine, my lord, but the queen's. I must return it or she will be unhappy with me."

And then Ramose was by my side.

"Lord Nakh-Min, so good to see you are still alive," Haremhab addressed the man who'd went AWOL on him. "What are you doing here?" As if he didn't know.

I thought Ramose pulled his contrition act off splendidly. There was an apologetic eagerness in him and a smile on his face. No fear, no guilt. Just a man glad to see an old friend.

"Visiting my aunt, the queen, and my cousins.

Taking a much needed time to rest. You must agree, my lord, that I have been stressed of late. Was not myself. Too many battlefields and too much death these last years. I am sorry for the words we had. Please forgive me. With time to think, I came to see…." He hushed his voice so no one else would hear and his smile evaporated. "You were right."

Brilliant move, Ramose, I thought. *Plead temporary insanity for leaving like you did and then pretend to go along with his plans.* It would give us time to escape.

Haremhab seemed to ponder over what his old friend had said. He grunted, nodding his head. "I am happy to hear that. We have been friends for a long time, Lord Nakh-Min. I will hold no grudge against you for your hasty departure from my camp. All is forgiven. This time." A stern warning. Haremhab was not the kind of man you crossed and lived to speak of it.

I'd expected the two men to come to blows but they hadn't. I'd expected Haremhab to call his guards and have Ramose arrested. He hadn't. Perhaps because there were people around us and Ramose was, after all, nephew to Queen Nefertiti. She still had her supporters. Not many, but some. Or perhaps because Haremhab wasn't worried any longer about Ramose or anything he could do to him now that Haremhab was related to Pharaoh. No one or nothing could touch him. After all, Ramose had no actual proof of Haremhab's conspiracy to kill Pharaoh. And without proof Ramose could do nothing to him. Haremhab was now too powerful.

Thank God the man couldn't read minds. If he

Egyptian Heart

suspected we were escaping that night with the queen and her children it'd be altogether a different story. We'd all be dead people.

Not that I trusted Haremhab *not* to kill us anyway when we left Pharaoh's Palace. Perhaps it was only that he didn't want anyone to know he'd ordered our deaths and there was a crowd of people around watching and listening. Assassinations were best done with secrecy.

Haremhab's gaze revisited me. "So she *is* with you, Lord Nakh-Min?"

"I am with the queen," I interrupted before Ramose could say anything and ruin the lies I'd woven. "As I said before, my lord, I am her seer."

I caught the look of amusement flicker across Ramose's face and just as quickly disappear. He understood what I meant and played along. "It is true. Queen Nefertiti has need of her tonight—she has had omens she needs deciphered—and sent me to find her and fetch her back. Now." Ramose took my arm, started to lead me away, saying to Haremhab, "We must not tarry any longer. You know how annoyed the queen gets when her commands are not obeyed."

Haremhab reached out and caught Ramose's other arm, keeping him from leaving. "You must obey the queen's summons, yet you and I must have a *talk,* my lord. Soon."

Ramose played another trump card. "Tonight, when I am done with this last errand for the queen?" *Knowing* Haremhab had a marriage bed to go to and a royal marriage to consummate. Crafty of him, I mused. How could Haremhab doubt Ramose's loyalty now?

The general hesitated, caught off guard. "No. Tomorrow morning will be soon enough, I suppose. It has been a momentous day and I can see the weariness in you as well. I understand how the queen would have need of her seer's counsel this night." I caught the gloating in his voice.

"I will send my guards tomorrow morning to escort you to my chambers here in the palace. Then we will talk."

"I will be ready, my lord," Ramose countered earnestly. His respectful tone reflecting Haremhab's new position in Pharaoh's court.

Ramose guided me out of Haremhab's sight, down the hall and out into the night, the noise of the partiers growing dimmer with each step. I was glad to get out of there. Too open. Too many people. Too many prying eyes. As we made our way towards the queen's palace, he peered back a few times in the dark. His face faintly lit by the half moon riding in the sky above us.

"You don't trust him, do you?" I was shivering in the cool night air. The wind was a chill touch on our hot skin. I let out a deep breath I'd been holding for what seemed like forever. Ever since Haremhab had caught me going out the door.

"No, I do not. He may have other things on his mind tonight, but he will not forget me. Us. I know too much and am a threat to him. I am worried that his forgiveness of my indiscretions back there was but a ruse. That even now he is sending out assassins to rid him of us."

My hand wrapped in his felt safe. I *felt* safe. I

Egyptian Heart

couldn't believe we *weren't* safe.

"You don't think he believed that you're on his side?"

Ramose shook his head. "I am not sure. He knows we will be with the queen in her palace shortly. Protected by her guards. It is getting there that I am concerned with. If he decides he is better off with me dead, he would be wise to have it done now."

"But you and he were friends for so long," I blurted out. "How can he just have you killed?"

"Because his hunger for power is greater than any friendship he has ever had before or will ever know. I cannot understand why I did not see that before. We were never friends. I was the queen's nephew and it suited him to play at being my friend and keep an eye on me.

"We should hurry." He pulled me along almost at a run. We left the path and took a short cut that Ramose knew of through a garden and behind the palaces.

Our flight reminded me of my first night in ancient Egypt running from Ramose's soldiers in the desert. This time always seemed to be full of dangers for me. Seemed I was always running from someone.

We arrived at Nefertiti's palace out of breath and after making sure no assassins waited for us at the entrance, Ramose announced to the guards who he was and we were let inside.

Nefertiti and her children were ready to depart. They'd shed their finery and their jewels, were scrubbed clean and dressed in simple clothes. She'd told the girls that they were going on a trip to see prosperous friends in Nubia. In this time it was a country that bordered on Upper Egypt; in my time it was called Ethiopia. Our destination was just inside Nubia. Still a very long journey and far enough away to hide from Pharaoh.

We were leaving at night, Nefertiti also told the girls, because she'd had a dream advising her to begin their journey under the light of the moon or something bad would happen. Good explanation. The girls accepted that as any superstitious Egyptian children would and were excited to be traveling anywhere. It was an adventure, riding out from the palace in the middle of the night to catch a boat for a cruise on the Nile.

Though I think the oldest girl, Neferneferuaton, didn't swallow the whole dream excuse. She'd seen her sister Ankhesenpaaten offered in marriage to their father and she knew of Meritaton's fall from favor. Saw her Aunt Beketaton given to Haremhab. She was old enough to sense her mother might be afraid of what might happen next to her and her children.

Sesehat was the only slave Nefertiti trusted enough to bring along.

It was strange riding through the night with a queen of Egypt and her daughters. The woman was an expert horseman and so were her girls. Ramose led and his men surrounded us. We rode hard until we got to the river and boarded a large menechou Ramose had retained for our river voyage.

No one seemed to be following us.

Ramose shepherded his aunt and cousins to the

captain's cabin and settled them in for the night as the boat left dock and headed down the Nile towards Nubia, its sails billowing and its prow skimming the water. The further we were from Amarna, gaining on our lead, the safer we would be, Ramose hoped.

I stood at the front of the boat as a steamy rain fell and gazed out across the river at the boat lanterns swaying and bobbing around us. *I've been here before.* Ramose came up behind me and put his arms around my waist. Laid his head against mine. *This time is better. We aren't fighting.*

"I feel sorry for her." He meant the queen. "She is a strong woman but these have been difficult years for her. She does not know what is to become of her and her children. I have never seen her afraid. She is afraid now."

"Do you think General Haremhab will come after us?"

"Of that I am certain. Nefertiti has the love of her people and could cause him problems if she rallies them behind her. She has the power if she wants to use it. My aunt is a smart woman who could rule alone. She is a great queen and a priestess. Haremhab knows this and fears her. As long as she lives, he will never be able to claim the throne completely. He knows this as well.

"Then there are Neferneferuaton, Setepenaton and Baqtaton. Royal pawns who carry Pharaoh's blood in them. They are as dangerous to Haremhab as their mother, if not more. Married to another of their bloodline, they could be queens of Egypt themselves someday.

"Haremhab will come."

"Do you think he will find us in Nubia?"

"I expect he will try. He has his spies everywhere."

There were other things I wanted to ask but didn't. I was tired after the long day and my mind wasn't working right. I'd had that feeling of disorientation again when I'd first come on the boat. I'd shaken it, but it'd unnerved me. I stroked the amulet around my neck and worried over what was happening to me.

All I cared about was being close to Ramose. Spending as much time with him as I could for as long as I could. The allure of ancient Egypt had worn off.

The love I felt for Ramose was the only real thing to me. All the rest, even my past life, was the dream.

"Do you know what will become of Nefertiti and her daughters?" Ramose pressed, watching the river traffic with me.

I knew he was talking about their futures. Something I would know about if what I'd told him about myself were true.

"No, I don't. It wasn't in any of the books I read. No one ever knew what became of Nefertiti and her younger daughters. I'm sorry. They just *disappeared.*" I smiled mysteriously in the moonlight. "But I believe she escapes Akhenaton and Haremhab and she and her three beautiful daughters live out the rest of their lives safe and anonymous with friends in a city in Nubia. They're happy, they all live a long time, have more children and die unknown. Just my belief, though."

Ramose remained silent for a minute or two.

Then: "What becomes of Pharaoh?"

I lifted my eyes and took in the stars, letting the rain gently splash my face. "He will not live much longer. According to the history books in my time he dies by age thirty- two."

"My *friend* General Haremhab?"

I almost didn't tell him, but what the heck, telling him wouldn't hurt anything. Or not much that I could see. Fate will out.

"Someday, for a very brief time, he will rule Egypt…after Smenkhkare and Tutankhamum…and Ay."

Smenkhkare was a son of Amenophis III and one of his lesser wives. "Tutankhamum will marry Pharaoh's widow and daughter, Ankhesenpaaten and also will only rule a short time. Then Ay,"—the non-royal father of Nefertiti— "will also marry Ankhesenpaaten and rule a brief span. Finally, history says that Haremhab will take the crown.

"If we haven't changed it by convincing Nefertiti and her daughters to abscond now. It's sooner than it should have been for them to drop out of sight."

We may have already changed history. Who knows? Would I be around to see if we have changed things? I didn't know.

"The Hittites? Will they over run Egypt and enslave our people?"

"No," I replied firmly. "Egypt will live on. Strong and powerful, intact, for many, many more centuries. The Hittites will not prevail."

"You know these things to be true, then?"

"I do."

Ramose was relieved. "I do not know if what you say will come to pass. I do not care. The queen and her children are safe and that is all I care about now.

"And we are safe. Together." He swung me about and kissed me as the rain fell softly. I slid my arms up around his neck and kissed him back. Many times. I was happy we weren't quarreling any more. Time was too precious, too short to waste it fighting. I knew that now. Knew it all too well.

Egyptian Heart

Chapter Fifteen

We traveled down the river for days. Each day hotter than the last; the sun, a ring of fire pulsated over us and the heat glimmered in the waves before us.

No more rain. No cool breezes. I would have loved to been able to wear a pair of shorts and a tank top, but I didn't have any in my luggage.

All my gowns and robes, even the nicer ones Tiye had given me, felt too heavy to wear on my skin. I was drenched with sweat from morning to dusk until Nefertiti took pity on me and lent me two of her summer gowns and I was grateful. Made of the best linen they covered my whole body but were light enough and loosely woven enough that they allowed air to cool my flesh.

She also gave me a jar of her special lotion to protect me from the sun because I'd run out of what Ahhotpe had sent along for me. Even with all the sun I'd had the last weeks my skin could still burn.

When I wasn't with Ramose, I'd spend the days with Nefertiti or with her girls. Parading the deck, remarking on the merchant crafts that passed us and the wares they carried; observing the dark shadows of the mountains in the distance drift by or pointing out animals, buildings or people on the banks.

The princesses were full of stories of Pharaoh and his court that I never grew tired of hearing. They were exceptionally bright and imaginative young women and I enjoyed their company, but I never said anything about our journey from Amarna or that we were in flight from their enemies.

I honored their mother's request that the girls not know they were in danger. They were children after all.

Ramose had my belongings loaded on the boat before we sailed and I faithfully recorded in my diary at the end of every day, under a makeshift shelter Ramose's men had built for us on deck, everything of interest Nefertiti or her daughters said to me.

It gave me comfort to write about my daily experiences. It reminded me who I was, an Egyptologist on the safari of a lifetime.

Sometimes, I drew miniature pictures in my journal of the river scenery or portraits of the people I was sailing with. Got a couple of good ones of the royal women and of Ramose. A few of the soldiers. Nefertiti was so impressed she asked me if I would draw her and her children again when we got to Nubia and she could get me better drawing materials.

Flattered, I said I would.

Ramose and I spent the evenings together, talking and sharing confidences; falling deeper in love. He wanted to know everything about my old life in the future, though he had trouble believing most of what I described could be real.

I entertained him with tales of cars and airplanes and computers. They made him stare at me in awe or laugh outright. Told him of my life at the University and about my family. It felt so good not having to lie anymore to him and I know we grew closer because of it.

I slept in his arms each night, knowing he wanted to make love to me, and I'd come to want the same thing. I loved Ramose and no longer doubted he was the love of my life, and I his. We both knew it. I no longer cared about remaining a virgin or holding back the passion I felt for him. No longer cared if the amulet might send me back home at any moment.

It made me want him even more, for our time could be short.

There was no privacy on the boat, sleeping among his soldiers and the sailors manning the menechou, so out of regard for me, he would wait to consummate our love.

Yet I wondered if we ever would make love. My dizzy spells were increasing. I hid them and what they might mean from Ramose. I didn't want to scare him, too.

It was enough for me to know we loved each other. All those years of hearing from my mother about true love and fate and how when you found the man with the heart and soul destined for you, you'd know.

I'd never believed her. I believed her now.

The days passed. We sailed with the currents, oared through the lulls and broiled in the sun. I acquired more of a tan even with Nefertiti's potion. Aside from being worried that Pharaoh's or Haremhab's soldiers would find us and drag us back to Amarna for punishment, I was happy.

I was the one who first became aware of the crimson boat with the washed out yellow sails dogging us. Usually I glimpsed it at dawn or early twilight silhouetted on the horizon. It tried to stay out of sight as it stalked us. Other boats fell away, passed us or vanished along the route. Day after day I waited and watched. The crimson boat was always there.

It could just be a merchant taking his goods down river. Going our way. Nothing to fret over. Not chasing us at all. Then I thought I spotted soldiers on board.

"I think someone may be following us," I said to Ramose on the fifth morning after I spied the boat again. "It stays behind just enough so it doesn't call attention to itself."

I described the vessel to him as we stood together at the bow of the menechou, his arm around me. We'd gotten up early to see the sunrise of exploding lemon and peach clouds scudding across the skies at the river's edge. Water birds had appeared and disappeared in the wispy clouds, their cries accompanying the dawn.

Ramose and I had kissed as the sun gave life to another day and I'd thought that no one in the history of the world had ever loved as we loved each other.

I had finally found the magic love people talked about.

Every minute with him was precious now to me for I'd come to believe my time here was almost over…just a strong feeling…and the lapses from reality I'd been having.

"It is one of Lord Haremhab's boats," Ramose had responded. "He has sent his soldiers after us.

He must have had spies who alerted him when we fled with the queen and her daughters. They have most likely been following us since we left the palace."

"They've come to kill us?"

He nodded.

"Why haven't they made a move yet? We've been on the river for days." I felt a stab of fear as my eyes searched for the enemy's boat. There it was, barely visible in the morning's mist behind us. It looked bigger. Closer. Gaining.

"The winds have been favorable. We have a fast boat, have traveled at night, and have not slowed down. They are biding their time. They know eventually we will stop. That is when they will strike."

"What are we going to do?"

Ramose had been staring at the other boat, his hand resting lightly on the hilt of the dagger at his waist. I'd seen that look before. He was strategizing. Preparing to fight. As we'd taken a curve in the river he'd had a good look at the other ship and had proclaimed it as Haremhab's.

"Tonight when the sun goes down we will drop anchor," he said, "douse our lanterns and torches, remain still in the water and the dark and wait for the other ship to pass us in the night.

"We will follow it and at dawn board the ship and kill them before they can kill us. I will not let them hurt my queen and the princesses. I will not let them hurt *you,* Mag-gie."

My heart wanted to protest, beg him not to put himself at risk, but I had no right. Ramose was a warrior and fighting—winning—was what he knew best. And all our lives were at stake. The queen and her children. Ramose and his men. Me.

The assassins, when they struck, could leave none of us alive. Ramose understood that. I understood that. I thought Ramose's plan was feasible.

The rest of the day Ramose made plans with his men for the coming skirmish.

He made clear to Nefertiti what he was going to do and cautioned her and her girls to stay out of sight and safe in their cabin.

If I am not successful, he instructed her, *I have given orders to the captain to sail you away with all speed and get you to safety. I will leave men aboard to protect you and the princesses. Have them sneak you off the boat at night if you must. May Aton go with you.*

In the dusk, Ramose came and put his arms around me and we watched the sun set together. We'd had a meal in the cabin with the queen and the girls earlier and I could see how scared the queen was. How vulnerable.

Without all her trappings of power and wealth around her, Nefertiti was only a woman with children running for her life and theirs.

I felt as sorry for her as I did for Ramose and myself.

I'd had a taste of being out of one's world, helpless and frightened and it wasn't an easy road to walk. Now there were men trying to murder all of us.

Night fell, lights were snuffed, the boat was

steered nearer to the bank and its anchor tossed into the river.

I stayed close to Ramose as he laid out final orders to his men, in whispers, because sounds travel far on the night river, and we waited for the other vessel to catch up and to pass us. Waited in the blackness, with all the river noises as the men prepared their weapons and their nerves for action.

The day had been sultry, the night had brought tepid temperatures and a heavy fog had flowed in to enfold our boat. The only light was a full moon but now the clouds racing across the sky flickered its light off.

In the darkness we sat, counted minutes and prayed to our own individual gods that we'd all be alive in the morning.

Ramose had no doubts. He was brave, moving among and reassuring his men as the lights of the distant prey floated nearer.

Haremhab's ship gradually passed ours in the night, not seeing us, and after a short interval the anchor was brought up, our sails were raised and we quietly slipped in behind the other craft. Everyone was silent, sitting cross-legged on the deck, listening, the only sounds were the cracking of the sails as they stretched and relaxed against the wind and the swish of the water as the oars dipped in and out.

We couldn't let the craft in front of us get too far ahead.

In shifts Ramose had his men sleep. I tried to sleep, but couldn't.

I ended up patrolling the deck with Ramose,

holding his hand. When no one was looking, he'd pull me into his arms and gently kiss me, tell me he loved me. Tell me that he would triumph against our pursuers. I shouldn't worry.

I'd a terrible premonition about the morning's battle and wouldn't let Ramose out of my sight. The thought of him being wounded or killed made my heart ache.

Before dawn the tension on the boat was palpable. No one spoke, no one moved as the sun began to come up and Ramose ordered the oarsmen to row faster. The crimson ship was ahead of us. There were many soldiers aboard.

They'd seen us, and the cry that we were behind them and trying to ram them rang out. Too late. We'd caught up, nudging our boat up against the other one's side, we hit with a jolt. It nearly knocked me off my feet.

Ramose's men had thrown grappling ropes at the other boat to secure the two vessels together. As I crouched half concealed behind the cabin—I'd refused to hide below with our guests as Ramose had told me to do—I saw the drama unfold and clutched the knife my lover had given me, in case.

In case we'd be overpowered and I had to defend myself. Or kill myself.

I could die today. We all could. Dwelling on it filled me with terror. *I didn't want Ramose to die. I didn't want to die.* Now that I'd found my true love.

I touched the amulet hanging around my neck. Would it let me die here in another time? It might. Perhaps this was my fate. If so, I couldn't escape it.

In my eyes, the battle was short but vicious.

Egyptian Heart

With a yell to announce the attack, Ramose led his men onto the other boat's deck, their weapons ready as they faced their pursuers. They were Haremhab's men. Over a dozen, by my count.

Later, Ramose would say he'd remembered some of them from other military campaigns. When they'd been on the same side.

He'd hated to kill men he'd once fought alongside of, but it was either kill or be killed.

The soldiers fell on each other with clubs and daggers. I'd never seen a real battle with real men. It was awful. The cries of the wounded and the stench of blood and raw flesh. I forced myself to watch as long as I could bear it.

I had to keep my eyes on Ramose fighting in the crowd. To see that he was okay and that he lived.

He fought well. His men fought well. I edged closer to the struggle and in the rising sun I saw Ramose fighting with one soldier as two others were sneaking up behind him.

I didn't think, just reacted. I flew across the deck and jumped over the chasm between the two boats. Stumbled over clay jars of what looked like incense oil. Righted myself and ran towards the nearest man who was advancing on Ramose as I pulled out my knife.

I cried, *"My lord, behind you!"* Ramose didn't respond fast enough.

I don't know how I did it but I found the courage to plunge the knife blade into the other man's arm as he was about to hit Ramose with a spiked club.

When the man's eyes fell on me, they widened

in pain and then in shock. He screamed something at me that sounded like *demon woman,* and swung the club at me; I jumped back but not quick enough and it grazed the side of my head.

I staggered, my hand going to where the blood was flowing. He'd got me. But I was still standing.

The man, though, had hesitated long enough for one of Ramose's soldiers to knife him. He slumped to the deck. I think he was dead.

Having heard my warning and glancing up, Ramose saw me and yelled, *"Get back to the boat now!"* I'd never seen him so angry or his eyes so desperate. I know he would have seen to me but he was in combat with another soldier by the time the words left his mouth.

I did as he said and scrambled back to my hiding place. Only then did I feel the astonishment of what I'd done. My head hurt from the blow. I ripped off a piece of my gown and used it to stop the bleeding from the wound.

How lucky I'd been that I'd moved when I did. Or I'd be dead, lying on that other bloodstained deck across from me. God had been with me.

I couldn't stop my body from shaking as my eyes took in the rest of the battle. What a chance I'd taken. Was I nuts or what?

No. I loved Ramose enough to fight, die for him if necessary. I didn't regret for one second what I'd done. Do it again if I had to.

A cheer arose from the other boat and Ramose appeared at my side, out of breath, sweating, with cuts and blood smeared on his skin. "Are you well?"

Egyptian Heart

"It's just a flesh wound," I muttered sheepishly. "I'll be all right. Could use a couple of aspirins, though." I tried a smile, but he only glared at me. He wouldn't know what aspirins were anyway.

Then I was in his arms and everything was better. He didn't even scold me, that's how happy he was to see me still alive. For us both to be alive and victorious.

"They are all dead," he said. "My men are burning the boat so no one will know what happened to them. By the time Lord Haremhab learns of their fate, we will be safely at our destination. He will not know where to look. The queen and the princesses will be safe."

"How many men did we lose?" I had to ask.

"Four. Two wounded being attended to even now. Three wounded including you." He took a peek at my injury, proclaimed it wasn't bad but that I'd probably have a sore head for a while.

The other boat was in flames as we disengaged from it and continued our journey down the river. I shivered in my love's arms, humbled and exhausted by what we'd been through, and watched the bonfire as we moved away.

The air was full of the stench of wood and burning human flesh.

There was sorrow on Ramose's face. He'd had to kill men he'd sat around campfires with and led into war. It would leave more than battle scars. Warrior though he was, he disliked killing unless he had to and in this instance he'd had to.

The last time I saw the boat with its funeral pyre it was a flickering flame on the water far behind us, dwarfed by the sun.

I said a prayer that now we would be left alone.

That now the danger was over and hoped someone was listening. I'd had enough excitement to last a lifetime. No, two lifetimes.

Egyptian Heart

Chapter Sixteen

Fourteen days later we sailed into Nubia. It looked a lot like Egypt to me but the people had darker skin and appeared to be more tribal. Barefoot and smiling shyly, they'd follow us along the bank as we floated by, mothers carrying their babies and small children waving at us; men with spears yelling at us to stop and trade. They seemed like a trusting people.

I hated leaving the boat in some ways. Except for the whole being chased, fighting, being wounded—and it had healed nicely—and burning up the other ship thing, it'd been an enchanting voyage.

I'd learned about Nefertiti and her children's lives and we'd all become friends. The queen was a woman, as any other woman, with problems and dreams of her own. Unsure who to trust and only wanting to be happy. Like me. I'd miss them.

Ramose and I had grown so close. We were still not actual lovers but it didn't matter. We loved and we knew that soon it would be consummated.

If I remained here.

"Will we be staying in Nubia with your aunt and cousins?" It was our last night on the ship. A balmy one, full of wonderful perfumes: wild river plants and grasses, the aroma of coming rain, and the enticing smell of roasting fowl.

We'd dropped anchor earlier that day and Ramose's men had gone hunting. They'd shot ducks from the skies with their bows and arrows and we'd had an end of the journey feast. My stomach was full and I was content. We'd escaped Haremhab's assassins and... I was still here. Still with the man I loved.

For a while, perhaps.

"I know we can't go back to your or your family's palace. General Haremhab will be looking for us there, I suppose?"

"He will be. And any other place I once knew. Egypt will not be safe for any of us for now or for a long time." Ramose looked across the dark water. "I've sent word to my mother and father to also go into hiding until it is safe again. Whenever that will be."

Most of his men were sleeping. The boat was quiet. A river creature splashed nearby. Then another. A herd of hippos, according to Ramose, swimming downstream.

"So we will remain in Nubia with the queen until, as you say will come about someday, Haremhab's reign is over."

"It could be a long time, my lord. Years. We'll stay in Nubia all that time?"

"Yes, or we will travel to Arabia and Persia. I have long desired to see these places, having heard of their beauty and intriguing people."

"How would we live?"

"My father and mother gave me funds when we were there that I had put aside for just such a desperate time as this. Their men will close up my palace in the desert and set free your slave friends, as I have requested. Until the day comes we can return home, my love. When Lord Haremhab no longer controls or sits on Egypt's throne."

I could see his smile in the faint torchlight as the boat swayed beneath us.

"Free the slaves? You're going to free Ahhotpe, her family and the others?"

"For you, I have determined to do this," Ramose explained. "A gift. There is no need for me to keep slaves there when we will be gone from our home so long. They can have their freedom. They will be given food and silver to begin their new lives. Papers to prove their freedom. Names of friends who might take them as workers into their households if they so choose."

I was touched at his great gift.

Speaking of Ahhotpe brought her sweet face before my mind's eye. I'd thought of her and the others often. My poor eager students who'd been so appreciative of any little kindness I'd shown them when their lives were so hard. Wondered how they were doing without me. If they were well and were being treated fairly. When the master was away I knew the soldiers might revert to their old ways.

I couldn't bear to think of any of the slaves being mistreated. Now I wouldn't have to worry about it any longer.

Thinking of my slave friends reminded me of Min, my left behind kitty, and then Geb, my beautiful horse, stabled at Chnum and Tiye's. I missed them almost as much as I missed my real family—mother, brothers and sisters and Snowball—who wouldn't live for another three thousand years.

I sighed and Ramose, as if he knew the reason for my longing, squeezed me. Kissed me on the tip of my nose and then my cheeks and chin until I laughed. Which is what he'd wanted.

"You are not alone, my love. You are never alone as long as we are together."

The love he gave me made up for the loss of everything else.

He kissed me on the lips then. A kiss of passion and of promise. Caressing the side of my face with his strong hand, he leaned over and rested his head against mine, and whispered, "Freeing the slaves is part of my wedding gift to you."

I stared up at him, soft light dancing around his handsome face, and my joy mingled with astonishment. "You still want me for a wife after everything I told you? Everything you know of me? That I might someday just vanish no matter what I want or do?"

"Yes. Is it so impossible to believe I want to marry you? I cannot live without you now, Mag-gie. These last months have shown me the truth. *I love you.* Whatever, whoever you are, and whatever time you come from, it makes no difference. You are here now, with me, and it is where you will stay. If the gods allow it."

I caught the plural, gods not god, and thought he must be covering all his bases, just in case.

"I could command you to become my wife, yet, out of respect and love, I am asking." His arms were strong around me. His lips so close to mine that if I moved an inch our lips would touch.

"I am *begging* you to marry me."

Egyptian Heart

Tears of elation, or of misery, threatened to fall. So many times in the last months I'd dreamed of being his wife. I'd never wanted anything in my life more. Not anything. Not my Archaeology degree or my job at the college or my book being published.

But I couldn't marry him.

I could be whisked back to the future at any moment. How could I marry him if I wasn't sure I'd be here from day to day?

Since the night I'd found myself on the desert I assumed I was on borrowed time.

Now I believed my time was short since lately I was having so many of these…*lapses.* I'd get dizzy, so hot I would sweat, then so cold I would shiver, and my reality here would blur.

It's like there was a door between this time and my time and I could *see* it opening, irresistibly beckoning me to come through. Sometimes I'd even smell the moldy dankness of Ramose's tomb where I began my incredible sojourn or feel the chill of its stone floor beneath my feet, not the warm deck of the ship.

It was summoning me. My own time—my family, my friends and even my beloved Boston—was calling me.

Come home. Come home where you belong, Maggie.

Three episodes last week and another terrible one this morning as I'd run around the boat, giggling, playing hide-and-go-seek with Setepenaton and Baqtaton.

I'd seen a transparent image of the tomb behind my closed eyes. I'd really thought I was going back.

I'd racked my mind trying to figure out how to stop the episode. What had sent me to Ramose's time to begin with, I asked myself? The amulet, yes, but I'd come to believe there'd been another ingredient in the brew.

But what?

What *else* had happened in those crucial moments before I was hurled into the past? The confrontation and struggle with Jehan Essenusi…the two amulets merging together…and what else?

What else?

And what would send me back and, more importantly, what would let me *stay?*

Part of me still wanted to return. I think that's why I was so susceptible to its siren call. People I loved were there. My old life. Cars, indoor plumbing, microwaves and electricity were there. Snowball and my cozy apartment. My career that I'd sacrificed and worked so hard for were there.

Ramose wasn't.

"Ah, you fear I will take other wives besides you some day?" His voice conciliatory and falling to a husky murmur, "I promise I will not. You will be my greater wife; my *only* wife. For always and forever.

"In life you will be my equal. Everything we will share. Gold. Power. Decisions. Our children will be taught your knowledge and of your past. We will raise them together with love and compassion, as you have taught me.

"I will treat my slaves, no, my servants, as I will have no more slaves, with kindness as you have shown me.

"When we die you will be buried beside me in my tomb so we will enter the afterlife and eternity together. Whichever afterlife it will be." His voice had grown anxious.

He drew away from me, his disappointment that I hadn't answered yet suddenly a shadowy presence between us.

The amulet was a hot ember against my skin and as I looked at Ramose his face began to fade...the boat, the night sky of ancient Egypt began to fade. Ramose's voice was so soft and far away now, I had to strain to hear him. Fight to stay beside him and feel his arms around me.

Ramose had sworn to marry me and the amulet was answering for me. It was going to really send me home. Now. I felt it.

Don't know how, but I did. I knew.

Our children. Silent tears had begun to fall at Ramose's words because, in that dark moment, I knew the truth.

I will never marry this man I love more than life itself. I will never have his children or grow old with him. Never make love with him because I would not be here. In all our time together he'd never insisted I'd make love with him, never forced me to, as much as I now wanted to, and now I'd waited too long. Stupid, *stupid.*

I was going home when I'd finally decided passionately once and for all I *didn't want to*.

I wanted to stay with Ramose. Marry him. Love him. Have his children. I'd never have regrets. My mother, sisters and brothers, had their own lives.

They'd miss me but they'd be okay in time. They had their lives. Even Snowball. He had Mom to love him and take care of him. *They* didn't need me like Ramose did.

This life here with Ramose was my true destiny, it had to be. My true life. Not the other one in the future.

"I love you, Ramose. I want to marry you!" I cried out, clutching at him and feeling only emptiness.

I couldn't see his face any more. I couldn't feel his body against mine. He was gone.

The boat was gone.

I was in a black tunnel rushing away from all I truly loved.

"No, I don't want to go back! *Don't send me back!*"

Sayed's words about the amulet returned to me. It was as if the man with the kind brown eyes, the man who'd known how lonely I'd really been and how much I'd ached for someone to love and be loved by, was speaking to me across the millennia.

The amulet is very old. Meant for you. It will protect you from evil magic and harm, from Jehan, and lead you to the one you love. Wear it always. Never take it off. Never take it off.

Unless you want to stay.

Was that the final ingredient in the brew? Taking the necklace off? Or, for the first time since it happened and since my head wound that had trickled blood down my neck, I remembered scratching Jehan's face, getting blood on the scarab. Was it the blood?

Egyptian Heart

In the darkness between worlds, as the tomb of Ramose began to form around me, solid and real this time, I found the amulet in my fingers and *I ripped it off my neck.*

The tomb was still materializing around me. It hadn't worked!

Please don't send me back. I love Ramose and want to stay with him. Please!

Then it came to me and I *knew*. It had to have been Jehan's blood. Blood had been the final ingredient. Blood had made the magic work. Somehow. A sacrifice. Perhaps the blood had sent me here and perhaps blood could keep me here. It was worth a try. Anything was worth a try.

I scratched the palm of my hand until blood flowed, and then rubbed the amulet in it.

Nothing happened. The tomb was solidifying. Ramose was a ghostly shadow before my eyes…fading…fading.

I cried out in frustration and, out of pure desperation because I didn't know what else to do, I viciously flung the amulet into the tomb.

"Here take it back. I don't want it any more. Don't need it anymore. I want to *stay!*"

It hit Ramose's golden sarcophagus and burst into flame. I watched it dwindle into nothing and disappear. The necklace was gone.

For a heart wrenching moment I wasn't sure it'd worked. All those months of being so careful to never take it off. All those months that I'd believed the necklace was my salvation and way back home. I couldn't lose it. Could never take it off. Had I been wrong? Had the amulet kept me tied to the tomb and my world or had it kept me tied to his world? Had I waited too long to get rid of it?

The tomb was around me, nearly concrete. I could see Ramose's sarcophagus and the stone walls full of hieroglyphs boxing me in. Saw Jehan's body lying in the corner, unconscious, where I'd left him.

As if no time had passed at all.

"Ramose," I sobbed at the wispy shadow, closing my eyes and crying out with my very soul as I began to weep. *"I love you. Don't leave me."*

I reached out for him until I could almost feel his warm flesh beneath my hands. Willed myself back to him across the ages. Strained with every molecule of my being to stay with him. My grief at our parting a physical tearing of my heart and soul that produced a pain so fierce I must have passed out, falling into a swirling black abyss.

****

When I awoke, it seemed an eternity later, I was in Ramose's arms on the deck of the menechou, the stars of an ancient Egyptian night glittering down on us.

The scarab necklace was gone. The tomb was gone. I was back with my love on the ship on the River Nile.

I'd been right. Getting rid of the amulet at that exact moment had sent me back to ancient Egypt. Had released me from its hold. Its magic.

I'd never felt such joy. I was choking on it.

"I've been sent back and I'm here to stay," I breathed. Ramose said something to me and I was relieved I could still understand him.

Crying and laughing at the same time, I molded myself into his hungry embrace, so relieved to be with him.

"Nothing will ever separate us again," I promised. "No matter how difficult our lives will be. If Lord Haremhab hunts us for all our days or not. Where we have to go or how we have to live. What the future brings. I love you and I'll marry you…tomorrow…tonight. The sooner the better. I'll be your wife—your only wife— and give you many children. Yes, yes, *yes.*"

The kiss Ramose gave me sealed our future. I heard Nefertiti and her daughters applauding and giggling behind us. They'd been listening the whole time. I wondered if I'd actually disappeared from Ramose's grasp and if Nefertiti or anyone else had seen it.

Well, it was dark and torchlight could play tricks on one's eyes.

I laughed again as Ramose lifted me into his arms and held me up high as if I were an offering to the sky, carried away with his elation.

Finally he was speechless.

And I was finally where I belonged.

With the man I loved in 1338 B.C. Egypt.

Epilogue

Sayed stood reverently above the two gilded sarcophaguses in the recently discovered and opened tomb. Two sarcophaguses containing two mummies. One man and one woman. A tall woman by the size of the second sarcophagus.

The electric lantern hung high above him on a pole, its glow lighting up the chamber that had until today been dark for over three millennia.

The old man examined the two exquisite coffins with a satisfied smile on his wrinkled face and a glint in his gentle eyes. In his hands he held a tattered and makeshift journal made of swatches of papyrus paper and tied together with thick string, that he'd found along with the tomb's *Book* of *the Dead*.

The *Book* of *the Dead* recounted the lives of two remarkable people, Ramose Nakh-Min and Magshepsut Nakh-Min. Ramose had been an Egyptian warrior and once the second in command of Akhenaton's armies, before he'd fallen from Pharaoh's favor. He'd also been a great humanitarian of his time.

In the other sarcophagus was Magshepsut, who'd been Ramose's greater and *only* wife. It was rare for a man of Ramose's wealth and renowned status to have had only *one* wife. Unheard of, really. The *Book of the Dead* also spoke of Magshepsut's strange and wondrous talents—it'd been said she could see into the future and she could paint a picture so beautiful it'd make a man cry—and of her goodness and love for her friends, family and servants.

The tomb was crammed with Magshepsut's paintings. Realistic and stunning renditions of the woman's life, her husband, their children and an unnamed woman who looked like a queen surrounded by three young women who looked like her.

Sayed went back to the *Book* of *the Dead*. It also spoke of the sweeping reforms the tomb's inhabitants had brought to their subjects. It celebrated Magshepsut's great and ever faithful love for her husband that never weakened their whole lives and the six strong and fair minded children they'd had: three good sons and three devoted daughters. Ramose and Magshepsut had lived a long and happy life.

Their *Book* of *the Dead* was the official record, written in ancient Egyptian, of all that and their secret friendship with Queen Nefertiti and her three remaining daughters. The same Queen Nefertiti who'd been married to Akhenaton and, having been set aside, had disappeared into history and never been heard from again. *Until now.*

Whereas the papyrus journal was written in modern day English, by a woman originally called Maggie Owen who'd found herself in a time she hadn't been born to and was the unofficial record of Maggie's, Magshepsut's, life.

Sayed had read this document with great interest and would hide it in a safe place. No one must ever find it—as if anyone would believe it if they did.

The journal diary was Maggie's own telling in her own words of being thrown back in time to ancient Egypt by a magical amulet. She wrote poignantly of being mistaken as a runaway slave, of meeting and falling in love with Ramose, the master of the house she'd been enslaved to, and of her and her lover's adventures trying to save the lives of Ramose's aunt, Queen Nefertiti and her three daughters. She wrote of deciding not to go back to her time because she loved and wanted to marry Ramose.

Wrote of the days after that, when she and her husband traveled to escape General Haremhab's wrath. Haremhab, having been the ambitious and ruthless final usurper of Akhenaton's throne.

Ramose and Magshepsut had freed their slaves—unheard of in that time—traveled for years and years and finally when Haremhab was dead, they returned to Egypt with their three children, had three more children, and lived happily the rest of their days in Ramose's childhood home by the Nile. Their children had grown up to be as compassionate and generous as they'd been.

Quite a *fairy tale*.

Standing up from the crouch he'd been reading in, Sayed took the handwritten diary and tucked it into a knapsack hanging from his shoulder.

The journal diary had been meant for his eyes mostly, he thought. A sort of thank you from Magshepsut, or Maggie. A message to let him know things had turned out just as he'd planned them.

You took my advice, Maggie, and you found your true love. Your destiny. You found happiness

Egyptian Heart

and made a difference in your time. Good for you.

What Maggie had never known was that *his* ancient ancestors had been descended from the slaves of Ramose and Magshepsut Nakh-Min. The story of his family would not have ended so happily, in fact he might not have ever existed, if not for Magshepsut's kindnesses to his long dead relations. So he had helped himself by helping Maggie find true love.

And all had ended well, Sayed thought.

He exited the tomb and the darkness returned to cover the sarcophaguses. Soon enough the whole world would know of Ramose and Magshepsut. Know of their magnanimous lives and their great love. The official version, that is. The rest—the magic—would remain a secret.

As it should be.

The End.

****

Please, if you'd be so kind...could you leave a review of this book on Amazon and Goodreads? I would greatly appreciate it. The author, Kathryn Meyer Griffith rdgriff@htc.net

Also, if you like ancient Egyptian stories be sure to give my other ancient Egyptian romantic adventure ghostly tale, **The Calling** *(*http://tinyurl.com/h9kmrpy*), a look; on sale everywhere and also in paperback and Audible audio book. Also, a little racier is my ancient Egyptian horror short story,* **The Nameless One** *(*http://tinyurl.com/nvgv3mr*), though in eBook only. Or, if you like thrillers, horror, romantic time-travel, or murder mysteries, you might try one of my other 27 novels or 12 short stories (all listed on next pages):* https://tinyurl.com/ycp5gqb2

Kathryn Meyer Griffith

About Kathryn Meyer Griffith…

Since childhood I've been an artist and worked as a graphic designer in the corporate world and for newspapers for twenty-three years before I quit to write full time. But I'd already begun writing novels at 21, over forty-eight years ago now, and have had twenty-eight (nine romantic horror, two horror novels, two romantic SF horror, one romantic suspense, one romantic time travel, one historical romance, five thrillers, one non-fiction short story collection, and six murder mysteries) previous novels and twelve short stories published from various traditional publishers since 1984. But, I've gone into self-publishing in a big way since 2012; and upon getting all my previous books' full rights back for the first time in 35 years, have self-published all of them. My five Dinosaur Lake novels and Spookie Town Murder Mysteries (Scraps of Paper, All Things Slip Away, Ghosts Beneath Us, Witches Among Us and What Lies Beneath the Graves) are my best-sellers.

I've been married to Russell for over forty years; have a son, two grandchildren and a great-granddaughter and I live in a small quaint town in Illinois. We have a quirky cat, Sasha, and the three of us live happily in an old house in the heart of town. Though I've been an artist, and a folk/classic rock singer in my youth with my late brother Jim, writing has always been my greatest passion, my butterfly stage, and I'll probably write stories until the day I die…or until my memory goes.

2012 EPIC EBOOK AWARDS *Finalist* for her horror novel **The Last Vampire** ~ 2014 EPIC EBOOK AWARDS * Finalist * for her thriller novel **Dinosaur Lake**.

Egyptian Heart

*All Kathryn Meyer Griffith's books can be found here:
http://tinyurl.com/ld4jlow
*All her Audible.com audio books here:
http://tinyurl.com/oz7c4or

Novels & short stories from Kathryn Meyer Griffith:
*Evil Stalks the Night, The Heart of the Rose, Blood Forged, Vampire Blood, The Last Vampire (*2012 EPIC EBOOK AWARDS*Finalist* in their Horror category)*, Witches, Witches II: Apocalypse, Witches plus Witches II: Apocalypse, The Nameless One erotic horror short story, The Calling, Scraps of Paper (The First Spookie Town Murder Mystery), All Things Slip Away (The Second Spookie Town Murder Mystery), Ghosts Beneath Us (The Third Spookie Town Murder Mystery), Witches Among Us (The Fourth Spookie Town Murder Mystery), What Lies Beneath the Graves (The Fifth Spookie Town Murder Mystery: sixth, All Who Came Before, coming in 2019), Egyptian Heart, Winter's Journey, The Ice Bridge, Don't Look Back, Agnes, A Time of Demons and Angels, The Woman in Crimson, Human No Longer, Six Spooky Short Stories Collection, Forever and Always Romantic Novella, Night Carnival Short Story, Dinosaur Lake (2014 EPIC EBOOK AWARDS*Finalist* in their Thriller/Adventure category), Dinosaur Lake II: Dinosaurs Arising, Dinosaur Lake III: Infestation and Dinosaur Lake IV: Dinosaur Wars, Dinosaur Lake V: Survivors, Memories of My Childhood and Christmas Magic 1959.*

Her Websites:
Twitter: https://twitter.com/KathrynG64
My Blog: https://kathrynmeyergriffith.wordpress.com/
My Facebook author page:
https://www.facebook.com/KathrynMeyerGriffith67/

Kathryn Meyer Griffith

Facebook Author Page:
https://www.facebook.com/pg/Kathryn-Meyer-Griffith-Author-Page-208661823059299/about/?ref=page_internal
https://www.facebook.com/kathrynmeyergriffith68/
https://www.facebook.com/pages/Kathryn-Meyer-Griffith/579206748758534
http://www.authorsden.com/kathrynmeyergriffith
https://www.goodreads.com/author/show/889499.Kathryn_Meyer_Griffith
http://en.gravatar.com/kathrynmeyergriffith
https://www.linkedin.com/in/kathryn-meyer-griffith-99a83216/
https://www.pinterest.com/kathryn5139/
https://tinyurl.com/ycp5gqb2
****

E-mail me at rdgriff@htc.net I love to hear from my readers.

Egyptian Heart *SOON to be in a brand new AUDIBLE AUDIO BOOK narrated by the amazing Nila Brereton Hagood, too! Look for it.*

Text copyright © 2015 by Kathryn Meyer Griffith
All rights reserved.
Printed in the United States of America.
Egyptian Heart

by Kathryn Meyer Griffith
Cover art by: Dawné Dominique
Copyright 2015 Kathryn Meyer Griffith

All rights reserved. No part of this book may be reproduced, scanned or distributed in any form, including digital and electronic or mechanical, including photocopying, recording, or by any information storage and retrieval system, without the prior written consent of the author, except for brief quotes for use in reviews.

This book is a work of fiction. Characters, names, places and incidents either are the product of the author's imagination or are used fictitiously, and any resemblance to any actual persons, living or dead, events, or locales is entirely coincidental.